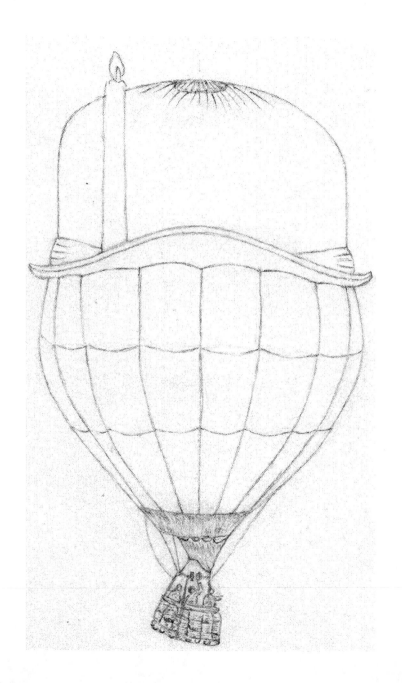

Flight of the Yellow Bowler

Written and illustrated by

Will Riding

author, also, of 'Ebenezer's Tale.'

authorHOUSE®

AuthorHouse™ UK Ltd.
500 Avebury Boulevard
Central Milton Keynes, MK9 2BE
www.authorhouse.co.uk
Phone: 08001974150

First published by AuthorHouse 5/2/2012

ISBN: 978-1-4685-0401-9 (sc)
ISBN: 978-1-4685-0402-6 (e)

Chapter One

Old Ebenezer smiled at his grandson. 'Ah well,' he said. 'Now you'll be wanting to hear what happened next to those two young boys I was telling you about last time.'

'Alec and Ben, do you mean?' said his small listener eagerly.

'Aye,' said old Ebenezer, 'Alec and Ben, that's right. A bit like you, bright sparks the pair on 'em.' There was a pause for breath.

Old Ebenezer began again. 'Well then, there they were, now all growed up lads, good friends, spending an afternoon off work, together out in the Dales and enjoying a picnic. Like picnics, do you? Grand fun. The little pebbles, green 'un Alec's, red 'un Ben's, that had come their way when nobbut two young boys, and kept safe ever after – took care not to lose 'em, see – lay quietly amongst t' sandwiches and such, on the flat stone they were using for t' picnic table. There they lay, t' stones, winking and flashing in t' sunshine. T' sun were reight hot, and the two friends, full of sandwiches, they were, cake and coffee, too, dozed off. Henry heron – you remember him, I expect, flew in and wasn't too pleased with the snoring!' Old Ebenezer himself stopped speaking and began to doze. But he stirred himself. This is how his story ran.

'Ay-oop, ay-oop, this will nivver do. Coom on you two lads!' came a voice bouncing across the picnic stone. It jerked Alec and Ben to their feet and wide awake in complete astonishment. They wildly looked around for some clues. Where could the voice (seemed a bit familiar) have come from? All to be seen at first was the rugged little hawthorn tree – twigs and branches criss-crossing everywhere – which overhung the picnic crumbs and held, deep within it, a bird's nest. How it remained there, in all weathers, anybody might have to guess. There'd been some canny builders for sure. Birds are very clever.

But was it a bird's nest? That was the question. Suddenly very curious, Ben decided to take a look. He carefully wriggled his head into the very prickly thicket. Didn't want to get scratched.

'Go on,' Alec called, keen to know whether what at least looked like a nest had anything inside. Any eggs would have cracked long ago, any fledglings flown. Very slowly, Ben edged his head forward. He discovered there wasn't in fact much of a nest at all. He detected a kind of sweet smell. Before his eyes were actually able to see right in, all began to change. The tatty bit of a nest was becoming very different.

'Look at this,' Ben called out. 'Can you see?' At that moment, the back of his head caught a hard, spiny branch. 'Wow, that hurt,' he said with a howl. Trying to calm down, he crouched and slowly, carefully, wriggled his way out again into the open.

'Could you see anything?' Alec said impatiently, before Ben could speak.

'Nothing much, but I'm not sure,' was the reply.

'Nowt much! Nowt much!' The two companions jumped as if they had been stung! A voice out of nowhere! Yes, surely. And there it was again, this time as definite as you like: 'Nowt much!' It seemed to come from the middle of the tree. (Well, of course it did!) The two friends were totally hooked. What was happening? Trunk and branches creaked, shook, started to change. Gradually, so gradually, the twiggy tangle caught in the middle started to change until, at last, no longer just a tumble of twigs and moss, but something like – yes – no question, a hat, and would you believe it, a flat-crowned, broad-brimmed, be-furred hat, remembered, half-remembered, from boyhood, way back. It instantly vanished.

All at once, from behind what had been up till then a more or less ordinary hawthorn, came the voice: 'Coom on lads.'

Round the back of the little tree shot the two by now very excited friends. As they did so it completely fell apart. A flicker, a sudden flash, there stood instead a widely-smiling Alva, their ostler friend of long ago, just brushing off a leaf and a twig or two from his waistcoat.

Yes, there he was, breeched, gaitered and hobnail-booted, looking out from under his wondrous hat. He stood in a broad stance, feet firmly planted, sleeves rolled up. Here was their old friend the horseman, strong-armed, alert and ready for anything. And how his belt buckle, "weskit" buttons, gleamed and shone. Articulus, his mighty piebald horse, might have appeared at any minute! And what would he have to say in his usual elegant manner? Make no bones about it, both Alec and

Ben were completely staggered and amazed. Memories of being flown across the Dales on the back of the great shire when they were boys remained crystal clear. It took a moment or two to gather their thoughts. Could this all be real? A tricky question.

Alva took off his hat, flicked away a hawthorn berry and said: 'How about a drop of Kendal mint cake?' Still the same old Alva! The two friends laughed, but remained staggered to see, so unexpectedly, their long-remembered and much respected ostler acquaintance once more. Strange to say, time seemed to lose its meaning at that point. Age, time in any form, meant nothing at all. Here stood, as far as Alva was concerned, just his friends Ben and Alec – 'and that were t' top and bottom on it.' And if it didn't bother Alva, it has no need to bother us! And he was going to call them lads, any road! He offered no special greeting, merely a wink and a warm handshake.

Knowing Alva and his fully-stocked hat from times past and what he would, could and did produce from it, the Kendal mint cake he offered could just as easily have been a cheese sandwich that the friends were invited to taste. And Alva saw them now, just as they had been at his first meeting with them. So long ago, it seemed, in his old barn on a wet Dales' day. All three were thinking the same way. Time had simply dissolved. The Kendal mint cake tasted grand, any road!

You might well expect lively conversation to have burst forth. It didn't. Alva turned away, looked into the far distance and scratched his ear. Was he listening for sommat? Was sommat afoot? He'd refused a picnic sandwich. Not even a rock bun would tempt him. Something was on his mind. What was it? The two picnickers followed his gaze, away to the far horizon. Time stood still. Imagination was fizzing all right!

The red and green stones, you won't have forgotten them, lying on the flat picnic stone, still gleamed in the warm sun. Alva drew breath, gave a sharp whistle from between his teeth, then gently called: 'Coom by'. Startled, the companions half-turned to look behind them – for a quick movement had caught their attention – they saw their two mysterious little stones leap into the air, fly and land straight into Alva's "weskit" pockets; red to the left, green one into the right. Instantly, in their place upon the picnic stone, scattering the few uneaten cakes and biscuits, sat two almost identical, cross-bred, collie dogs. Neither dalesman could quite believe his eyes. Alva thrust his thumbs into his belt, gave a chuckle – my, how that belt shone – and said: 'Let's be off, then.'

The two dogs wagged their tails with great excitement, jumped off the stone, sat down, cocked their heads on one side and, with shining eyes, looked enquiringly at Alva, eager for his next command. A whistle from him, the two dogs raced off on an outrun of lightning speed. Alva, along with a rather stunned Alec and Ben, (who made short work of clearing up the picnic table, scrambling the remains into their rucksacks) followed on at a brisk pace across the lovely, wild-flowering grassland ahead of them.

Such energy! The dogs, with their young, lively legs, began to leave the threesome behind. Alva whistled sharply once more. The two collies halted, stood still for a moment, then turned, poised, a front paw half lifted. Eyes shining, dripping pink tongues sliding and dancing in and out between brilliant white teeth. What a picture!

'Ay-oop, Liz, ay-oop, Kim,' called ostler Alva between cupped hands. To the casual eye, these glorious animals were so similar in their black and white coats, even to the tips of their tails. But closer inspection would reveal Liz's golden cheeks and Kim's brindle eyebrows, which gave her a kind of permanent look of surprise. The two dogs raced back and lay in the grass at Alva's feet. He, Ben and Alec had stopped and decided to sit down, take a breather and see what might be going to happen next. Alec asked after Alva's horse, Articulus – their well-remembered flying, talking friend – who had flown them on his broad wings into so many interesting places and experiences. He hadn't so far materialised. Would he, they enquired, do so?

'Ah well,' said Alva, 'he's not that far off and will be here reight sharp if we need him.' Alec wasn't too sure whether or not he had seen something fairly large moving between some trees. Earlier, had Alva been watching for a noble head to rocket over the far horizon?

There now seemed lots to talk about on Dales' and other matters. Weather, of course. Alva, not surprisingly, perhaps, was very well informed about his two friends' activities since last he saw them: Alec's archaeological lecturing and Ben with his guided tours among the hills. Oddly, it didn't seem all that long since they first became friends. Time really had evaporated. But Alva had remained aware. Maybe he'd been feeling that the time had come for another jaunt, and knowing exactly how to set it up!

Both collies had settled themselves, eyes half-closed, moist noses twitching and alert, content to enjoy the day and the soft grass. There was just the occasional, gentle, rather optimistic snap at a passing butterfly, which missed. Collie Kim briefly stood up and began slowly turning in a tight circle to make an even more comfortable couch for herself. After all, the day was blissfully warm, the company friendly. Pausing in her efforts, she rather thoughtfully sniffed the air. Quickly, now, she stood bolt upright. And, in a moment, so did Liz. Both dogs lifted their heads, noses held high, twitching madly. Tails wagged wildly. Alva, Alec and Ben were left in no doubt that something was afoot. (You may depend, Alva was in no doubt at all.) Each animal started to prance back and forth, running away a little then returning, encouraging everyone to follow them.

First, Ben caught it, then they all caught it, laughed and looked at each other and in one voice shouted – 'cooking!' And so it was, the undeniable smell of cooking carried on the summer air. Such cooking! Irresistible. Who was the chef and where was the source of such a great aroma? That was the question. The two collies were in no doubt. Throwing a look at Alva, as if asking his permission, they began to move away, heads tilted back towards him for a word of command.

'Reight then, lasses, off tha goes,' he said. Liz and Kim bounded away, then back they shot, circling round behind the three companions. Round and round they went, all excitement, then off again, scampering and encouraging, clearly determined to drive the three in the direction they should go. Well, what else would you expect a brace of expert collies to do?

'Coom on you two,' said Alva, getting to his feet, heaving his friends to theirs. He had things in mind, other than who might be cooking a meal. There were things he wanted them to see, and that was his reason for returning. Where would the dogs land them up?

Ingleborough was not all that far off and this seemed to be where the two animals were heading. Was someone with a barbecue on the summit making merry in a chef's hat, fanning sausage-rich vapours downwind? Was some shepherd in his hut having a reight good fry-oop, leaving his window wide open? Fried egg and bacon adrift on the open air? Ah, bliss! Hikers brewing soup – was that it? Maybe a mountain rescue team, somewhere boiling up, just in case. The guessing went on. Alva's guests had their own ideas. Alva himself didn't join in, but smiled a good deal and kept his eyes on the dogs as they raced to and fro, disappearing one minute, rushing back the next. Maybe there was little need for their encouragement. Benefits of the rather basic picnic eaten, it seemed, ages ago, had rather worn off. The two friends were right now ready for almost anything, as long as it was food.

The day continued to be beautiful, fleecy clouds swirling across the very blue sky. But, ah, the gravy on the breeze! Both dogs halted every now and again, pointed and sniffed. Ingleborough became nearer, but then the land began to fall away towards a tumble of turf and rocks. A moment or to and the seekers were there. The challenging entrance to the vast and famous pothole – Gaping Ghyll – lay before them. They were now completely enveloped in the smells of cooking! Might their old friend, Gilbert, appear at any moment? Wonderful smells of cooking, gust after gust, rose up all round. Just what was this giant of a man cooking down there in the great pothole that was his home? You might very well ask. Not Lancashire hotpot, you may depend!

The party stood where they were and breathed in. Oh, yes. And again! Alva smiled, thinking of what might lie ahead. A rather familiar voice roared up from below: 'Nay, don't mither about, coom down, coom down.' How are we to manage that? thought Alec, somewhat staggered, like Ben, at this turn of events.

'Well now, you two lads,' said Alva, 'seems to me Gilbert has something particular for you.' Food, archaeologist Alec hoped. Surely not old remains. He knew what remarkable discoveries of all kinds the area could produce. But something special would do. Meeting Gilbert again would be special. Ben agreed, whatever might lie beneath. But how they were to get down into the mighty pot puzzled him.

Reading their thoughts, Alva said, 'I'll have a word with Gilbert.' He promptly vanished. Left with the two faithful dogs, both peering intelligently after their master, the two friends sat down and talked to them. Felt bound to ask just what they themselves thought. The dogs merely tilted their heads first one way, then the other and opened wide their eyes. Did one of them say 'Search me?' It was, so far, turning out to be an altogether remarkable day. A merlin floated overhead, catching their attention for a moment or two before swooping away.

Alva reappeared. 'Gilbert is waiting to see you,' he said.

'Aye, it'll be reight grand, coom straight down,' boomed a deep voice from below.

'Come with me,' Alva said and began walking away from where they were all standing. The two friends followed him a short distance and found themselves in something of a gully, partly grown over. It was quite unfamiliar.

'Look through there,' Alva said, pushing aside a branch of a stunted tree. 'Give those rocks a shove. If tha can.' Alec could see a jumbled, weedy heap of limestone, mossed over and lolling against a gentle slope of stone and scree. Why has Alva brought us here, he thought. Only one way to discover. Setting about the job, he steadily shifted the mysterious heap, stone by stone. 'Give us a hand, Ben,' he called.

'Watch thi fingers,' Alva warned. Ouch! Too late. They were amazed at what they saw. Revealed, a curious opening at an angle, tilted into the slope and supported by business-like pieces of the natural rock.

'Go on, one of thi, tak a look,' said Alva. A rather more than encouraging nudge from Ben, Alec stooped and looked right into what they had exposed. They couldn't believe their eyes. They found themselves looking at the wide mouth of a great tubular slide which now lay open before them. Both were stunned! Just about able to speak, 'Look at that, Ben, look at that,' Alec croaked. Ben already had. His eyes had nearly departed his cranium.

And what's more, there were two bristling mats at the mouth, all ready for take-off.

'Give it a whirl, why not?' said Alva with a smile. He turned twice and disappeared. Good old Alva! He'd obviously known about it all along. A right joker was our Alva, and that was what he'd had in mind when he materialised a while back by the old hawthorn tree at the picnic. Who could have guessed? So here were both friends totally stunned, right flabbergasted, Alec described later.

Mick the shepherd appeared nearby. He had caught the sound of voices and didn't seem at all surprised at what he saw. 'Off tha goes, lads, Gilbert's waiting,' he said. He sharply called the two collies to him. It was time for a bite to eat. Might there be something waiting for him (and them) in his frying pan? He gave a brisk whistle, called them once more: 'Coom by,' he said. The two dogs ran to him. Together, off they all went and disappeared up to his hut in the hills.

The two young dalesmen watched them go. Then, quietly, Ben said rather dubiously: 'What about it then?' The two looked at each other, gave a laugh.

'Give ower mithering about,' echoed up through the tube. There was nothing for it but to give it a go!

Chapter Two

The mats were waiting and certainly eager to give it a go. Alec seized the moment. Stooping into the mouth of the tube, he grabbed the nearest mat and sat on it. Whoosh! His trousers had hardly made contact – he was gone. His involuntary 'Whoopee' filled the entire slide, it hung in the air like chimney smoke trailing behind an express steam locomotive. Ben suddenly felt very alone. 'Come on,' he said to himself, 'can't hang about.' As soon as he made the entrance to the slide, the second mat almost sprang to meet him. No chance of sitting. Before he knew it, he was swallowed into the tube headfirst and went streaking down its silvery throat. He couldn't see much in what was an eerie half-light. But he found he was twisting over and over, like water swirling down a plughole, the slide, surely, was like a great corkscrew. He was travelling at speed. How would he end up? Didn't like to (could hardly) think about it. Breathing rather occupied his mind at the minute! What a ride the two friends were having. Rip-roaring, I'd call it. So might you if it was happening to you. Hair-raising and heart-stopping it was (especially when friction caused the mats to smoke a bit as they hurtled down into the mighty pot). Worth every moment, both pilots declared at a later date. And hoped they were believed!

The tube levelled out as it ran to its end. Arriving at the finish of the mind-boggling launch, mats, plus pilots, were sent one after the other, whizzing across Gilbert's pothole floor, to land in a bit of a heap and a great laugh at the awaiting Gilbert's great feet. There he stood, enormous hair awry, heavy tweed jacket, waistcoat, breeches, thick woollen socks firmly gripping massive calves plunging into serious hiking boots. He was just as large-scale as he had been when, as young lads, they had first met him.

'That was reight grand, wasn't it?' was Gilbert's first remark. 'Welcome, gentlemen.' Two rather breathless mouths opened and weakly gasped – 'Yes.' It had been rather more than just grand, more like the experience of a lifetime. 'Hang t' mats over there if you will. They'll be needed for next time, happen,' Gilbert said. The two pilots looked at each other and all round in amazement. How many "next times" might there be, they wondered. 'Oh,' went on their host, 'and tha can put tha rucksacks ower there if you like. But it's time for summat to eat, I doubt you'll be ready for a bite.' Neither voyager argued about that! 'Well, now then, tak a seat,' said Gilbert.

It was now possible to take in everything around them. First, Gilbert's great oak table and sturdy, high-backed chairs. At the table head stood Gilbert's own chair, a vast, high-back carver, snug inside with a magnificent white fleece to rest and warm his back and shoulders. The chair's broad arms had been crafted to carry the strain of weighty forearms. About the floor, along each side of the table, lay handmade rag rugs of many shades. On the table, flickering light from slender candles, elegant in candlesticks of polished brass, danced and reflected in its highly-polished surface. Such sparkle from bright cutlery laid ready for the next meal! From the merry candle flames at table and brackets high above them, weird shapes and shadows flung themselves around the pothole walls and mounted tapestries. The whole area was both savoury and comfortably warm.

Gilbert slowly and courteously took Ben to his place at table. Moving round and settling Alec in another splendid chair, he suggested a glass of wine. Red or white, was the question. 'I can recommend the red,' he said. He filled his guests' and his own glass to the very brim. 'Drink oop, lads,' he said. Sitting down at the head of the table, he raised his glass and proposed a toast: 'To thee lads,' he said. And with a wink that seemed to convey he knew more about their future than they possibly could (how might they?), he repeated: 'Welcome, and here's to a grand holiday to coom.'

With this, he got up and moved swiftly out of sight through an overhanging archway in a far corner of semi-darkness beyond the table. A warm glow radiated from somewhere. Who knew where? The savoury smells that had started the search, this was, surely, where they'd arisen. Now they increased to full force, blossoming out to fill the great chamber here below. In not many minutes, here was Gilbert back with two loaded plates of Yorkshire pudding and gravy, setting one in front of each of his guests. Again, off he went, to be back in a jiffy with his own steaming platter. He sat down with it at his own place. 'Coom along, lads,' he said, 'eat oop.' They all did, right sharp.

Finished, Gilbert left his chair to put the empty plates on a mahogany sideboard glowing just a little in the half-light against the wall. To his kitchen, next, coming back with two plates of roast beef and every kind of vegetable. There was even some horseradish sauce for Alec. It wasn't long before he had his own meal before him at the table, sat down and led the charge.

Gilbert's hospitality was not to be forgotten. Strangely, his guests when trying to remember, looking back much later in their lives, realised that they had lost all sense of being smaller than their host the moment they landed down in the great vault.

Relaxing at Gilbert's table, enjoying the delicious food and fine wine, there was a lot of laughing, remembering the great Yorkshire pudding that had bounced and skipped all the way down from Ingleborough to fill Gilbert's stomach in times gone by. There was much to talk about – fishing, fell-running, sheep trialling, how many potholers had got stuck this season. It was a grand chat. Prodding at his roast beef and chasing a brussels sprout from under a parsnip,

Gilbert enquired after Alva's great horse, Articulus, who had been so helpful to him in times past.

'We haven't seen him for some while,' said Ben, 'but he's sure to turn up again when least you expect it. It's been good to meet you again, Gilbert.'

'It was grand to see Alva, when he told me about you two lads being back in these parts,' said Gilbert. 'Allus been a good friend to me, has Alva. Grand lad wi horses, allus has been – brilliant wi old Articulus.'

'See much of Henry the heron these days?' enquired Alec.

'Not a reight lot,' replied their giant host, 'but I did meet him up on Ingleborough not long since – flew down for a chat. He said I might be seeing you two lads again before long.' It was good to hear that Henry was still fit and well informed.

Away went the empty plates and Gilbert disappeared again to his catering department. He was gone just long enough for the two friends to wonder between them as to what might be going to happen next. Might they find themselves back up on top of the moors, directly? But Gilbert returned, managing to carry three generous helpings of fresh apple pie and cream. On a side table lay a major fruit cake cut into large wedges. There was an Ingleborough-size chunk of the most lovely cheese sitting on a great blue and white charger. By its side, a handy-looking knife. 'Cut heavy,' said Gilbert, 'whenever tha likes.' Soon, there wasn't much left to be seen of apple pie and cream! Gilbert raised his glass for the umpteenth time. 'Really good to see thi, lads,' he roared. And turned to the cheese. His voice shot up the tubular slide and out across the fells. A number of young birds being taught to fly over Ingleborough and one or two over Penyghent, hit by the sudden turbulence, almost crashed to earth. Henry heron, flying near Whernside, felt it too, knew what it was, made the necessary corrections and glided on, smiling. Gilbert's guests raised their glasses and, though now well tanked up with wine, cake and cheese, managed to shout – 'Same to you!'

All was going well, very well indeed! The meal had been quite splendid. Gilbert was a spectacular chef! 'Well now, lads, if you don't mind.' As he said this, he began to clear away. His guests were invited to leave it to him. Soon the great table was bare except for the candles, which continued to burn bright, and wonderfully mirrored in the deeply polished board.

The atmosphere, delightfully gravy-laden up to this point, began gently and pleasantly to change. It assumed a breath of the Dales. Well, what else might you suppose? Temperature, however, remained comfortably warm. Had Gilbert operated his air conditioning system? If you wondered what this was and how it functioned, I'm afraid you'll have to ask him, or maybe work it out for yourself. Oh yes, I know exactly, because Gilbert told me! You would have been so interested to see his cooking arrangements. Gilbert was pleased to show his guests his beautiful, brilliant, black-leaded cooking range (the oven door was still warm), and all his pots, pans and kettles. Boggling, would be the best way of describing his entire range of kitchen equipment. Apart from the oven door, there was no other real evidence of cooking. None at all of washing up. Pristine – said it all.

Leaving the kitchen in a state of complete wonderment, Gilbert's guests were invited back to sit again at the great oak table; or the "girt" oak table, as Gilbert put it. What might be going to happen now? A very good question.

The giant man appeared to be dozing. Not so – lost in thought, perhaps. He said quietly: 'Let's have some fun.' Glancing all round, he raised an arm and loudly clicked his fingers. Immediately, every candle bracketed round the walls blazed right out to create an arena of light beyond the table. A small figure emerged from the shadows, made a deep bow, then leaping into action put on a show of such high-class tumbling that made both Ben and Alec think they ought to have paid to come in! There was no music, just a very light breath of sound as the performer's feet met the floor at the conclusion of every high somersault and spin. Such was the speed of movement, it was hardly possible to identify the performer or costume. But was that a suggestion of a "weskit"? The performance lasted for several breath-taking minutes. Suddenly it was over. A swift bow. No time to applaud. The performer had gone.

Two contortionists appeared, put on a staggering act of lifts and attitudes, in which gravity had no part whatsoever! Apart from one or two "allez oops", this performance, too, shot through in silence. The burning candles offered a flickering impression of harlequin-like figures who, with a final bow and flourish, catapulted out of sight. Complete in flawless white tie and tails, a conjuror appeared. With a smile and slight incline of his head, he set up his little table, produced countless rabbits from his top hat, doves from his coat tails, cards from his cuffs, multiplied countless bottles, produced miles of coloured strip and razor blades from his mouth, tangled and untangled umpteen shining jingling rings, cut and repaired yards of rope. A burst of red fire, flash of magnesium, he was gone.

The candles displayed above flickered, bubbled quietly, then ceased to burn. From their sleeping wicks, lazy spirals of blue smoke drifted high into the roof. The only sounds to be heard were one or two deep chuckles from Gilbert. 'Did tha like that?' he said. His guests, both perhaps now trying to recover, were a little lost for words.

'Great surprise, pretty spectacular, thank you very much,' Alec at last managed to say. For a while after this, there wasn't much conversation. Well fed, well entertained, the company started to relax, maybe doze. Even the candles at the table seemed to feel the mood and burnt less brightly. Zzzzzz.

'Na then, what's to do?' Gilbert, on the alert again, had been thinking. He went on —'It's all been reight grand, but mebbe there's yet more for you to see.' What was there yet to see, thought the two friends. All had been so extraordinary so far, it could be anyone's guess, but feeling pretty well fortified right now, it was almost a case of "bring it on!" But what? We shall see. Gilbert rose quietly, moved from the table and away from the quiet candlelight in its brass candlesticks. What was going to happen now? There was nothing to do but wait for him to come back, and hear what perhaps he had in mind.

Gilbert took quite a time to come back, long enough to raise a little concern. When he at last reappeared, he was carrying two rather familiar rucksacks. He handed them back to their owners, who were delighted to receive them. He sat down in his great chair and sank back into its deep, luxurious sheepskin fleece. He remained resting for a few minutes in contented silence. His guests sat, poised, and together felt, surely, something was about to happen. Drawing a deep breath, the mountain of a man slowly heaved himself to his feet. 'Coom on, lads,' he said,

drawing the two friends towards him with a broad sweep
of his arm. At this, his two guests left the table, slung their
rucksacks over their shoulders and moved towards him,
ready for who knew what. They had long since noticed
that the shining shoot that had shot them down into the
vast pothole was nowhere to be seen. The three of them
headed away from the table towards a far point in the lofty
banqueting hall. Gilbert had clicked his fingers. There was
light again from the walls.

On they went, stopping at fairly frequent intervals to
admire the many tapestried wall hangings. Who would
have worked them, Ben wondered. They were obviously
of some age and had been finely crafted. Along the way
stood one or two old chests and coffers and, at one point,
one of the tallest tallboys Ben had ever seen. (Well, a
little 'un would have been no possible use to Gilbert!) The
gentle meander away from the table ended at a twist in
the wall. Gilbert led the way round. There hung such a
tapestry as you might never expect to see. 'Na then, you
two,' said Gilbert. Reaching out, he drew back the lovely
hanging. There, revealed, a broad steadily rising staircase
cut into the rock. At that precise moment, two of the most
surprised young dalesmen on the planet simply gasped!

'It's time to go,' Gilbert said quietly. 'Glad you could
come and share a bite wi me.' He took the hand of each
of his guests, one at a time, and thoughtfully, warmly,
shook them. Alec thanked him and said how amazing
it had all been and how much he had enjoyed it. Ben
agreed, thanked Gilbert and said the meal, entertainment,
the whole experience would not be forgotten in a hurry.
Above all, how good it was to meet him again. Gilbert
seemed touched. In times ahead, his guests often wished
they had asked about the origin of the tapestries and fine

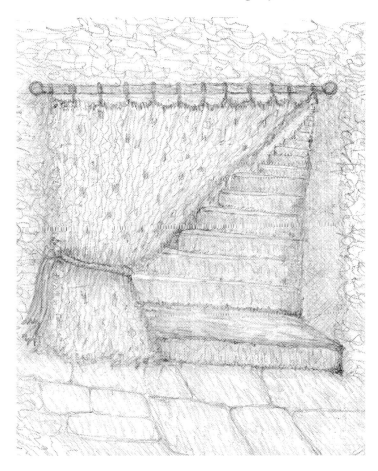

furniture. (What might the chests and coffers have held?) 'Na then you two lads, off with you,' Gilbert said. It was, at last, time. Tightening their rucksacks and offering final thanks, the two smiled, turned and, with a wave, took to the stony stairs.

Climbing the rugged staircase, fairly steep in sudden turns and places, with not much support except for a stout old rope anchored here and there to the wall, was an adventure in itself. Marks of tools used to hack out the treads and risers so long ago, left only wonder at the skill and scale of the achievement. Every so often, niches had been cut into the rock, no doubt to hold some kind of light, maybe of rush or of animal fat, to guide the masons, whoever they were. Who could guess? What drew the climbers on was a strange light that shafted into the stairway from above at different angles, hitting the walls at intervals as the spiral progressed upwards. From time to time there was airflow. Could that be birdsong faintly brought with it? It was a fairly eerie climb and it wasn't all that warm.

There was a good deal of headroom, which of course there had to be with Gilbert in mind. Every now and again, the work levelled out to form a platform. You could say a staging point where tiring stone cutters could rest awhile, eat an onion, bread and a bit of cheese. Maybe swallow a drink of some sort – water? – wine? Who knows? They would certainly need something before labouring onwards and upwards. Alec's archaeological eye thought it caught sight of a skull underneath a rocky overhang; remains of an unfortunate man or possibly some kind of prehistoric animal? Imagination can play tricks. There were no tricks about the clear symbols and motifs cut into the rock at one or two places. Marks of the craftsman's trade?

A gargoyle-like face with bulging features grinned from overhead. It was partly amusing, partly disturbing. Somebody must have had a sense of humour and energy to spare and taken a break from the main task, had a bit of fun, maybe amused his mates. Not far off, it was almost possible to make out a date. No luck. It was not possible to decipher it. Who were the craftsmen and how might they have lived, Alec wondered. Anyway, the climb continued.

It seemed to be going on for a very long time. How long, it was hard to tell, neither of the two friends carrying watches. They could only guess. They were beginning to feel hungry.

'Let's rest awhile,' Ben said as they arrived at the next halting area. Alec said he'd taken the words right out of his mouth, and it would be good to put some food into it. Both sat down, leaned against the surrounding walls and stretched their legs. Maybe there were some edible picnic remains in their rucksacks. They unslung them to have an optimistic rummage. They needn't have worried. Out of each rucksack came bread rolls, cheese (and some chunks of that beautiful cake), apples, along with a small bottle of wine. Good old Gilbert. Thanks very much. No glasses? Well, well, that would be no problem at all! The stop for refreshment was brief, because the warmth from climbing quickly ebbed away. Chill set in. Soon they were off again. Apart from a few random scratches and gouges, there were no what you might call significant or personal mason's marks to see this time. But in a still moment, a pause to listen, it was almost possible to imagine sounds of hammer, maybe mallet or chisel. At one point, Ben wasn't sure if he hadn't seen a dark shadow, felt an odd chill.

By way of encouragement, light now filtering from above became steadily, if slowly, stronger. And yes, surely, curlew cry, there it was again and increasingly easy to hear. Doggedly, the steps were tamed, inch by inch. Conquered was perhaps not quite the word. At last the flight began to level and reach out. Its risers became shallower, treads more spreading. After what seemed an age, the upward journey became almost achieved. And air was changing, improving. Wasn't that a whiff of the sea? Wherever were they going to emerge? Morecambe? Surely not. Well, why not? Why not indeed? Fish and chips sprang to mind. Egged on by such ideas, effort was spurred on.

Sweating, slipping, tripping, now, as over-eagerness and anticipation kicked in, led to a certain amount of recklessness. But who was going to miss a bit of skin right now? A great blast of air! They had made it! Where? Morecambe? No, pushing up through a scrag of stone, heather and grass, into a fairly wide turfy crater, here they were on the slopes of Ingleborough! Triumph at last! Laughing and staggering out, blinking in the light of a beautiful early summer morning, they had no idea how long it had taken them, but they were there!

Both climbers were pretty exhausted, not having hung about much on the way up. In spite of Gilbert's generosity, they were on the hungry side and more than a bit grubby. But above all they were fascinated to discover where they had surfaced. It could have been anywhere. Or could it? They were certainly very delighted, for here was a commanding view of the countryside and they could contemplate almost anything.

Ben suddenly spoke. 'By gum,' he said, 'we'll have a job convincing people when we tell them how we got into Gaping Ghyll and what happened there. They'll never believe us, but I can't say I'm too bothered. We enjoyed ourselves. As for the grand staircase, they'll never swallow that. We'll be able to dine out on that for weeks! Food right now, head for Ingleton or Clapham, d'you think? A good meal, major wash and brush up, what a thought.' Emerging into the open had brought the travellers within workable distance from the top of Ingleborough.

'Come on, young Ben,' laughed Alec, 'so near, let's make it to the top. Here, have an apple,' he said with a laugh.

'Right,' said Ben a little wearily, 'let's go.' Arriving a rather slogging twenty minutes later, they stood on the summit and sat down to consider their next move.

Chapter Three

'Well,' said Alec, getting to his feet. 'If it's a good meal we're after we'll have to make a move from up here and sooner rather than later, I reckon. Right?'

'Can't argue with that,' replied Ben. 'It'll take us a while. Better get on if we want to find a good place open.'

Discovering themselves on Ingleborough's wide expanse began to stir a few boyhood memories, faint but very persistent. Roman soldiers wandered into Alec's thoughts, one in particular who had welcomed them at the gates of his fortress. Or was this only re-living a school history lesson? And why were one or two Vikings hovering in the back of his mind? These were some of his thoughts as he and Ben trudged in some haste in the direction of a good meal. They went as fast as they could manage.

As they hurried, neither of them noticed it at first, but their attention became drawn to a heap of stones standing a little way off. Was it a tumbled cairn, perhaps? Curious things, cairns. Just a neat heap of stones to some, but to those who build them, something rather more. Interested, the two seekers after food decided to look. The sky remained blue, fleecy clouds dashed about and a stiffish breeze kept the curlews happy. With every stride, the companions closed on the lonely, stony pile. With a way still to go, Ben thought he detected something jutting out from the far side of it. Ah well, couldn't be much, maybe debris left by hikers. And there are always enough untidy ones to spoil it for the rest of us. Nearer now to their object, the two friends began to wonder what they might find. They arrived and, would you believe it, they certainly couldn't: right alongside the stone stack, for all to see, leant a sturdy, bright purple tandem bicycle! There it was, complete with bells, pump, saddle, saddlebag, panniers, front and rear lights. Extraordinary. And what's more, gears for every situation and tyres pretty well pumped up. Ready to go! It had been the racing handlebars that had jutted out to catch the attention. But why should such a machine be here, seemingly abandoned? First Ben, then Alec, called out in case the owner was lost or in some distress. They made a wide search. Nothing. But then, how could anyone get a tandem up here, anyway, where they found it, or be unwise enough to try? There was to be another surprise! Suddenly, their attention switched.

At some distance away, up from the valley below, rose a bright yellow hot air balloon, crowned with a shape like a bowler hat with a candle lodged in the hatband, as with potholers of long ago. Higher and higher it soared and made good progress towards the great mountaintop. Now, overhead, it was huge! From its basket, suspended underneath, emerged the top half of its pilot, on his head an old flying helmet and goggles. Leaning perilously out of the basket, and waving a gauntleted hand, he called out, 'I've arranged a little fun for the pair of thi. Ah, I see you've found it. T' tandem is yours if you'd like it. You're welcome. This is my new flyer. Horse, Articulus, is back home in t' barn. I'll give you a trip sometime if you let me know.' He gave a quick burst on his burner and the balloon drifted serenely away on the breeze. It was soon a mere speck in the distance. 'By gum, Alva,' was all that two young dalesmen were able to manage.

What to make of this remarkable turn of events was hard to judge. If finding a smart tandem high up on a very high hill wasn't extraordinary enough, an odd-shaped balloon turning up and half a conversation with its very singular pilot certainly was! But the aerial craft was now out of sight. It was time to relieve cricked necks and turn attention once more to the original needs of the inner man. It was, however, good that there remained no necessity to look for any cyclist in a state of distress.

The tandem was inspected once more, pulled up from where it leant and wheeled round in a trial circle. Solidly built, it felt reasonably heavy. Had either dalesman ever ridden a tandem before? They had not. Have you? I have, and it takes a bit of getting used to! It seemed to be a splendid, remarkably generous gift, this twin-saddled phenomenon. But up here? There was a lot of laughing and falling about as attempts were made to mount the machine. It is not entirely easy, at first, this tandem riding, as I suggested, especially for the rear passenger. The fixed handlebars defy all attempts at steering. Anyhow, after a brief rest, it was decided to give the machine a proper go.

It was obviously going to be easier without rucksacks getting in the way. Maybe they could be crammed into the saddlebag. It was pretty big. Handy that almost everything from Gilbert had been eaten, so both were more or less empty. Panniers each side of the back wheel looked pretty useful, too. Alec took off his rucksack, undid the saddlebag's straps and looked inside. Yes, it would be big enough. 'Let's have yours, Ben,' he said. He removed a brown paper bundle the saddlebag already held. 'Look at this, Ben,' he said with a laugh. 'What do you think?' He took the paper off and laughed again. 'You'll never guess,' he said. 'A full packet of Kendal mint cake. Well I never.' (Or perhaps he did.) Who, after all, was that pilot? An all-day English breakfast was still the priority, but mint cake would help. A mouthful or two was great, the remainder wrapped up and secured in a side pocket, to join spanners and tyre repair outfit. There was a silent hope that no adjustment or repairs would become necessary, especially as there were no tyre-levers amongst the spanners. No hope of finding a couple of kitchen spoons on the open road, perhaps, either.

Both rucksacks carefully stowed and secure, trouser bottoms tucked into socks, the tandem was rather thoughtfully wheeled into an open position. Push-bikes are great. But tandems for beginners high up and faced with the rugged fell? Oh well, try it gently at first. Taking a firm grip on the front handlebars, Alec slung a leg across the frame. Astride the machine, holding it steady, feet firmly on the ground, Ben joined him astern. Both stood for a moment, braced, ready for the off, feet in the clips of the raised pedals. Push down, scramble a bit, maybe, shove feet on the opposite side into their clips, away we go! Crazy wobbling in a mad zigzag line over the bumpy terrain gave way to reasonable stability. This was great – a piece of cake – this was going to be a breeze, OK? Confidence, that's it. Progress became excellent until an unseen stone found the front wheel. What a surprise! Tandem and crew went flying, legs all over the place. The whole outfit came to a jolting stop. Alec thought he'd split his jacket. Ben lay on his back on the ground where he'd been kind of pitch-forked, and just laughed. 'By gum, that were a good 'un,' he said. 'Come on, let's have another go.' They did, first relieving the machine of bits of mud and grass. 'Right,' he said, 'let's take off.'

Feet rammed once more into pedal clips, the machine held steady, a firm shove and away they went in another proving run. It was wonderful. Alec got into the spirit of things and, taking an extra firm grip, crouched low over the racing handlebars. Lowering his head and shoulders to assist streamlining, he found a helpful gear and they were away! On impulse, he rang the bell. What a shock! It didn't produce the result he expected. It let out the most piercing whistle like an express train. Immediately taking control right out of Alec's hands, legs and feet, the machine shot forward like an arrow. Well, there was no stopping it now. With the two adventurers holding on for dear life, feet and legs revolving like frantic fly-wheels driven by high-powered dynamos and with pedals flashing in the sun, the tandem flew round in ever widening circles. It slowed right down after this, causing its riders to wobble about and almost lose their balance. But there was no getting off.

The machine clearly had a mind of its own. A brooding power trembled through its purple frame demanding that its crew "stuck with the ship." It began to circle once more, quite slowly. You could say it was trying to decide upon a plan. To make up its mind. There was not long to wait. Speed ratcheted up. The tandem took a straight line, went faster and faster until, travelling at break-neck speed, it tore across to the far extremity of the Ingleborough summit. Alec went pale. Ben shut his eyes and held on. They were heading for the most severe drop to the regions below.

No stopping now. No brakes – they had ceased to function. Two pairs of knuckles clung on and went white. Here was the edge. Over went the whole outfit – men, machine – whoooshhh! I can't say that either rider shouted "Geronimo," but there was a shout mounting to a shriek, which, ripping, echoing right across the countryside, found its way into local folklore. It was time to abandon contact with pedals, fling legs out sideways and if possible enjoy the trip. Strangely enough, following the frightening launch, the downward journey at hair-raising speed was remarkably smooth, despite everything the terrain had to offer. Exhilarating! Here was a machine and a half. With dirt, dust, stone, shale, it seemed half the countryside, mud and water, flung up in turn or all at once, down shot the purple tandem no matter what, until sliding, skidding to a dramatic stop below, quite near to a small church. They had arrived in Chapel-le-Dale, a little village near to Ingleborough's foot. A passer-by merely bid them 'Good day' and after advising them about services, and saying the vicar was a grand lad, simply continued on his way following the sign to Ingleton. The two riders could hardly speak. Not surprising!

You might imagine the travellers and their steed would have offered a sight to cause comment. Not at all. The two riders and the purple wonder presented the kind of reasonable and respectable appearance you might ever hope to see anywhere, not least in the vicinity of a place of worship. Clothes were a little dishevelled, true, but otherwise in good order. And the purple paintwork was as smart as ever. It would be fair to say the cyclists were rather breathless and decidedly unbelieving when looking up again at the great fell and their route down from the very top of it. But generally they were in good form. Maybe rocking a little, as you might be after one of the more imaginative theme park rides. They were still hungry.

'By gum, I wouldn't want to do that in the dark,' Ben said. 'I don't suppose anyone will believe us if we ever tell them about it. Can't really credit that we did it at all. What a lark. Talk about a Cresta run.' The sun now shone warmly, accompanied by a slight, very welcome breeze. Managing to dismount, the friends propped the tandem against a nearby wall which offered a bit of shade. They sat down, their backs against its mossy stones, legs stretched out in the soft grass in front of it and considered their position. The meal. Ah, yes. After something of a breather, they remounted their machine and, following the signpost, pedalled towards Ingleton, keeping an eye open for any advertisement that indicated food. At last, "All day breakfast" announced an establishment. The time had arrived. They got off, parked the machine and went inside. What a pleasure it was to exchange saddle for a comfortable chair, quiz the bill of fare, order, rest awhile and prepare to set to. Bliss!

The little café looked like many another you might expect to find. You've seen them with their menus hanging, peering through the steam in the front window. The place was fairly well filled with holiday-makers at closely-set tables, each complete with its own cloth, cutlery, pepper, salt and sticky sauce. It was warm inside. A very slow, old, electric fan creaked round up in the ceiling, hoping it was helping.

Alec and Ben's order arrived. Egg, bacon, sausage, mushrooms, black pudding, tomato and fried bread, so much looked forward to, lay before them. A cup of tea put the finishing touch. The meal was terrific. As it gradually drew to a close, there were questions as to what it might be fun to do next. All might depend on ideas their oddly determined machine might hold in its purple frame.

The two late breakfasters sat back and relaxed, but before long it really was time to move. The bill would have to be settled. Ben got to his feet and, weaving quite unnoticed between the tables, made his way towards the till, perched high on the end of a counter loaded with sauce bottles, squash bottles, glasses, sheaves of straws and packets of biscuits. A highly ornamental glass cake-stand filled with every kind of stickiness, mercifully more or less covered with a glass dome (a bit cracked) stood in command.

Arriving in cakeland, Ben cleared his throat to draw anyone at all's attention from the far reaches beyond. A rosy, smiling figure, topped by a chef's hat, appeared. Before Ben could speak, the face from under the hat gave a broad grin and said quietly: 'On the house.' With this, figure, face, grin and hat were gone. Hadn't that face seemed a little familiar? There was no chance really to respond, but Ben called out a surprised and grateful "thank you." Pondering somewhat, he weaved his way back to Alec, to tell him what had happened. Again, despite jogging the odd elbow, for which he apologised, shoving someone's forkful of spaghetti way past the expectant mouth, his home run as before was entirely unnoticed. Alec was pleased and amazed at the unexpected generosity of the management. 'Lucky old us,' he laughed.

Outside once more, in the sunlight, it was great to have a good stretch. Ben gave a huge yawn. Recovering, he said without any hesitation – 'Morecambe, we must head west to Morecambe.' He was rather surprised to find himself suddenly saying this. A small sound, and he noticed their two-seater had shifted itself just a bit along the trunk of the shady tree they'd parked it under, out of the sun. Was it restless, like a racehorse pawing the ground impatient for the starter's flag?

'Morecambe?' Alec laughed, 'Why Morecambe?' The whiff of fish and chips they'd caught, drifting to them on top of Ingleborough, had long since been forgotten. 'Morecambe?' he said again. 'Alright then, what d'you reckon is our best way?'

A small stationer's just up the road seemed likely to be of assistance, being full of that magical kind of stuff any good stationer provides. Maps, that were it, maps! Inside, the shopkeeper, a solid, cheerful little man sporting a fine weskit and chain, was immediately helpful in pointing to a stand full of maps for almost anywhere you could imagine. Ben thanked him and gave the revolving display a gentle spin. Loaded as it was, it lurched and creaked a bit as he worked it round. He was distracted for a moment by packs of deliciously coloured pencils and shiny sticks of sealing wax eager to be melted and blobbed to feed signet rings and seals. Suddenly, there flipped out, hit the floor and fell right open – "Easy routes to Lancaster and Morecambe." Here was their map, the very one they wanted! It wasn't all that expensive, in fact a real bargain price, so much so that Ben bought a couple of colourful, scenic postcards, too, without any idea to whom he might send them. Alec smiled, he knew Ben of old. But finding the right map was tremendous.

The two of them sat on a seat under the shady tree sheltering the tandem, to look at their bargain, which they opened right across their combined knees. They had to juggle with it a bit. And hoped it would be easier when it came to folding it up. But their route, yes, there it was of course – make for Lancaster and then head for the sea. Sounded simple enough.

The purple machine gave a great lurch and nearly parted company with the trunk that supported it. Had it slipped, or just wanted to be on the move? Don't think it was bothered much about maps.

'Are we ready for off, then?' said Ben, gathering what seemed like acres of bargain chart, struggling a little, finally folding it up and stowing it in a saddlebag pocket. 'We'll take our time,' he said, 'enjoy the trip.' They wheeled the tandem out into the sunshine and comfortably climbed aboard.

'Ready?' said Alec, 'off we go then.' Deep breath, steady pressure on the pedals, machine and passengers moved smoothly out to the open road. Well, you might have imagined Alec would have learnt his lesson, but feeling really great now, he delightedly pinged the bell. Whoa! With its riders hanging on for dear life, the tandem shot off down the road, careered round a couple of corners and headed at break-neck speed to the great beyond!

On this beautiful day, for such it was, the journey with the combination of physical force, purple intent, and a following wind, simply flew. Add the surrounding scenery and run of the road, it was at times little short of spectacular! On, on, head through Lower Bentham, on to Claughton and down to Lancaster.

There were a number of tense moments when it became necessary to hold on with utter tenacity as the

road rose and fell and shot round every conceivable kind of bend. The machine jolting and bouncing over bits of road awaiting repair, the spanners in the saddlebag frantically rattled and clinked quite alarmingly. At certain bone-shaking moments, the two riders could only hope the tyre repair outfit would be allowed to remain unused. And just as well each saddle was relatively kind! Willy-nilly, on flew the racing partnership – men and purple machine, squirting up all manner of grit and wildly splashing through abandoned puddles. Other traffic on the road was more or less skilfully avoided. A few narrow squeaks were sometimes unavoidable when surprise vehicles appeared from nowhere. On one occasion, rounding a bend, there all of a sudden was a vast tractor and loader, farm trailer trundling at a snail's pace. What a relief when it turned into a stackyard!

On, on, scattering shrieking chickens wandering and pecking across the road (no doubt trying to get to the other side). A horse quietly leaning over a dry stone wall, tossed its mane, snorted and galloped away to the safety of a distant meadow. There weren't many people about. An old man (a one-time mariner, perhaps, in his thick, dark blue seaman's jersey) sat on half a wheelbarrow in a gateway and smoked his pipe. Hearing the approaching whirlwind, he leapt to his feet, almost lost his cap, blew out a blue, coughing cloud of tobacco smoke and promptly sat down again with a bump. His pipe shot out of his mouth, hit the ground and rolled into a clump of nettles. 'By gow,' he exploded to his faithful collie dog, who just thrashed his tail about, looked up at him and laughed. On, on! But hold it! Lancaster in sight. Must surely go steady through the town. Stoppppp!

Fair to say, the journey to Lancaster had at times been hair-raising, yes, but a great lark. Calm down and collect a few thoughts for what might lie ahead. Any townsfolk seeing the smart purple tandem now smoothly and considerately pedalled through their streets, politely halting at crossings, rightly stopping at traffic lights, could hardly guess at the frantic exploits that had gone on before. But as far as the friends could tell, no one took any notice at all! There was no time really to ponder, certainly no time to visit the castle, which was a pity all round. Heigh-ho – forward to Morecambe.

Chapter Four

Arriving at the seafront, it didn't seem too bad an idea to ease off a bit. So, tandem parked out of the way, protected from sand occasionally gusted up by the salty breeze, its crew walked a little, eased their legs, loosened up their shoulders and looked around. After a bit, they discovered a couple of vacant deckchairs along the promenade, moved them to a spot in the sun, sat stretched out and, almost lost amongst the gaudy stripes, contemplated Morecambe's great cockling bay – the tide was out – spreading away into the distance. Time to relax, let go. Warm, salty airs wafted them into deep, deep contentment. Time stood still. Dozing.

'Ay-oop, ay-oop, gentlemen.' Ben, Alec, were instantly awake, trying to place the voice. 'Pay oop at t' kiosk if tha please, afore tha goes,' said a retreating figure over his shoulder. He had lodged a couple of tickets in the top pocket of the sleeping Alec's jacket. There had been just a split second to take in half a face. The voice seemed oddly familiar. Now, fully alert – better react, grab the tandem, head for "t' kiosk". Pay and try to find out. Pushing the machine along the promenade, seagulls wheeling and squealing (one swooped down and pinched a small boy's sandwich) was very jolly indeed. Children and adults jostled everywhere clutching windbreaks, sun hats, buckets, spades and babies, in every direction. Joyous shouting. There was, too, much activity down on the sands. One person struggled with a monster kite shaped like a shark, all gnashing menace. One minute it almost dragged him off his feet, the next diving, thrashing, threatened to gobble up every holidaymaker within reach. Fun all round!

Ah, here was "t' kiosk". Prop the tandem against it. Alec fished out the tickets. The beaming proprietor said nowt at all about t' brass. He just smiled and promptly offered two small dishes of cockles. (After all, it was Morecambe.) He pulled out his watch, on a long golden chain, from his waistcoat pocket, looked at it, smiled and said: 'Time's going on, I'm thinking.' Smiling again, he reached up, pulled down the overhanging shutter, murmured 'good afternoon' and closed for the day. He was gone before either biker could say anything at all. Ben wasn't keen on cockles. Alec grinned, finished the lot! That voice, so familiar!

The day was delightfully fine. Why not a spell down on the beach? Surely it would be fun to cycle across to Grange-over-Sands or, perhaps, try somehow to make it to Cartmel, see the remains of the old abbey. The tandem was leaning against the cockle kiosk. But not quite where they'd left it. For some reason this didn't seem odd. Taking hold of it, they bumped down the nearby steps, arrived on the beach and, dodging more than one mad kite, got back on their saddles. Trying to avoid lagoons and creaks left by the retreating tide, they pedalled off across the bay.

Everything was going very well indeed. So brilliant out in the seaside air. Why not stop awhile, enjoy the fabulous view? Yes, and have a go at the sausage rolls, squash and bags of crisps bought from amongst the sticks of rock, bags of sweets and shrimping nets at the promenade shop. It really was magnificent being out in the warm breeze. There were several great greedy seagulls to agree. How big some of them looked at close quarters, parading and prodding about looking for absolutely anything to eat!

But what's this, sky beginning to darken? Breeze was chilly now. Sausage rolls and such were going down really well, although eating a bit awkward, perhaps, straddling the tandem at the same time, but it had seemed best not to lay it down on the sand. Squash bottle poised in mid-swig, Ben suddenly gasped. The whole beach started trembling, shaking, shuddering, heaving. This was not imagination. Movement was violent now. Then everything stopped, leaving just an eerie silence. It lasted no time at all. From a shallow creek just ahead, two madly-blinkered, ghastly grey coach horses' heads reared up, flinging sand from their manes and snorting it from wide, gaping nostrils. Then their whole bodies, out they came in full gleaming harness secured between great, prancing, brass-tipped shafts.

In a burst of sand, cockles and lugworms, here, shaking itself free in all its black and gold livery streaked with sand and seaweed and leaping on powerful old springs, rose the great coach itself in all its decorated magnificence. With lamps burning, coachman with his whip, reins in hand, what a sight to marvel at! And what might that be emblazoned on the doors? Hanging on behind clung a white-faced guard, trying to dislodge sand from his post-horn and vigorously shaking head and shoulders free

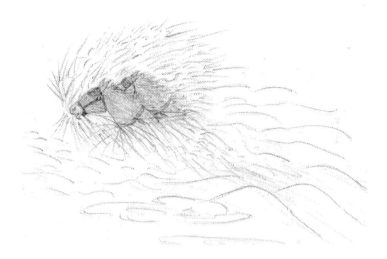

of the salty particles still clinging to his heavy coat and cockaded topper. The coach windows were shut, but as its red brocaded curtains stirred, was that a gaunt face peering from inside? If so, to whom might it belong, and would there have been other passengers? The straining horses dragged the coach clear, gathered themselves and raced off with it, sand flung out from the flailing spokes of its red and yellow wheels. A bold flourish of the whip, the whole spectacle disappeared into the distant gloom. No trace, no sound, nothing.

It was some time before any sense of reality returned. Very thoughtfully, Ben slowly completed his swig and closed his mouth. He turned to Alec, who'd had a sausage roll in mid-bite. His jaw had ceased to work. Everything began to function once more. The few crumbs to fall to the sand, he'd leave for the seagulls. Still a bit stunned, he, too, found it difficult to speak. Ben left their machine and walked to where he was sure everything had happened. Imagination? Huh! But there was nothing to see.

Absolutely nothing. The area was completely undisturbed. He walked back. At last able to speak, 'What d'you reckon to all that?' he said to Alec.

Handing control of their machine to Ben, a very disbelieving Alec went and looked for himself. Returning, 'Search me,' he said, 'but there are local legends hereabouts, saying what, over the years, the quicksands have swallowed up.' The two bikers stood for some time, looking round and peering into the distance. Suddenly, Alec said: 'Can't hang about, let's push on.' After stowing away the remnants of their refreshment, they did, making rather wobbly progress into the bay.

The sun had come out again and all round people could be seen busy about their own business in such a way as to suggest they had seen nothing, been aware of nothing that the two companions were quite certain they had witnessed.

Neither rider was concentrating much, minds still very full of what they were convinced they had seen. No one was going to make them think it had all been imagination. What of their purple tandem? They'd become rather used to it. But were they taking it for granted? From time to time, it had done strange things. What might it be likely to do next? Almost immediately, the going became harder.

Suddenly, there was a challenging shout. In the far distance, a man in dark blue seaman's jersey and trousers and wearing sea-boots, was waving wildly. He came half-running towards them, arriving breathless and in a great state of agitation and alarm. 'Quicksands! You don't want to be out here, look yonder, t' tide's coming in. It comes in that fast, people get cut off and so will you. Trapped, lose lives, lose everything! Some folks say, they do, a coach and horses went down in these here quicksands a couple of hundred years ago. Heading for Grange-over-Sands, they were, but never made it. Can't say I believe it meself. Some folks will say anything if there's an audience and they've a mind to scare 'em. But don't stop here. Look sharp, let's be off. Follow me, known the place since a lad. Call me t' sand pilot, they do.'

Judging by his appearance, it seemed very likely that he knew what he was talking about. Best take his advice, he certainly didn't hang about. After a few strides he looked back and, seeing no immediate response, shouted: 'Come on you two, no time to waste.' Off he went again, waving his arm towards the distant promenade. The tandem was turned round and pedalled off to join him. But after a few yards, there was no going any further, progress came to a jerking stop. Both riders almost fell off as their front wheel, grabbed by wet sand, rapidly started to sink and very soon was down to its hub. Half falling, half scrambling, first Alec – almost thrown over the racing handlebars – and then Ben straddling sideways, abandoned their saddles. Their would-be rescuer and guide turned again. Shocked by what he saw, he shouted: 'Leave t' owd bike, leave it and save yersens!' People on the promenade, although a considerable way off, heard the shouting, stopped what they were about and looked anxiously across the sands. Someone panicked and alerted the offshore lifeboat. A kite-flyer became tangled in his kite string, sending the object of his endeavours into a loop and dive, frightening the life out of an unsuspecting party of picnickers.

Trying to wrestle the tandem clear failed immediately. The front wheel being sucked out of sight was dragging the rest of the machine down with it. Efforts to stop this were hopeless. The tide was beginning to race in, spreading out and deepening at an alarming rate, just as had been warned. Creeping and bubbling across the sands, it was now starting to swish over the rather inadequate shoes of its victims and in through the lace-holes. Efforts to free the handsome purple tandem were really frantic now. The battle was fast being lost. Both bikers heaved and struggled, only making things worse.

'Stick with it, we can do it,' Alec spat out from between gritted teeth. Why wasn't he at a comfortable dig somewhere, unearthing even a run of the mill mosaic, he thought to himself. 'Come on Ben,' he urged. Ben was doing his best, not only to save the machine, but very definitely the panniers rigged each side of the back wheel and the saddlebag hanging on behind, together holding uneaten food and their worldly belongings. Strained to bursting, a button shot off his shirt. He tried to shut out thoughts of a pie and a pint at a favourite pub with a party of students. His ankles were almost submerged now. Half a dozen cockles rose up, swirled round, turned over, sank and disappeared. Help!

Drifting slowly, high out of the sun, appeared a hot-air balloon, all poise and commanding calm. A quaintly shaped, yellow hot-air balloon. Now, you're going to say, what could possibly be new about that? The ballooning world is full of such. Well, here was a good 'un, wearing a bowler hat – a glorious bowler chapeau with a candle stuck in its hatband. On, on it drifted in complete silence. Starting to descend, its shadow began to spill across the stranded travellers and their rapidly sinking purple machine, unable this time to respond and take charge as it had in times past.

'Stuck?' whispered down a quiet voice. The two increasingly desperate young men stopped what they were trying to do, twisted round and looked up. They were astonished as they took in the bowler-hatted wonder, and leaning out of its basket, its pilot's head and shoulders – helmeted, goggled, flying jacketed. There came a wave from a gauntleted hand. The aviator smiled widely and gave a chuckle. The two adventurers, stuck in the muck, so to speak, were mightily relieved, I can tell you.

'Think on lads,' said the balloonist as his craft floated down, its basket hovering, slightly spinning over the hazardous wetness below. 'Hook oop,' came the command. 'Hook oop,' came again. Two hooks, each on its own rope, snaked down from the side of the basket. They accurately dangled just over the stricken tandem. What's all this about? Confusion. Who? What? How? But now, quick thinking! Ben grabbed one rope, Alec the other and, as best they could, attached them to what they hoped would be a point of balance on the frame of the purple machine. 'Right lads, hop aboard,' came the invitation. More amazed than ever and by now very nigh exhausted, the two lucky escapers managed to heave themselves up and over into the basket. Saved! Ask questions, work it all out later.

'Well done, lads,' the pilot laughed, turned to his burner and gave it a blast. His great balloon rose slowly and majestically, the two ropes tautened, the two hooks tightened. One purple tandem was gradually and safely drawn from the deadly danger sucking it to destruction. It was made secure, outboard along the basket side. The whole purple frame, looking entirely untouched by the drama, gleamed in the sunlight and would be ready for who knew what. A thin trail of sand and seaweed dripped from its perfect tyres and blew away across the wind.

The sea-booted, would-be rescuer, who had tried so hard to help, clambered back to the promenade, looked up and waved to the departing flyers.

'Was there much happening on the beach today?' asked his wife when he returned home.

'Just a bit of kite flying and a few kids messing about,' she was told. He seemed to have no recollection of any drama whatsoever. (Or, maybe, he was just not telling!)

Flying high in the safety of the balloon's basket and carried smoothly across the sunlit countryside was, especially after the quicksands scare, pretty wonderful. Periodic bursts on the burner to maintain balloon height were the only things to disturb the peace. An occasional, enterprising bird arrived and perched on the side of the basket for a minute or two, peered in looking for crumbs. The pilot didn't say much. He was pretty busy flying his craft: checking altitude, wind-speed, drift, compass reading, one or two meteorological details. The two survivors rested in the bottom of the basket, but from time to time got to their feet to look at the countryside below. They hadn't the slightest idea where they were heading.

You might suppose they would be keen to consider their saviour, but just relaxing and enjoying the flight was, at the moment, enough. They vaguely became aware of breeches, gaiters and hobnailed boots below the flying jacket, but really gave very little thought about anything right then.

Opening one eye, Alec took in a waistcoat (weskit?). Spanning across it, from pocket to pocket, winked a gold watch chain. A fob shaped like a horse's head dangled and spun. Peering over the basket-side to scrutinise some object in the terrain below, the pilot raised his goggles for a clearer view.

'Kitted good and proper, Alva,' Alec said, 'but by gum, you saved our bacon!' His mind shot back to the proprietor in Ingleton who had provided their map. And how about t' cockle kiosk? What of the golden watch chain seen there too? Alva again? Alec scratched his ear and tried to remember. He looked towards the pilot and gave Ben a nudge.

'How are you, gentlemen?' Alva said. The balloon flew on, rising and falling in response to blasts from the burner, air pockets, thermals, up-draughts and odd moods of wind and weather. Morecambe became a distant dot. A friendly gust, bowler hat and passengers soared in stately fashion right across into the Yorkshire Dales.

Chapter Five

There was grand chat in the basket, as you can guess. Ben said he'd had no idea that Alva might come to their rescue. Jolly grateful to be hauled to safety, though. 'What a stupendous balloon,' he said. The whiz of a trip down the twisting tube and Gilbert's banqueting arrangements made a good laugh. Grand surprise finding the ancient staircase up to Ingleborough. 'Never thought I'd ride a tandem,' Ben said. 'Didn't expect to find one on Ingleborough.'

'Forget about ballooning, Alva, try a high-speed bike ride down the side of Ingleborough,' Alec said, laughing. 'Give you an appetite.'

'You'll be glad to have landed safely at t' bottom,' Alva replied. He had by now replaced his flying helmet and goggles with his more interesting and familiar flat-crowned, wide-brimmed, be-furred hat. 'By gum, it must all have been reight exciting,' he said quietly. Conversation by now really on the go, Ben told of Ingleton and of the free, full English breakfast. Not a great deal was made of the stationer's map, but their wild, reckless, bone-shaking, break-neck career down to Morecambe was described in graphic detail. Alva's canny smile made it reasonably clear that he had known what the two friends were in for from the start. What else might he have in mind?

It was a bit of a struggle, but Alec leant out of the basket, reached the tandem, managed to grab sausage rolls and one or two bags of crisps from one of the panniers, and handed everything round. He couldn't be sure this sort of fare would suit Alva. But it did. Enjoyed it. The balloon went on waltzing and floating for a while. Time had serenely ceased to matter very much.

'We're about there,' Alva said, taking a bite out of his sausage roll. He leaned out and took another squint at the ground below. Where could this be, thought Alec. He peered over the side of the basket and began to fully take in the scene below.

'Ah yes,' Alva murmured: 'Ingleborough.' He made one or two technical adjustments, brought the balloon to a hover, then gradually took it down.

This kind of flying had been something new for Alva's two passengers. Excited, but a little nervous, they braced themselves against the basket side. Their pilot had chosen as flat a spot as he could. Slowly, the balloon floated to earth. To the two inexperienced flyers, it was positively rushing up to hit them! Spotting their concern, Alva assured them that he had done all this before, many times, declaring, 'There's nowt for either of you to fret ower.' He wasn't sure if they believed him, but did his best with a laugh of encouragement. There was a bump and another and another as the basket danced and skipped, jolting to rest in a lively tilt. The two passengers tumbled over each other, just managing to stay in control. They recovered, scrambled clear, rolled over and stood up. 'Did tha like that?' laughed Alva, brushing himself off and rubbing an elbow.

'A lot of fun,' Ben managed to say.

'A great buzz, the whole flight, sorry it's over,' Alec said with a kind of wild laugh.

'Grand,' said Alva, uncoiling a mooring rope hooked into the basket. 'Fasten this to yonder hawthorn, you two lads, now, will tha please?' he said. He'd spotted the old stunted tree when beginning his landing. After a bit of a struggle between the thorns, basket and balloon were safely anchored. 'Give t' basket a bit of a shove,' called Alva. 'I want us to be off directly. We shan't need t' tandem.' The basket was heaved upright to his satisfaction and ready for lift off. Just this minute landed, thought Ben, and we've to be off again. What and where could this mean? But the sun had gone in, light beginning to fade. There was really no point in trying to guess the future after all that had taken place.

Alva remained in the basket busy with technical matters. Looking up and leaning out, he said: 'I've some things here you two lads should have.' From his left-hand weskit pocket he produced a very familiar-looking little red stone. 'Ay oop,' he shouted and with his thumb and forefinger expertly flicked the little object to Ben. It flew through the air in a high arc. Ben stretched and caught it with the skill of a cricketer fielding at first slip. From the opposite pocket, out came the green stone that Alec had treasured since boyhood. It flew to him like an arrow. He closed his fingers on it before really knowing what he was doing. Those were the stones, you will remember, which in the blink of an eye had released two border collies a while ago. Alec certainly remembered. But where might the dogs be now, was the question. No time for that at present, he smiled to himself.

'Right, lads,' called Alva, 'how about another trip? Set t' purple fella back where tha found it. It'll do for t' next, happen.' Next? Who might be next to take on the wild machine? Someone was in for a surprise, for sure! 'When you've done, let t' rope off and climb back aboard.' The tandem was unhooked and wheeled on its still perfect tyres to where it had first been found. It was carefully propped back against the same pile of stones. Ben undid the saddlebag, retrieved their two rucksacks and handed them to Alec. He couldn't help looking in the side pocket which held the noisy spanners and repair outfit. There they all were, so was the brown paper packet with the pieces of mint cake they had not eaten when the tandem was first discovered. He put the packet back and strapped it up. Someone (who?) would be glad of it some day, he thought. It would do for t'next, as Alva had put it.

Ben paused and looked admiringly at the sleek machine. It was going to be odd, walking away from it, after everything that had happened and after the way both he and Alec had survived. The friends turned away and paid attention to Alva in the waiting balloon. They briefly turned back to the tandem for one very last look. Was there just a movement, a shift in the purple frame? Could there be more than a glint from those silver spokes? Maybe the setting sun was merely teasing them. An ancient figure in open-necked shirt, jacket, plus fours, long socks and white, old-fashioned tennis shoes, appeared and, taking the tandem by its handlebars, very slowly and quietly wheeled it away. A very keen ear might just have detected the tiniest ting from the bell. But that was all. Suddenly, the tandem shot back into view, white tennis shoes furiously pedalling in front, dignified old lady clutching at her hat and grimly holding on behind; all to be swallowed up into the far distance in a cloud of pebbles and grass. The two lads were almost speechless. Alec looked at Ben. Ben looked at Alec. 'What d'you make of that?' they said at last, almost together.

Back in the balloon, pilot Alva called rather urgently to his two passengers: 'Na then lads, shall we be off?' Neither of the friends, a little lost in thought, perhaps, had intended to hold up the balloon's departure, but just had no idea how long they'd been away from it. 'Let go t' rope, lads,' came the shout, 'and we'll fly.' Together they released the line from the stunted little tree, which had served as anchor. No need to do very much else for, released, the rope leapt free with a mighty "twang", zipped through the air on its own and made straight for the balloon, where it settled itself in a series of neat hanks on a peg at the side of the basket. Well!! The two friends fairly sprinted for that basket, I can tell you, and flung themselves in before it might rise beyond their grasp! Alva gave a surprised laugh, reached up and gave a quick burst to his burner, sending a spurt of eager flame leaping into the billowing, slightly sagging envelope above him. He shouted, 'Here we go.' Swiftly, balloon – now glowing cheerfully in the developing dimness – basket, Alva the ostler, Alec and Ben rose up into the evening sky with not much else but the burner to light it. But what was that intermittent signal flashing way across to the west?

As if drawn, the balloon, after spinning a little, began heading westwards. No doubt about it, helped as it was by a gentle but insistent current of air. Down below, lights winked and twinkled from households and dwellings.

Here and there, brightness broke free – seemingly glad to be released – from front doors opened at last for people to emerge into the night. Voices in conversation were easily heard in the surrounding stillness. 'Not much moon yet, then?' floated up as clear as you like. Balloon and balloonists drifted on and on. And as if to contradict the talkers below, the gleaming disc stole out, full-faced, from behind a trail of misty cloud, which finally parted to release a million stars. All was peace in the basket. Pilot Alva stirred himself and his burner at shrewd intervals. His two passengers, who had subsided to the basket floor and drifted into an easy snooze, slumbered on. The gentle voyage continued.

There came a freshness to the air. It was now becoming quite light, and chilly with it. Rousing himself and trying not to disturb the still sleeping Ben, Alec slowly got to his feet and looked out from the balloon. Such a saltiness met him. Very quickly, he was wide awake, and what's more, decidedly hungry. The basket taking a sharpish tilt and an upward jerk woke Ben and brought him, too, to his feet. His eyes opened wide. In the distance was the sea with its lighthouse, which they were approaching at increasing speed. Alva smiled. Looking for a landing site, he spotted a wide, smooth grassy stretch spreading right across the cliff top and began skilfully to bring his balloon down. A large herring gull (very large at close quarters), turning up and attempting to land on the edge of the basket, caused Alva great surprise, the burner to receive an unexpected burst.

'Sorry,' said the gull. 'Call me Sam if you like,' he confided. 'But you weren't too far off one or two family nests along the cliff there. Might I suggest you try landing in that field – no nests there, just the odd camper's tent, perhaps, much more easy to miss, I would say.' The handsome bird flew off.

'Well then, we'll try again,' Alva remarked. He flew his craft in with Sam's directions in mind. Not too easy, for a stiffish breeze had sprung up. In fact, the whole rig started to rock and buffet as it drew closer to the ground, causing Alva's passengers to guess anxiously at the potential impact with the earth when finally (very shortly) they landed. Both braced themselves and held on very tight. In the event, the whole aerial apparatus, in the most skilful of hands, serenely floated and touched down as gently as you like. The two adventurer balloonists heaved a huge sigh of relief and finally felt able to release their fierce grip on the side of the basket. A glance between them said, quite clearly – whatever next!

'Now then,' called their pilot, 'reckon that surprised thi. Grand landing, eh?' He went on: 'Caught your thoughts a while back. Getting a bit peckish, if I'm not much mistook. Hop out. Explore a bit, see what you can find. I doubt you'll have much bother.' He chuckled and was pretty certain his passengers would discover a good deal more than the square meal he had in mind. Caught on the shoreline breeze, was something distinctly savoury. Alec slung a leg over the high-sided wickerwork and jumped to the ground.

'Come on, Ben,' he said, 'let's go.' He was soon joined outside on the grass. They both turned, looked up and said almost together: 'Great ride, Alva, thanks for the trip.'

'Right lads, I must be off. Leave you to your own devices,' was Alva's brisk reply. 'But – wait on.' At this, he bent down, obviously to locate something in the basket. Straightening up, he called, 'Here you are, lads, don't forget these.' In each hand he held a rucksack. 'Look out, here they come,' he called, as he lobbed them out. They were easily caught. He laughed and shouted, 'Well held. Cheerio, gentlemen, and all t' best.' He gave his balloon a quick "burn". Alec and Ben leapt aside, falling over each other and laughing as bowler and basket rose from the ground. A wave from Alva, his whole contraption sailed way up into space. Soon, all to be seen was a distant speck as he and it rose ever higher, diminishing now almost to a mere thought.

'That was a bit quick,' said Ben, picking himself up.

'It was that,' was the laughing reply as Alec rolled to his feet. 'But at least we've got the rucksacks back. I say, it's a bit nippy,' he went on, flinging his arms wide apart, then back again, thumping them hard across his body. 'By gum, that's better, brrrr! Alva must have had one or two things in mind, to shove off so quickly. But you never know what he might have up his sleeve. Keeps us guessing, doesn't he? Wish the sun would come out, though.'

Two noses trembled like compass needles seeking north. But the twitch was directed toward wafts of food that had been radiating definite signals the very minute – even before – the balloon had landed. Food, where was it? That way, was the shout. The two friends headed off across the landing ground, made for a gap between some brightly-painted beach huts, burst through and found themselves on Morecambe's promenade. Alva had set his course westwards, but said nothing about destination. The brisk, salty breeze bowling along the seafront offered encouragement to run flat out, get warm and hit the main target. Food! And what was more, the sun now began to appear. At last. Bulls-eye! Fifty yards ahead. Pace quickened, stride lengthened! No temptation to buy sun hat and shrimping nets, kites and the rest, offered for sale on the way, not much thought, either, for sticks of rock and postcard views. Not on your life! A last gasp, a final stride, there it was – the prize. "Fish and Chips. Proprietor Brenda Battersby." Funny, all at once that name seemed to ring a very familiar bell. Memory from their Dales village of childhood?

Hissing, bubbling, chuckling, the deep fat churned and heaved, gilding the fish and chipped potatoes that swam in it and filling the shop with such hospitality. The two hungry and slightly winded wayfarers stepped into Battersby's chip shop and its wonderfully warm "Frying tonight" (except it was daytime) embrace. Both gazed up at the bill of fare pinned against the wall.

'What'll it be, then?' said the very ample rosy figure leaning generously across her glass-fronted counter. Ignore the meat pies, fish cakes, crisply battered sausages trying to tempt. Next time, maybe. The request was for straightforward fish and chips, resulting in two grand pieces of fish and a mountain of the most golden chips. 'Salt and vinegar?' Brenda offered above the crackle of fat. They were quietly refused. 'Well, we're all different, I expect, aren't we?' she said. 'Enjoy everything.' Two finger-nipping-hot bundles of fish and chips, swathed first in greaseproof paper (optimistic or what?) then wrapped in newspaper, were smilingly handed over.

Remembering, pondering, it was impossible in later years to explain why no money was ever exchanged 'Pay me when next you're in. You're welcome,' had rolled across the counter. 'Must fettle me pigeons at the minute.' The jovial rosiness had turned and swayed out of sight towards the back of the shop. There was a fleeting moment to offer a "thank you", but that was all. And when might the fish and chip eaters next be in? They couldn't possibly guess. Out of the shop they went and wandered a step or two across the quiet road, to sit down on a low wall fronting the promenade and facing the sea. To make matters completely perfect, the sun came full out, skies looked bluer than ever. White clouds swirled and flew. Time to open the bundles. The food tasted good, very good. Even better eaten out in the open in the freshness of keen seaside air. There wasn't much talking. A clattering draught of wings. A seagull flashed in, stole a chip poised to enter Ben's mouth and was gone. An angry "oi", Ben was on his feet and shook a despairing fist. Settling way off on the beach, the bird plodded about as if trying to look innocent. There seemed every chance his thoughts were turning to another chip (maybe chips!). Bit of a character was our herring gull, Seagull Sam.

'Can't trust 'em gulls,' said a voice. It came from a figure of a man, not noticed before, a man of some years, sitting not far off on an old cask. Peaked cap, dark blue like his seaman's jersey, also his trousers tucked into stout sea-boots, here surely, was a man of the sea. There he sat, puffing on an old pipe. 'Ah,' he said, 'allus got an eye to the main chance, they seagulls. Grand day. On holiday, are you?' He fell silent, thoughtfully puffing away in a cloud of tobacco smoke. This suited the friends, busy as they were with their meal. He began again. 'Name's Davy, lived here all me life I have. Lighthouse keeper I was. Ever been on a lighthouse, have you?'

'No,' Alec said. Lived round here all his life, he must know where we could get a cup of tea, he thought to himself. I wouldn't mind a look at a lighthouse some time. He bundled up his, by now, empty fish and chip wrappings, stood up and cast round for a litterbin. 'Come on Ben,' he said, 'over here.'

A sudden shout from a distance away caught his attention just as his and Ben's empty bundles fell into the bin. The old seadog, where was he? Not sitting where he had been. Didn't see him go. But there he was, trudging his way right across the shore. 'Come on,' he shouted, 'if you're after a cup of  tea.' (How did he know?) 'My mates in the lighthouse will have the kettle on.' Cup of tea – tea in a lighthouse? That could be something special! Not far from the water's edge now, Davy was standing next to a sturdy clinker-built rowing boat, beached and comfortably tilted on its side as it lay close to the water, ready for action. 'Come on,' he shouted again, 'if you're after a brew.' A rather long-distance cup of tea seemed to be developing, but there was nothing for it but to give it a go.

'We're coming,' Ben called. Hoping their shoes would hold out, the two friends hiked through the sand, shingle and seaweed to the waiting craft.

'You'll have to give me a hand to shove her clear,' came the comment. 'I'd take your shoes and socks off if I were you. Sling 'em round yer necks.' Shoes quickly found themselves dangling as directed, and trousers rolled up. The three men pulled the boat upright, heaved, skimmed and swished her into the sea. As she began to float, Davy jumped in and began to ready the oars. The water became deeper, beach shelving away. It was above the knees, now, and the boat began sharply to rise and fall as the motion of the waves took over. First Ben, then Alec, grabbed at the gunwale, managed to scramble aboard and sit down.

'Here you lads, an oar each. Let's have your rucksacks, they'll only get in t' way.' Off came the items, quickly to find themselves stowed under Davy's position in the stern. 'I'll tak t' tiller,' he said. Not without a little difficulty, the two novice members of the sea-boat's crew mastered their individual rowlocks, adjusted their oars and sat down just a bit exhausted, it must be said, on their respective thwarts. 'Grand, grand,' said their helmsman. 'Give way together.' Alec and Ben began to row.

It was soon discovered that rowing at sea was a good deal tougher than on any old boating lake ashore. A bit hit and miss at first to keep their blades covered. Rhythm of stroke had to be worked out, to avoid painful collision between oars and bending bodies. Ben, rowing mid-ships, Alec in the bows, at first received one or two thumps to his back when Alec reached out to take another stroke. Every now and again, something of a chuckle combined with a 'well done' came from the tiller, but after a while his crew began to wonder just where they were heading. Could it be to a floating teapot, was Alec's waspish thought.

Rowing was becoming a little less amusing than when they first set out. The sea was now a bit choppy, boat jarring every time it dipped and butted into oncoming waves. And the sun was really starting to turn on the heat. They hadn't been rowing all that long, but it just seemed like it. And rowing back to front, as it were, you can't very well see where you're going. But just then: 'We're steering for yon lighthouse,' came from old Davy. At least that was a clue. The sea had become more agitated and rough. No one was feeling queasy (certainly not Davy), but at one point as spray was flung across his face yet again, Ben, bouncing off his thwart, trusted he and Alec were not actually in the hands of the Davy Jones of legend, and about to meet him in the dark depths below!

Seabirds wheeled and shrieked. Occasionally, one came down to bob and float on the sea. One actually swooped down to the boat to perch for a moment on the gunwale. It looked oddly like Sam the seafront chip pincher! Struggle against the lively sea continued. Davy, serenely in charge of the tiller, was clearly enjoying himself. Perhaps the only one on board? But the sea suddenly began to calm, surprisingly so. It turned almost to a millpond. The sun burnt less hot, disappearing in and out behind kindly clouds. It changed to a beautiful day.

'Steady, lads, steady, we're coming round, unship your oars,' came a stream of command. No longer propelled, the boat rocked, drifted and wandered. Responding to the tiller, it smoothly connected with some kind of soft sea-weedy underwater buffer and came to rest with a glancing bump. At last, able to turn round, something the companions first saw made them positively gasp. Standing proud, and would surely remain unmoved by any sea, was a magnificent lighthouse. The tall, shapely column reaching skywards – the pair could hardly believe their eyes!

'Jump ashore, one of you lucky lads,' commanded Davy, 'make the painter secure.' His two oarsmen very carefully stood up, a little stiffly, and tried to get their balance. Ashore, turned out to be the massively rugged platform the lighthouse stood upon. Steadying himself and managing to turn round, Alec spotted the painter stowed up in the bows, grabbed hold of it, steadied himself once more, placed a foot on the gunwale and jumped towards a mighty iron ringbolt jammed into the great rock Davy had pointed out. Fat bunches of slippery seaweed covering everywhere, didn't help much. Alec wildly slipped and scrambled, banged his knee (he has the scar to this day), but finally succeeded in making the boat secure. Don't ask what knot he used, maybe a round turn and two half-hitches remembered from Boy Scout days. But it held. 'You're next, young man,' said Davy. Ben balanced on the gunwale for a moment, gathered himself, then flung his body into mid-air to join Alec, who'd begun to make his way up some tricky, rather treacherous steps to the massive beacon. Davy smiled and slowly began to fill his pipe.

There was a chance, now, fully to take in the situation. The lighthouse stood some thirty metres high, twelve metres at its base, and was set on a dramatic, forbidding crag, as far as could be judged between thirty and forty metres in very rough uneven diameter, swirling and rising from the sea.

Anyway, it seemed about the biggest thing Davy's crewmen had ever had in their back pocket, so to speak. "Staggered" just about said it all, as they clambered and stumbled across its harsh, spiteful platform rising outrageously from the depths of the sea. Patches of seaweed doggedly clung on in wild attempt to soften it. But it remained formidable enough and Ben marvelled how the lighthouse could ever have been achieved to survive there. Seabirds had obviously defied the odds, and left their mark.

It was an extraordinary feeling, on arriving up close, to lay a hand on the massive stones that bonded so tightly together to form their commanding, cylindrical wonder, towering above. Standing in a doorway about ten metres up, at the top of a series of seriously iron rungs set into the stones, stood a man. As far as could be seen, he looked remarkably like Davy in his dark blue rig and tough sea-boots. Even at a distance, his face appeared similarly bronzed through long acquaintance with weather and sea. 'Ho, you down there,' he shouted, 'come up.' Ben looked up, the challenging climbing arrangements suddenly seemed to be longer and higher than ever. He looked at Alec with a look that seemed to say – what d'you think?

'Ahoy there,' came from Davy, who was now to be seen sitting comfortably in the stern of the rowing boat, leaning back on one elbow and puffing at his pipe. He'd unshipped the rudder and taken it inboard. His boat would rest easier, moored and waiting for the return trip. He'd pushed his cap a little to the back of his head and looked rather pleased with himself.

'Can the lads come up?' shouted the man at the top of the ladder.

'Aye, it'll be right,' Davy shouted back 'Go on, you two lads, look lively.'

Not really wanting to be first, but anxious not to be seen dithering, Ben stepped forward to the steepling rungs. He put his foot on the first, stretched up, took firm hold of the best within reach, heaved himself up and started to climb. Don't look down, his mind advised him. Taking a deep breath, he paused for a moment, gritted his teeth, grinned at Alec, then went for it, hand by sweaty hand! Not looking down took a bit of doing, I can tell you. Alec shouted a few words of encouragement. Rung by concentrating rung, Ben made it to the top, how long it had taken he hadn't the slightest idea. Didn't matter. The welcome relief at the top was something he was never to forget. Straightening up at last, he let out a great gust of air, he'd had no idea how tightly he had been holding his breath during his climb. Now released, full of courage after his triumph, he yelled down – 'Come up, there's nothing to it!' but didn't really expect Alec to believe him. There was a moment, now, to look round, take in the fantastic scene and the ever-changing colours of the sea.

Now it was Alec's turn. 'Oh, really?' he'd shouted back, when told there was nothing to it. Stepping up closer to the challenge, he gulped in a chestful of air, reached out, took hold of the cold iron, placed one foot on an early rung and began to climb. Time for him seemed to stand still. There was little noise other than the sea slapping somewhere against the massive rock which held the building. How remote this became to him, the higher he scaled. Even the seagulls kept as quiet as they could. He missed his footing once or twice and barked a shin. With just the merest glance below, he shook off a bead of sweat and went on. He even managed to admire the remarkably precise stonework, pondering the skill, guts and time it had taken to complete the build. But, by gum, the sea looking absolutely miles below (and deep) seemed at that moment to be more important than anything else. He wasn't used to climbing at this height, certainly not like this – hugging his first lighthouse – an experience denied most of us, I would expect, in our entire lives. Sticking with it, he made it to the top and, wonderfully relieved, scrambled into the building.

There was brief applause from Ben, the Davy look-alike and two other keepers. Chest still heaving, Alec thanked this reception committee and did his best to appear reasonably unconcerned as they gathered round to congratulate him, thumping his shoulders just a little too much, he felt!

'Come on in, then,' came the invitation. Leading off a pace or two from where they were all standing was a cheerful room with, amongst other things, a wooden table and chairs. On the table was a cribbage board, its little bone pegs upright and ready for action, dominoes spilled and tumbled about. A fat candle in a solid brass candlestick stood ready to light battle, after dark! Nearby shelves offered a number of books and charts. From stout, wall-held pegs and hooks, hung oilskins and sou'westers ready for rough times. There were storm lanterns where they could be grabbed at a moment's notice. Just a few framed pictures of family and rural scenes hung about the walls. But best of all, perhaps, was a very quizzical, wise old grey parrot, which tilted its head first one way, then the other and winked a bright, piercing eye as it took a leisurely stroll back and forth along its free-standing perch. 'Well, how are ye,' it kept repeating in a rather startling manner. Could this be a welcome, Ben thought, or was the bird demanding how he and Alec dared to barge in. A kettle could be heard just coming up to the boil. 'Fancy a cup of tea?' snapped the parrot. Maybe it was a welcome after all.

'Fancy a cup of tea?' echoed Davy's double, and promptly disappeared into a small galley nearby without waiting for an answer. He soon reappeared with mugs filled to the brim. After such a climb, the answer to his question was easy. It was good to sit down, relax for a spell, help legs to stop wobbling. Mugs of tea were pure genius.

'I'm Jack,' said the tea provider.

'Nathan, that's me, tea boat alongside!' said one of the other keepers who had just appeared, smiling broadly. 'Our other mate is Joshua. Josh, we call him. Know your names, we do. Been on a lighthouse before? We'll show you the big lantern directly.' Know our names? The two friends stared at each other. The proposition to inspect the light was just what both of them wanted most of all.

'Can't wait, thanks very much,' Ben said, mug halfway to his mouth. To make it to the very top of the lighthouse – wow!

'Well, when you've finished your tea, we'll mek a start,' was the suggestion. Finishing the tea didn't take long. Ben stood up and rather noisily scraped the legs of his chair across the floor, causing the resident cat, dozing in a corner, to jump to its feet. 'Sorry, puss,' Ben said. He needn't have worried, the animal calmed itself, stretched, yawned, padded slowly to him to begin purring loudly and rubbing his handsome jet-black fur round Ben's legs.

'Got a mind of their own,' said Jack, shaking his head. 'Can't never fathom 'em, specially not that one. Never mind, let's mek a start. Ah, but happen it'll be a bit draughty up top for you two young fellas. Wait on.' He stumped over to a cupboard partly built into one of the walls and opened both its double doors. Standing on the floor jostled two or three pairs of sea-boots. Neatly folded on wide shelves above were various items of warm clothing. Suspended on hooks inside the doors and handily framing a seaman's almanac on one side, a maritime calendar (looked new enough, but dated eighteen hundred and something) hung hanks of codline, excellent for almost everything, but certainly for tying round and holding together oilskins worn in rough weather. Jack briefly rummaged in amongst one of the shelves, smiled, then said to himself – 'These'll be grand.' Turning to his guests, he said 'Try these, lads.' He held out two seaman's thick woollen jerseys. After a real struggle to find ways into sleeves, shove heads through neck 'oles, and finally pulling down, fit was perfect. Twice. The two friends hardly knew how to thank him. But they did, and felt very nautical indeed! 'Up we go,' came the command.

One of the keepers led the way, which took the little party up a series of stairways past different and very interesting chambers at ever-higher levels. There was much to see within, but all seemed secondary to visiting the mighty lantern right up above, meeting with the great life-saving light, which would guide to safety mariners who in every weather had to grapple with the ever-changing night-time sea. There would be chance to delve into other matters, they thought, on the way down. And three cheers, the journey down would be more leisurely and less exhausting than the way up. At last, there!

'Lantern room, this,' said the keeper, 'and I'll show you t' lens gallery.' The friends walked round and were amazed. 'Powered by whale oil, that lamp,' said their guide. 'Clockwork turns it. Has to be wound up every half-hour. I'll show you that, too. Used to be candles,' he went on. 'Come outside now.'

Ben followed the keeper through a small door leading out into the open, to discover the great iron-ballustraded gallery, circling the lantern in its overhead dome. Wind whistled more than a bit, I can tell you. The view was spectacular, awesome!

'Come and take a look out here,' Ben called to Alec, who was at that moment being let into the secrets of this gigantic building. Both outside, now, the two young men explored the lofty gallery, every now and then leaning over its balustrade, as far as they dared, to enjoy the swirling waves washing and slapping against the lighthouse's massive rocky platform below. As they gazed out across the horizon on this beautiful day, it seemed to them the sea was beginning to quieten just a little, its waters gently heaving. Just enough energy to topple occasional white crests, spreading out and bubbling away into nothingness. A seagull, dropping, perhaps, for a rest on the easy sea, rocked slowly, peacefully with the rise and fall. It was Sam, quietly dozing.

But shock! Sudden, dark clouds. Sun shut out. Black darkness. Thunderclap to knock your head off! Fierce lightning, razor sharp, ripped and flashed about the sky. The whole lighthouse trembled as seas whipped to a frenzy thrashed against its walls. And the light not yet lit! Caught for once, the other two keepers went about their business and fought to ignite the life-saving beam. Some way off in the desperate dark glinted just a dart of light from the stern of a square-rigger, close-hauled, crew trusting its timbers, fighting hard to remain afloat. This was only the briefest glimpse offered to the two friends, drenched good and proper, salt water keenly smarting their eyes.

Chapter Six

There was no sound now. Alec raised himself on one elbow. Dear me, this shingle is uncomfortable and a bit damp. His companion seemed to have overcome all problems. Ben was asleep on a small patch of pebbles caught in the sun near the breakwater. Getting to his feet, Alec stretched and looked round, first at the sea, then at two people with their dog strolling across the beach. He turned, looked up and his gaze took him a little along the seafront, to its houses and shops. If he stood on tiptoe, he could just about see the name of that welcoming chip shop, set a little beyond the low wall fronting the promenade. "Bertha" something, was it? A beady-eyed seagull hovered for a moment, then flew off. Chips! On an old cask sat a man of some maturity, wearing a peaked cap, dark blue like his seaman's jersey, also his trousers, which were tucked well into his sea-boots. Every inch a mariner, life at sea had bronzed him good and proper. An aged pipe was clenched in his grizzled old jaw. A final puff, the blue smoke trailed and spiralled away. The old seadog slowly extracted the pipe from his mouth, inspected the bowl, flicked the stem free of spit, shook his head and heaved himself to his feet. He looked around and out across the sea as if searching for something, lifted his chin, sniffed the air and promptly disappeared. Alec stared, open-mouthed. His mouth closed very, very slowly. Recovering himself at last, he gave the slumbering Ben a shake, but not knowing in the least what he was going to say. Before he could frame anything remotely coherent, his attention was captured by an aerial object some way off. It was Alva and the balloon.

No doubt about it: just leaving the horizon and heading this way – a hot air balloon topped with a bowler hat. It slowly, very slowly, so slowly, floated its unhurried way towards the watchers on the shore. There was no sound for a long, slow time, as the balloon drifted closer. It was just possible, at last, to catch the harsh roar of the burner as Alva gave it a burst from time to leisurely time. Not a single member of the public, spread about the beach, so much as glanced up at Alva – now leaning right out of his basket – or his singular balloon. For that matter, they paid no heed, either, to Alec or his sparring partner.

Alva hovered overhead. His whole rig looked enormous. And still, neither man, woman nor child at play, picnic or paddling, was remotely aware. They were, however, admiring two or three seaside kites erratically plunging about just near the basket right over their heads.

Slowly, silently, Alva brought his craft down, to crunch gently on the beach, bounce up again a metre or so. He pushed up his goggles and took off a glove. 'Hello you two,' he said, reaching out a hand in greeting. 'How has thi been getting on? But wait on,' he said, throwing out a rope, 'mak this fast to yon breakwater, one of thi.' The two friends did it between them, making use of a stout and much barnacled old upright. That should hold it, they thought.

What on earth were the two friends to tell Alva, d'you think? They weren't even able to explain to themselves just how they came to be on the beach at this moment. Had they imagined the great lighthouse adventure? As to how their two rucksacks came to be hanging neatly from two red-rusted bolts sticking out of the breakwater timbers draped with bladder wrack and silky green angel's hair, completely defeated them.

Alva said, 'Now then, you two lads, tha looks just grand in thi seaman's jerseys, the pair o' thi, not seen them afore.' The "two lads" had already been wondering how on earth they came to be wearing them. Mind you, the dark blue jerseys were comfortable enough and really rather smart, they thought, with "Trinity House" emblazoned right across the chest. They still have them.

Anyone with anything of a weather eye at that moment, might have scanned just beyond the breakwater and seen an old seadog, clad in dark blue from head to toe, puffing on his pipe, whilst hunched on the gunwale of a rowing boat, beached and comfortably tilted on its side, where it had last left the sea and scrunched to a standstill. But then they might have been imagining, don't you think, in the dense coastal mist beginning to roll in? What do you reckon? Alva smiled. There were certain things only he knew. He wasn't about to explain. Not half the fun!

There was a good deal of activity all along the beach: picnickers, kite-flyers, frantic family cricket, volleyball, and people trying to change discreetly behind polite towels. See the empty deckchairs billowing, flapping, straining out into the breeze. Sail round the lighthouse and back in time for tea? Any minute now. But what lighthouse? Snorers, mouths wide open, lost to the world, couldn't have cared less. Nor the sun-worshippers, hardly a stitch on, still lying flat out on gaudy "terry", hoping to capture a tan. To be lobstered, more likely, and the sting that went with it. Ben loved it all. The more so, as it was quite clear that Alva, "his boys" and his balloon were entirely invisible. But, by gum, what about a snack? Not fish and chips, perhaps. A cup of tea and a biscuit seemed about right.

"Bertha Battersby's Fish and Chips" still declared themselves boldly over the shop. Bertha herself waved cheerfully at the passers-by. A voice from an elderly holidaymaker said to the party he was with: 'Used to be a fish and chip shop hereabouts, Bertha somebody, pity they knocked it down. Still, the garden's nice.' His group sat down to remember.

Bertha was out on the street, now. She shouted, 'Fancy a cup of tea, you two lads?' How could they refuse? Down they sat on a couple of chairs outside her shop. Soon they were enjoying a mug each of Battersby's finest. With an Eccles cake thrown in. 'Things about t' same, back in t' village,' was Bertha's first remark. Alec asked after John the blacksmith and was told he kept busy. There had been a letter from Mrs. Smurthwaite, who had given her all the latest news from that village just below the gentle hill called Oxenber. From there, if you were lucky, you might spot a distant signal from the Roman fort high on the top of mighty Ingleborough. There had been a party of hikers in the village, aiming to go and explore the vast pothole Gaping Ghyll, whilst the weather held. Hope they hadn't bothered Gilbert too much, down below there in his establishment, came the thought. There were many vivid memories for Bertha and her guests to enjoy. And her guests they were, for again she would not hear of any payment.

All at once, Alva waved from his balloon. 'Coom on, lads,' he called, giving his burner an awakening burst. 'Finish supping tea. Time to be off.'

'By gum,' said Bertha, 'tha'd better look sharp, but grand to see thi both.' The two friends thanked her, then shot off to the breakwater, two rucksacks still hanging there.

'Let go t' rope,' Alva called. Released from its mooring, the balloon joyfully began to rise. What a struggle it was to grab hold of that rope, speedily becoming out of reach as the balloon soared.

'Steady,' shouted the two crewmen together, rather frantically, whilst the rope snaked and swung right out over the sea. Alec swarmed up as best he could, almost losing a shoe. Carrying his rucksack, quickly unhooked from the breakwater, was a right nuisance, cluttering him up. He hadn't time to look for Ben, but finally scrambled up and fell over into the basket. Rescuing his own rucksack nearly did for Ben. And he left a bit of skin on at least one barnacle. Up he went in his turn. Wet, seaweedy fingers didn't help and the saltiness stung.

'Come on,' came a shout from above, 'it's easy.' Ben managed to keep his mouth shut. A last desperate effort. He arrived, flung his rucksack into the balloon's basket and pitched in on top of it, exhausted.

'Grand,' was all Alva said, and gave his burner a long burst. His whole contraption sailed sky high. Down below, the elderly holidaymaker and his party chattered and remembered in the garden, with its flowers and trim lawns. Some of them dozed off, dreaming of fish and chips of long ago. Alva and his crew, with a sniff of salt and adventure in their nostrils, headed west.

Not much sound, now, except for occasional roars from the burner. Lighthouse? Had there been a lighthouse? But what about the jerseys? Trinity House? Exactly. Such conversation, head-scratching and laughter amongst the balloonists! The jerseys were real enough. The very slight knock on the leg Ben had acquired collapsing into the basket, made him inspect his trousers. Nothing amiss, but there was a tiny tuft of hair caught in the seam. Cat's hair. And it was jet black. Now, there had been a jet black cat .....

Balloon and basket suddenly began to swing, together at first but then, with a jerk, in wild uncoordinated corkscrew dances. Not comfortable, but, wow, exciting! 'Brace thaselves,' shouted Alva, as his craft bucked and twisted. Glory be, at last it calmed, settled, floated, drifted, as before.

Chapter Seven

Not over the sea, now, countryside spreading out below. And something was definitely going on. Furious sounds of cheering crowds and the harsh whine of machines leapt and hit the basket. The racket was not constant, but reared up in surges. Pilot and crew held tight to any handhold they could find, looked down to the ground below and tried to guess what was going on. Their balloon flew on along the coast of an island steadily opening out below them. Pilot Alva decided that no matter what, now was the moment to attempt a landing.

Some way off, a fine castle stood at the coastline. There were a number of Viking ships, some moored nearby, others further off, afloat and riding gently at anchor. One or two, their squarish, boldly striped sails well set, were ready for who knew where. Life-like dragons' heads carved high in the bows would give any enemy food for thought. Men were very busy in some of the vessels. Sun glanced off a helmet here and there. Alec and Ben were riveted. Were hoisted sails ready for imminent departure or merely drying and awaiting repair? Where might some craft have recently been voyaging? There was serious activity between shore and some of the long-ships. Bundles and baggages were being heaved aboard. Could a fresh voyage be the reason? Exploration, trading, maybe, but supposing a little raiding were to be the very next.

Something a long way off caught Ben's eye. An individual could just be seen running at a furious pace along the ribbon of a road. Could this be a messenger of some sort? Vital news? Obviously hugely athletic, maybe he was merely training. But here was a sprinter running so fast he appeared to possess not two legs but three! He disappeared behind some trees just as Ben was going to point him out. Could it be important despatches were heading for the castle? Maybe vital navigational details were required by one of the long-ships still busily being loaded. It was shorter and broader than some of the others. Maybe a long trip lay ahead.

Daring to assume they would all be reasonably welcome, Alva began to bring his balloon down. 'Ever been to t' Isle of Man, have you?' was his question. 'Reckon you must have guessed, long since, where we'd arrived at?' He had it exactly right, of course. Both his passengers knew, Alec very early on. Long-ships from this Viking island had sailed importantly into his professional archaeology, years ago. The balloon was coaxed towards an empty-looking jetty, a little way off from the castle. An odd bale and baulk of timber would be no obstacle to a landing. As to the jetty itself, it looked sturdy enough. So, allowing for wind and the balloon to drift a little, its pilot brought his craft to earth. You could say basket and jetty met with just the suggestion, a hint, of a jolt, but Viking jetty-builders obviously knew their business. The structure held with barely a grunt. It probably grinned. Bowler hat balloon?

What the? Tethering the whole apparatus to one of the uprights would be more than safe. Alva and his passengers heaved themselves out from the basket and between them did the job. A sharp call, a rattle of feathers – Sam seagull flew in, approved and, dodging the worst of the barnacles, settled on top of the chosen timber.

Relaxing for a minute or two and stretching a few legs, the three flyers sniffed the sea air, took in a whiff of seaweed and looked about them. The castle, a little distance away, looked handsome indeed. Interesting sounds from it burst out across the breeze. Menace, alarm, outrage? Which might they be? Such noises could have meant defiant castle-dwellers ready to fight the shocking, unbelievable, unearthly aerial invader landed amongst them. But looking all round, nobody, but nobody busy with the ships, seemed bothered about them or the bowler hat at all. Had they even been spotted? The castle was intriguing. Flags flew, cavorting triumphantly from masts set high, each in its own appointed turret. They all combined in riotous colour, flung out by the stiffening breeze. More than one three-legged motif did its best to leap from its banner, leg it down the nearest country lane. So inviting. The surrounding countryside was attractive for sure, but not quite what the two Englishmen were used to. It might be said – a tree is a tree, is a tree, but the way they were set here was unfamiliar. So were the buildings scattered amongst them.

Anyway, here were Ben and Alva and Alec, balloon safely anchored (if sagging a little from exhaustion), and rather wondering what was going to happen next. Well, the passengers were, but Alva himself smiled at what was afoot.

But now, food! That was it! Supplies of Kendal mint cake stowed on board hadn't exactly run low. Alva could have produced it at will from his old, familiar, be-furred hat, now replacing the flying helmet. But, of course, there's a limit to how much K.M.C. anyone can eat at a stretch! Cheese sandwiches were always likely to appear from under the hat, but might it not be good, if possible, to try something different? Bertha Battersby's fish and chips were only a very distant delicious memory. Something really new would be fun if it could be found. But before anything else, the bowler hat needed attention. Without a fairly speedy burst from the burner, sagging could well become collapse.

Alva spoke. 'Now then, you two young lads, I'm going to float off for a bit, look after t' balloon. When you need owt or ready for off, give me a signal. You know what to do wi' t' stones. He nimbly leapt into the basket, changed his hat for helmet, pulled down his goggles, gave the burner a good go and shouted 'Cast off. Catch! These will put you on for a bit.' Two large cheese sandwiches, to be eagerly grabbed, flew through the air. With Ben's help, Alec let go the rope (not too easy, one-handed) and, almost before they knew it, basket and bowler balloon shot skywards, trailing a length of seaweed and rapidly disappearing into the clouds.

The two companions, munching away, set off on a leisurely stroll, their attention drawn towards the ships they'd seen receiving goods and provender. In fact, some of these activities were still going on. It would be good to take a closer look. A Viking crewman put down the box he was carrying, looked up and came towards them. This was a bit of a surprise, as up till now the aerial arrival had so clearly seemed to have gone un-noticed.

'Hello,' said the cheerful young man, closer now. 'Welcome. Jossund's the name. Saw you arriving. Good trip?'

'Grand, right grand,' Alec found himself saying. Language barrier? None. 'A bit rough for a spell a while back,' he went on, 'basket and balloon swinging all over the shop. And a fair old racket coming up from below. There were people shouting and some kind of engine noise almost to split your eardrums.' He gave a laugh. 'It made us wonder, as you might say, what the heck was going on. It shook us for a bit.' Jossund smiled and gave an enquiring look. Alec guessed what was in his mind. 'Ah,' he said, 'you'll be wondering who we are. Well now.'

Before he could go on, Ben stepped forward and, giving Jossund a cheerful look, shook him firmly by the hand. 'Ben,' he explained.

'Good of you to drop in,' said the Viking, smiling. 'And with that fair hair of yours, you could be one of us!'

Better introduce myself, too, thought Alec. Giving Jossund a vigorous handshake, 'Alec,' he said. 'We've come over from the Yorkshire Dales. Grand part of the world. Best in all of Britain, I would say.'

'Yorkshire Dales, eh?' said Jossund, his face lighting up. 'Know all about them,' he said. 'Plenty of our folk over there. Did you ever come across one of our chaps called Ulvik? Good friend of mine, haven't seen him for a while. Bit of a lad, our Ulvik, living in that cave of his, you would enjoy meeting him some time.' Alec gave a laugh and glanced at Ben, who looked surprised and amused at one and the same time. Jossund was told of their actual meeting with Ulvik in his cave when they were boys, his spiriting them away to Norway, their meeting with a certain P. Gynt. And they vividly remembered not only the dazzle of sun and snow, but the keen cold that had almost completely frozen their lips and eyelashes.

Curiously, none of this seemed so long ago. 'Small world,' Jossund murmured. 'Would you like to step aboard one of our ships?'

He began walking towards one of the waiting craft, picked up his box and waved an arm to the two companions to join him. They'd seen the loading which was still going on, it looked important. What and where might the next voyage be? They made to follow the fast diminishing young Viking. Stopped suddenly. How is it we really do understand each other's language? Does it matter? No. Laugh. Follow that Viking! They did, and eagerly looked forward to what they might see.

Inspection of the ship would have to wait, however. Tearing towards everyone, in a positive whirl of legs, came the fastest runner you're ever likely to see, who screeched to a halt in a spray of perspiration. He'd become very red in the face and stood, chest heaving. Was he the one they'd seen earlier, from the air? Viewed at close quarters, this fellow clearly had the regular number of pins! Between gasps, he managed to call out – 'Joss, your guests are invited to the castle.'

'Right you are, young Douglas, thanks very much,' shouted Jossund. 'Tell them we're on our way. I'll walk with you, you two lads,' he said.

'Phew,' said the young messenger, swivelled round and bent low in sprint-start mode. Jossund sharply clapped his hands. Limbs whirled. The runner was gone. Three legs, thought Ben. Three legs, surely! This speedy young Douglas looked for all the world to be possessed of three legs, as his lightning feet propelled him, streaking away to become a fast, disappearing dot. Extraordinary! It was to be hoped the messenger, on arriving at the castle, would be able to stop before crashing into a flying buttress or some such. Anyway, it was time to head for the Viking fortress. A cat emerged from a pile of sacks, sat down, blinked, washed its face, turned and softly padded off. 'Gracious,' Ben observed – 'no tail!'

Walking to reach their destination was going to take some time, but striding through the countryside was pleasant enough. There were no exact clues at first as to what might have set balloon and basket pitching and rolling whilst flying over the scene beneath. Alec began to have extraordinary thoughts, but dismissed them as mere imagination. A few flags were waving along one stretch of the way. Lines of multi-coloured bunting romped between gaudy banners hoisted everywhere among the trees. One or two local residents generously giving the travellers a wave, didn't seem entirely steady on their feet! Grass skirting the route was pretty flattened. There had obviously been a significant event of some sort. Jossund smiled to himself, but kept quiet. One or two bushes seemed disturbed. And, here, a tree had lost a strip of bark. Some very telling ruts ran along the way. Looking how they swerved and skidded crazily along the track, Alec's imagination really began to go into over-drive. In fact it started to race good and proper! Could he sniff oil? How could he? He said nothing. Were mad ideas taking over? After all, carts and horses left ruts. And a cart out of control will damage the land, carve into bushes and maybe slice into trees. The three walkers moved on.

The castle was becoming closer. It would be so interesting to see, although an early chance of food – it had to be admitted – was minute by minute becoming the more urgent thought. Conversation between Jossund and Ben was going extremely well. There was much to talk about and to share. Ben raised a laugh or two for everyone with accounts of some of the people he'd met in his job as a Dales guide. The young Viking had a keen sense of humour and laughed a good deal. 'You should see some of the people we get round here,' he hooted. 'Tell me about your great flying basket.' (So they had been spotted!) 'Not seen anything like it before. What d'you call that great thing on top that carried it, and what about the man who was flying it?'

Explanations were going to be difficult. Balloons of all sizes and shapes, ballooning. Where could one start? Talking about pilot Alva would be fun, certainly, trying to describe his other form of transport: Articulus, his flying, talking piebald horse, where might one begin? (Where might you? A young Alec would have told you.) The two Dales balloonists did their best, recalling their adventures when they were boys. They wondered what would be the reaction if Alva actually re-appeared at this very moment, astride his remarkable animal.

For no reason, Alec glanced back along the way they had come. He was astonished at what he saw, or what he thought he saw, just for a fleeting moment. What was that faint, but now rapidly increasing, high-pitched mechanical hum, teasing his ear? He opened his mouth to speak. Nothing came out. Blinking his eyes, he turned and looked again, looked closer. In the misty distance, yes, no doubt about it – a motorbike. In pursuit? Looked like it. Now it was here. In a flash, the machine roared past, swerved, turned at an angle and disappeared behind the castle, now right out in front of them. Streaming out from under the crouching rider's helmet – a plume of fair hair.

The massive building reared right up above them. Impressive, threatening, massively stone-walled, towered, turreted, terrific, it was! Exciting and forbidding all at once. Startling to hear the whip and slapping of banners stretched out, splitting, almost, in the stiff breeze.

Humming, thrumming, knocking, thwacking at their masts, their halyards determined to join in. It seemed almost too dangerous to stand nearby for any time at all.

'Impressive, isn't it? Castle and a half, I'd call it. I'll see if I can take you in,' said Jossund. 'Wait here.' He walked off and, after talking to the entrance guards, disappeared inside. After a few minutes (that seemed like hours), he re-appeared, waved an arm and called: 'Come on, you two, I've fixed it.' Jossund took his two new friends in and through to an outer courtyard. What might be going to happen next?

They arrived to discover the blonde, helmeted motorcyclist, goggles now shoved up, getting off his bike and slowly pushing it towards a distant archway. With an effort, he made it through and moved out of sight. The smell of engine fuel and warm exhaust lingered within the courtyard's sheltering walls. Alec caught it at first sniff. T.T., Manx T.T? Viking, Manx T.T? Is my imagination right out of control, he thought. He'd seen the legend "Viking King" emblazoned on the motorcyclist's petrol tank. Just caught it as the machine was braked and throttled back. He was sure he'd seen it. He stood for a moment, transfixed. Isle of Man ..... Viking King ..... T.T? Really?

'Come on,' called Ben, 'do catch up.' Recovering, Alec turned to see his friend along with Viking Jossund, at a distance across the courtyard and just about to vanish through a great, heavily studded door. Whoever, really, was on that bike, was the question Alec asked himself. Viking King? Viking King? Find out. Half running to join the other two, he headed towards the door. He made it quickly enough, but of Ben and Jossund there was no trace. And there was only just enough of a rapidly narrowing space left for him to squeeze through. He certainly wasn't, if he could help it, going to find himself shut out, oh no. Miss all the fun or whatever might be happening or about to be happening within. He cut it pretty fine, however, in his frantic efforts barking his knuckles fairly painfully on the doorpost. The great mass of studded timber swung closed behind him, with a shuddering thump. The draught knocked him flat.

Complete darkness. He was more than a bit shaken and it took him a while to recover his breath and stand up. Slowly, his eyesight began to adjust. He could almost, he thought, detect a faint glint of light a little way off. All was very quiet. Where might his companions have disappeared? He shuffled forwards a bit at a time, feet sliding across a stone-laid floor. As he edged along, the faint glimmer grew ever stronger, becoming reflected in the stone-flagged way that ran before him, worn smooth and a little slippery by many feet over many years. Alec groped forward, step by step, finding a bit of support with fingertips against the wall of the chamber in which he now seemed to find himself. On he went. The light became stronger. He could see it now, it came from a flaming brand held firm in an iron bracket set at an angle from a stone pillar. He walked right up and stood beneath it, felt its warmth on his head and the back of his neck. A lively spark detached itself, giving his hair a bit of a fizz. Another one gave his neck a red-hot nip. He quickly ducked – smiling ruefully – moved away half a pace and looked about him. Had he found his way into some kind of armoury? The fiery brand's unsteady tongue jumped and swirled to reveal, here and there, sharp glints of metal from mighty swords, ranged and ready. Helmets, too, burnished and prepared for action. Vivid colours, blazoning great shields, suddenly leapt out before darkness again overcame them. Alec peered about him into the shadows. He thought he could see one or two metal-banded chests or coffers. What they might hold, he could only guess. He was unwilling to leave the light, such as it was, preferring, for the time being, to accept the flame and smoke fitfully swirling about him. But he must get on. Jossund and Ben would be wondering how they'd lost him and where he'd got to.

Standing there in the smoky silence, Alec was considering the same question and wondering which way to strike. Maybe, if he followed the wall at his back and ventured into the gloom beyond, he would find another light to show him where he was. This is a bit of a do, he thought, hesitated for a few minutes, took a deep breath then struck off to his right and plunged into the dark. He steadily felt along the wall an inch or two at a time, but trying to get bolder. The stone felt very cool and a bit damp to his fingertips. All of a sudden, they lost contact. He felt a sharp blow to his right shoulder and almost lost his balance as he cannoned into an unseen buttress. Catching his breath, he looked about him. In the far distance he detected something of a glow. What if it was another flaming torch and he could persuade it out of its bracket, hold it to light his way? Can't stand here, he thought, must get on. Try it. He groped on towards the light.

He hadn't gone far, his ear caught the sound of voices. Not very clear, you understand, just the odd snatch. And surely a faint note of laughter. A bit of a breeze now began to fan along the wall. Alec walked on, light just starting to peel the darkness from the stone. If it would flare, not flicker, I'd know where I was, he thought. But what was this carried on the air? Surely, the undoubted smell of food! His pace quickened, cutting the distance between him, the light, perhaps a meal and, he very much hoped, Jossund and Ben.

The path before him started to slope away. He had begun to sense a change in levels some minutes before. Just a bit further he could see the wall still curving to his right. Hurrying a little, he followed it round. There, before him, stoutly bracketed in the stonework, was a fine brace of torches, well afire. Their flame and smoke spiralling up for ever, lit the scene all around. Alec saw at his feet a long flight of steps stretching down and away. Definite smell of food, joining with echoes of voices, swirled up from below. There could be no holding back, but could he chance the steepness plunging away into empty space? No time to hesitate. Well, no, but ….. He leant forward, foot gingerly feeling for the first step. Glory be, there was a tough old rope, held to the wall by trusty iron rings, looping its way down and out of sight into the darkness. What a bit of luck. He took a firm hold. Down he went. The rope was rough to the touch, except where it seemed to be a bit greasy. Could this mean regular use? Maybe he was on some sort of back stairs for cooks and scullions. Smells of cooking became definite and Alec fancied he could hear the clang and clash of pots, pans and crockery. Sounds grew louder, cooking smells more beautiful. Suddenly, completely broadening out, the stairway took a sweeping right-hand turn. All at once, the seeker was in a blaze of light and a warm, comfortable cloud of rich cooking, rolling and billowing through a wide entrance, door flung open as if to share the delights from within. Now, Alec felt ravenous! Unable to help himself, all fears gone, he walked right in.

Here was a wide, lofty, mighty kitchen. Generous bunches of herbs hung from walls. Piles of logs, some in baskets, some stacked loosely, stood by, ready to stoke oven fires. A great wooden table stood proud in its place of command. All manner of cooking utensils were spread about it as preparations for an obviously considerable meal were under way. Amazing to see the gleaming pans, earthenware jugs, pots and basins of every shape and size. Alec wondered at the strength and endurance of the many cooks and their helpers, busy creating something undoubtedly greater than a mere sandwich! Such weighing, measuring, stirring, pummelling, chopping, slicing, boiling – perspiring! Water-filled pans sat bubbling and spitting in the great heat from the fire at the kitchen's magnificent hearth. There were other pans, too, suspended on chains above, prepared and ready. Alec marvelled at the variety of knives, steels, ladles and every other kind of culinary equipment in use everywhere. He was amused by some mighty water jars which stood contentedly glugging with the gallons of water it was their job to hold ready.

But above all else, it was the large animal carcass impaled on a great horizontal spit straddling the hearth and slowly rolling, turning, to cooking perfection. Here was a real live (if the term can be used under the circumstances, the animal's especially!) wild boar-roast. Just visible through the haze of cooking, a small man could be seen close to the iron spit. Operating a simple mechanism, it was he who kept the carcass leisurely revolving. Every now and again, he reached for a giant, long-handled ladle, which hung on the side of the great fireplace. From a swimming pool of a drip pan situated beneath the spit, he from time to time ladled melted fat over the carcass, on its way to becoming perfectly done.

The little man sweated more than anyone else about the kitchen. He seemed rather tired. Not surprising in all that heat close to the blazing fire. The boar was enormous and took a deal of turning. Now and again he had the chance to rest on a small seat half hidden in a nook by the chimneybreast. But hardly had the little fellow crept to the shadows for a break, a loud call would come for him to return and begin again, turning and basting. The crackle of fat, its fierce hiss when it splashed back into the "swimming pool", cut right through the shouts of cooks and their assistants. They took no notice. It made Alec jump, I can tell you. Nobody took any notice of him, either. But then one of the cooks looked at him, gave something of a nod towards a large green vegetable. Startled, Alec found himself picking it up and handing it over. At that moment, it seemed, he was on the staff!

Here's a bit of a do, he thought, and couldn't help wondering how Ben and Jossund must have been scratching their heads as to what had become of him. But here he was amongst all the chopping, mixing, stirring, heaving, measuring, filling, emptying, boiling, baking, fending off great waves of heat making every effort to burst out through the oven's iron doors. One of the obviously senior cooks stopped what he was doing, drew one of the others to him and had a word in his ear (the only way he could make himself heard). Shortly, he wiped his hands on his apron and left the kitchen through a side door. Alec received a nod from one of the cooks, as before, silently inviting him, this time, towards the mighty roast. Trying his hand at turning the spit, he found it tougher than he had imagined. The little official spit operator thrust the monster ladle into Alec's hand, then faded into the shadows. Fascinating, sweaty fat-basting. Alec was beginning to wonder, after what seemed to him to be quite some time, just where everything was leading. Permanent employment? But here was the cook, back from his errand, bringing with him a messenger. A command shouted to the little man in his corner, his rest was at an end. Out he came, looking just a bit sad. Alec knew he would have to hand the job back to the expert. Half a pity. He was just getting the hang of it. And he'd been given a lovely, crispy piece of fat-soaked bread, which had tasted very good indeed. The messenger spoke. It was time to go. Alec abandoned the spit and handed back the ladle. He licked his lips, thanked the little man, tried a wave towards the entire workforce, joined the messenger, who then guided him through the side door. There were some stairs. To where and what might they lead?

Now this was the real poser. Had he been in a Viking kitchen? He wasn't at all sure. Didn't really care. More to the point, what next? Anyway, such fun it had been in the great food hall. And that chunk of wild boar-fat-soaked bread was just right! Could easily take to cooking. Give up archaeology?

Alec's thoughts and queries rumbled on through his head. What about the Viking on the motorbike? This was a Viking castle, he felt sure. What about the long-ships being loaded on the quay as Alva brought his balloon down? Jossund, he felt pretty sure about, but there was really too much to take in. These were some of the questions spinning around Alec's mind as his guide, who reminded him of an old seaman (odd?), conducted him up the steps away from all the cooking and clamour. The way led up several flights of stairs and along a series of dimly lit passages, until finally coming up short behind a heavy tapestry curtain suspended from above by stout cords. Just enough glow from a red-shaded lamp overhead revealed its rich design and the gold thread tracing itself right through it. Alec's guide was able, with a bit of an effort, to pull the heavy curtain a little to one side. Behind was a very solid, panelled wooden door. With his clenched fist, the curious old individual gave it two solemn knocks. Nothing happened. Standing in the shadowy crimson-lit passageway gave Alec an eerie feeling. Silence. There was no noise at all; well, not to speak of. The old fellow took one or two breaths and in between wheezed very quietly. He stirred his gravelly throat as if about to say something. Alec thought he could hear, somewhere beyond, distant voices. Not very clear, rather muffled. At intervals, there were brighter sounds, which he took to be laughter. Well, he told himself, nobody seems to be missing me much. His guide drew a deep breath, which sounded rather alarming, squared himself up, took firm hold of the curtain, pulled it to one side and gave the door a determined thump. A mighty scraping of bolts. Groaning at first, then whispering a little, the door steadily eased and shifted till it had swung right open on its heavy hinges.

Chapter Eight

Alec stood, transfixed. A voice called 'Come in, come in.' A little blinded by sudden brightness, in he went to find himself in a chamber of some size. Daylight and sunlight flooded through openings in rugged walls. There, to his surprise, were Jossund, friend Ben and a broad figure he did not recognise, who was seated at a long, wide table, which at first glance was strewn with maps and charts. But the fair hair did strike a distant chord. Had it not, or something like it, been seen streaming out from under a motorcycle helmet? Alec thought hard. What was he trying to tell himself?

Jossund was the first to react. 'Ah,' he said, 'you've found us at last, come in and join us.' Alec walked forward, as he did so the big man slowly rose from the table and without a word reached out to offer greeting. He was about two metres tall, rugged and weather-beaten. With flowing blonde hair and heavy moustache, he made a striking figure. His broad, muscular chest seemed as if it might any moment burst from his open-necked, decoratively woven tunic, just held in by a wide, buckled belt. His large, practical hand grasped Alec's hand in a long, very firm grip. Such could seal a friendship for life, assuming the bones recovered! Smiling, the quiet, impressive individual returned to his seat. Alec tried to take in what he saw stretched out across the long table. Maps and charts. Now, what were they all about? What had the big man, Ben and Jossund been studying? Beckoned across by Jossund, Alec looked closer. There was no real conversation, just a few murmurs and a nodding of heads from the two Vikings. After a brief shuffling, one chart came to the fore, the others pushed aside. The big man traced a broad finger across the one selected, glanced confidentially up at Jossund and this time gave a very firm nod of the head. He seized the favoured chart, swept it from the table, briskly rolled it up, thrust it under his arm, gave a brief bow and quitted the chamber, noiselessly closing the door behind him.

'That was Guthrum, the Viking king,' said Jossund very quietly. 'This is his castle – Castle Rushen.' His two new friends looked at each other in amazement.

Glancing round, it was not the chart table that Alec had first noted. It had been a side table offering fruit and rough bread. There was a great chunk of something, which he just hoped might be cheese. Occupying a big dish sat a leg of cold meat, which could, he thought, be hog from some other roasting. It, or what was left of it, tilted sideways amongst thick slices, earlier removed by a heavy knife, now lying half-smeared, half-glinting, alongside.

'Come on,' said Jossund, 'time to eat.' He took the weapon, skilfully impaled two slices of meat on its dagger point, transferred them to a wooden platter, added a hunk of bread and offered the food to Alec. Jossund gave a laugh.

'Thought you'd be about ready. Thought we'd lost you.' Alec started to explain, but with a smile was waved into silence. Jossund moved swiftly to gather another meal, first for Ben and then himself. 'Sit down, gentlemen,' he said, 'ah, but you'll need a drink.' From a handsome ewer, he filled three drinking horns, which he brought to the big table. He set them ready, one for each of his guests and one for himself. 'Castle mead, gentlemen,' he said, 'the best, here's to you – drink up.' They did.

There was plenty of room on the wooden benches alongside the chart table. Soon, everyone, comfortably seated, set about Viking hospitality. For a while, there was not much conversation, but, in between mouthfuls, Ben was keen to know what had happened to his friend after losing contact with him, after he and Jossund had slipped through the castle's great courtyard door. 'What on earth happened to you?' he said. 'You took too long wondering about that motorbike. I asked Jossund about it, he said he'd explain later.'

'Dashed to the door as fast as I could,' replied Alec. 'Only just squeezed through. Look at that!' He laughed and held out his right hand. 'Caught my knuckles on the doorframe. D'you think I'll live?'

'Shouldn't think so,' said Jossund, grinning. All three companions laughed.

As well as he could, Alec recounted his shadowy journey through what seemed to be an armoury, with its swords and helmets just visible in the half-light, and how he had groped along a shadowy way, half-lit with flickering torches. He told how he just about made it, holding on to the greasy rope down a plunging stairway, suddenly to find himself in the hot, bright, heaving activity of wild cooking in a magnificent kitchen. What surprises! It was an experience he never, ever forgot through later years. He had but to see a plate of ham, memory of wild boar leapt right at him. And there he would be, sweating on the handle of the mighty spit! He had Ben and Jossund's rapt attention. Whether it was his account, or the delightfully stimulating liquid with which the three of them had lubricated their meal, he was never quite sure. But he quite forgot to mention the aged guide who'd led him from the kitchen. But I reckon Jossund would, in any case, have known all about him, wouldn't you say?

Jossund finished eating, quitted the table and moved to the chamber's outer wall. For several minutes he looked through one of its wide openings and out toward the sea. What was in his mind? Standing there, he thoughtfully sniffed at the brisk wind starting to blow. He took note of leaping "white horses" topping the steeply rising sea, beginning to fling itself to shore. Clouds of spindrift whipped across the heaving waves. Jossund took one or two deep breaths, his eyes half-closed in concentration as he gazed into the distance. His two guests, who had also finished the meal, looked across to their host, then to each other. Something was afoot! Wondering and guessing ended. Jossund turned to them.

'Let's make a start,' he said. 'The sea's getting up. Let's go.' He pointed across the chamber to the door through which the Viking king had previously disappeared. 'This way,' he said. Ben and Alec left the table and quickly joined him.

All three headed to the door, Jossund held it open and they passed through to an upper walkway open to the sea. Wind cut across, carrying a smatter of stinging wet. Through another door, they found themselves under cover. An enclosed stairway took them down a series of flights into a wide, sheltered area. Glancing round, Alec could see one side was divided into sections. Were they workshops of some kind? Certain objects stood in two or three of them. Hidden under wraps, it wasn't possible to say what they might be. There was, however, a rather familiar whiff. Alec's imagination took off. Motor oil? Petrol? On now, through a wide open area. Some way off, a number of men could be seen milling round, busily occupied. Voices were out of earshot, but some discussion was clearly going on. Such were their movements, exactly what they were dealing with was fairly obscure. Not quite. Alec got half a look. His eyes nearly popped out of his head. Jossund caught sight of him, took in Ben's equal wonderment, and cracked out laughing. But before his two friends could ask anything at all, from behind there came a mighty sound. "Stand back," it clearly roared. The startled three did exactly that, leaping aside just in time. A very powerful motorcycle shot past, its rider crouching low, head and chin almost at one with the handlebars. Out from under the helmet streamed a mass of wildly flying blonde hair! There was a split-second glimpse of lettering on the petrol tank. "Viking King" wasn't it? Both Englishmen were spellbound.

'Come on you two,' Jossund said, rather suddenly, bringing both of them back down to earth. 'Must get on, weather may be closing in, follow me. Get ready, we're coming,' he shouted to the men clustered in the middle distance. The threesome set off towards them. They would soon discover what was going on.

If Alec was surprised, earlier, his eyes almost exploded when the little party arrived at their destination. On command, the gathering of men stood back. Exposed to view – three brilliantly sporting motorbikes, gently ticking over! Two mechanics, ready and waiting with helmets, goggles and gloves, attended each machine. Everything fitted perfectly. As you may have gathered, Alec was not unfamiliar with such vehicles. Not so, Ben.

'I've hardly sat on anything such as this,' he said, 'd'you reckon I can handle the powerful beast?' He noted a number three bolted to what was to be his machine. Glancing across, he could see the one assigned to Alec carried number eleven, and Jossund's carried a number seven. Three words shot into his head: "Manx Grand Prix." Crikey! Now, no kidding, Alva had landed them (in more ways than one?) on the Isle of Man. I suppose the penny had long since dropped. The tri-legged banner flying over the castle had triggered off early thoughts. But Vikings racing on motorbikes? What was going on?

There was no time for any more questions. 'Hop on,' was the invitation. Ben found himself doing just that, after putting on his helmet and dragging on his gloves. Goggles pulled down, he gripped his handlebars, finally located the throttle, somehow found a gear and, without really knowing what he was doing, let in the clutch. He received an encouraging rap on his helmet, with a spanner, from his mechanic (felt more like a sledgehammer). Off he shot, legs flailing out sideways for a few yards, in clouds of exhaust, before finally gaining some kind of control and definitely hoping for the best. A few seriously sweaty moments – he began to enjoy it. Alec and Jossund, calmly, efficiently, smoothly rolled away.

'We must make it to the quay,' Jossund shouted above the din. 'Follow me down the old race track.' Well, it was pretty exciting, I can tell you. Viking King Guthrum, long out of sight, the others pressed to follow. Ben, chancing his arm on a motorbike for more or less the first time, still slipped and slid a bit, from time to time flinging out a wild leg as he corkscrewed along the route left a bit slippery from overnight rain. 'Stick it,' shouted Jossund, 'you're doing fine.'

Alec joined in. 'He's hardly ever ridden a motorbike before, you see,' he said, as close to Jossund's ear as he could manage. The Viking threw back his head and laughed. Found it difficult to stop.

'Good lad,' he yelled out to Ben, as encouragingly as he could. In fact, each man was thoroughly enjoying himself. At one point, they came across an old seaman mending a chequered flag. Quite big it was, and attached to a handy stick. He was leaning against a battered wooden board lashed to a tree. The board said "T.T. FINISH." It just caught Ben's eye. He nearly, really, fell off his bike. There'd been another figure in dark blue. Racing with grim determination, he had overtaken everything and anything. How he'd kept smoking his pipe without losing it from his mouth had to be wondered at.

Travelling the rough track, past trees and bushes and dwellings of many kinds, more than one bystander just gawped. At least one shepherd had, desperately, to hustle his sheep out of danger as the three careered along. On, on. The track ran out at last. Here was the sea, the welcoming, salty sea. Almost skidding to a halt, two of the bikes came to rest against a few sacks and bales. Ben tried, but kept going till, slamming on the brakes, he came to an abrupt stop, back wheel lifting off the ground, front wheel just about hanging over the edge of the quay, him leaving the saddle, nose heading for the front tyre. Whooaa! With an effort, he hauled himself back. 'Watch it,' shouted his fellow riders. (A bit late for that?) He sorted himself out, switched off and scrambled clear to join the others. He was grinning from ear to ear.

'I enjoyed that,' he said.

'I'm sure you did,' they replied, relieved. All three riders dismounted and, with engines switched off, wheeled their machines into a nearby shed. They removed helmets, goggles and gloves, left them neatly on empty saddles, and returned outside.

Down below them, the Viking ships tugged at their moorings. On the deck of one of them stood the impressive figure of Viking king, Guthrum. 'What kept you,' he called out. 'Come aboard.' A number of his crew were busy about the ship, preparing it for sail. The vessel was manoeuvred a little closer to the quay. The sea had become a bit choppy, obliging the craft to heave up and down. Jossund made a quick move and, choosing a moment when the deck rose sufficiently to take a chance, nimbly jumped aboard. 'Come on, next,' he called. No one should have assumed the two landlubbers were dithering. Let's say they were considering – carefully. All right for experienced seafarers, of course!

'Wait for it, wait for it,' Alec cautioned, 'Now,' he shouted. Ben leapt and made it aboard, slipped a bit, grabbed a helpful rope and recovered. Grinning, he glanced back at the quay. 'Come on,' he said, 'it's easy.' Alec weighed up possibilities as the ship's deck continued to rise and fall. Decision was taken from him. Suddenly, robbed of his footing by a patch of seaweed at the edge of the quay, he was flung, spread-eagled into mid-air, to land in a heap aboard the long-ship. Embarrassed? Yes, but that was all, he even managed to join in the laughter. And he hadn't torn anything, either. Guthrum shook his head. 'We'll make sailors of both of you, once we've put to sea,' he said. 'Cast off, bear away,' he shouted.

Shoved clear, the ship, with Guthrum at the helm, made for open water. Driven by the great, striped sail, it met the plunging waves head on, dragon's head at its prow taking the lively sea smack in the teeth. Spray and green water swept across the vessel, momentarily drenching everyone on board. Not much concern about this, you might guess, for the Viking crew, but as the craft heeled over, the two Englishmen braced themselves on any part of the rigging that might offer a hold. Becoming wet through was hardly important. Flexing, thrusting into the sea, the long-ship told its own story. (Hear it, feel it, thrillingly, right through every fibre.) Gradually, conditions quietened. Enjoyment of the voyage surged wonderfully. Able to take a calmer look at the vessel, now, Alec reckoned it must be over twenty metres long, beam about five. He'd seen one of the ships drawn up ashore for repair when first landing from Alva's balloon. He'd admired the shallow-draughted, graceful, clinker-built hull, its slimness at stem and stern. He could imagine how it would ride and slice through the sea. Guthrum's command was doing it now.

The crew busied themselves about the ship as it scudded on, powered by the stiff wind. Its two passengers stood holding on close to the mast, steadying themselves as best they could, and hoping they were not getting in the way of the twenty or so men handling the craft. All wore sturdy, bright woollen jerkins and woollen trousers, colourfully criss-cross-braided close to the leg. Feet were in leather boots or any form of shoe to suit the individual. All manner of headgear served. There were some typically rounded helmets. One worn by a very seasoned crewman was more than slightly dented. What story might there be to tell? Ben thought it could be more than interesting to find out! Standing, holding on and taking in the vastness of the seascape was great. There was not much seating, anyway, just a few sea chests belonging to the crew and maybe best left to them. Three or four seabirds came and went. One fat gull perched on the gunwale near Ben, giving him a rather knowing, beady stare for a minute or two, before taking off. It circled once or twice, offering a particularly sharp call before heading out through the spray.

Dipping and joyfully rising, the long-ship with Guthrum astern skilfully at the steering oar, made fast progress up through the North Channel. Now leaning over the side, Alec enjoyed the changing colours, occasional phosphorescence, in the bubbling, churning waters alongside. Pale sunlight glinted back from the shapely hull. Just where was the ship heading? Where might landfall be? The questions were lost in the excitement of battling the sea. And Guthrum offered no clue. That distant shore on the port bow. Must be Ireland, Alec thought to himself. Might we be going to land? He wouldn't mind if they did, but steadily the ship bore away leaving the exciting prospect well astern. Anyhow, it was good to be at sea. The sun was gaining strength and Alec enjoyed the liveliness of the vessel as its bows rose high – almost to take flight – before smacking back into the sea. Spray, whipping aboard, added to the fun. Tongues tingled, licking lips from salt. The crew's skilful working of the ship gave it excellent speed. But in later years, Ben mischievously wondered – could there have been mechanical assistance deep in the stern of Guthrum's ship? Hidden propeller? After all, he was the Viking king. It said so on his motorbike! Of course not!

'How are you two lads feeling, aboard?' enquired Guthrum at a well-judged moment. 'Fine ship, isn't she?' He'd had a weather eye open on them all along. At that particular point there was only one answer – 'hungry'. 'Oh well,' he said, 'we must do something about it'. Erik, an experienced steersman, was called to take the oar. Guthrum drew his two guests over to the mast and invited them to sit on a nearby sea chest. 'Wait,' he said, 'see what you think of this.' He flung open the lid of a smaller chest and presented to each of the two Yorkshiremen a large piece of dried fish. 'Try a bit of that,' he said, half smiling, 'you'll love it.' Some attempt was made to nibble, chew, then swallow some. At the startled reactions, the Viking king let out a loud guffaw. 'Tasty, eh?' he enquired. Reply was unspoken, but clear enough right across two pale, rather green faces. 'My apologies,' he said, 'hand them back.' The fish was replaced by goats' cheese and rye bread. That was more like it. What a blessed relief! Ben's eyes had stopped watering and he had even begun to smile. Back again in the "larder", the dried fish would doubtless come in handy when Guthrum himself felt a bit peckish. He was glad that his two guests looked rather more cheerful as they enjoyed their meal, washed down with beer, which he'd drawn from an earthenware jar and poured into drinking horns. There was mead, too, which Alec remembered for a very long time.

Daylight began to fade. Was it the mead or the hour? Alec wondered. Anyhow, he and Ben were invited to make themselves comfortable under an awning rigged in the stern of the vessel. 'Shake down there if you like,' said Jossund, 'you'll find it comfortable enough. Grab some of those animal skins, they'll keep you warm.' With the comfort of the thick fur and the easy motion of the ship, sleep quickly overcame the two Englishmen. There was hardly a whisper of a breeze, the sea a gentle swell. Night slipped in, lit by a bright moon scudding and dodging between straggling cloud. With a murmur to Erik at the helm, Guthrum took over from him. Looking into the clearing sky, he set his course by the stars, trimmed the broad sail and headed north. What, you might wonder, was the Viking king's plan? He was pretty sure his passengers would be intrigued – and surprised – if they knew. The dragon ship quietly sailed on, not in the least disturbing the fat seagull, now returned and dozing above on the yard. Soothed by the gentle motion of the ship, Alec slept well enough. But at one point, jerked awake by a creak in the rigging, he glanced towards the stern. Of course, it was Guthrum at the helm, wasn't it? For a split second – unbelievable – it's the old seaman. Did he not seem a bit familiar in his cap, those sea-boots and style of dress? Propping himself up on an elbow, Alec focussed hard. No. It was Guthrum all right. Must have been the cheese – or the mead! He and Ben slept on.

Very gradually, morning came. Mist surrounded the ship. Olaf, one of the crew, gave the pair a shake, invited them to stretch their limbs, move about a bit and start the day. They were both glad to oblige. Though warm enough during the night, leg muscles had become a bit stiff. 'When you're ready,' Olaf said, 'have a bite to eat.' Bread, cheese and mead went down very well, I can tell you, on that damp, chilly morning. Closed in by mist, all was very quiet, almost creepy. There was nothing to see. The only sound came from the sea slapping against the hull as the craft idled forward. Guthrum was almost motionless, too, hardly moving as he steered his ship. He was keeping a sharp eye open, sniffed and breathed in the merest whisper of a breeze, no wind. He was listening, watching. His crew moved very quietly about their business. Each man found a brief spell to eat a little breakfast: bread, cheese and some of that dried fish, all to be washed down with a gulp or two of beer. Alerted by movements on deck, particularly the catering, the seabird awoke from his roost on the yard and flew down for crumbs. You know seagull Sam never missed a chance. Satisfied, for the time being, he flew off to find clearer air and a wider prospect.

Visibility improved very slowly and to help his all-round vision, Guthrum commanded the sail be fully reefed. The vessel continued to roll and dip in the ghostly, misty stillness. So quiet, unnerving. But the sea had no intention of resting for long. After all, there was a new day ahead, full of opportunity. And the long-ship had made it through to the Atlantic. The crew were at the ready, making sure everything was in good order, setting things up for whatever the day might bring. There was not long to wait. The ship could not be allowed to drift for ever.

'Man the oars, look lively,' shouted Guthrum. A rattle of timber, and fourteen duty members of the crew took hold of the oars, seven a side, and thrust them out between the pairs of thole pins set along the ship's gunwales. 'Two more places to be filled, come on you two lads,' shouted Guthrum to his passengers. Ben took one, Alec the other. Sun began to break through, but as if lying in wait, the sea began to heave. 'Give way together,' came the order. Bending their backs, the sixteen oarsmen – now including the two dalesmen (trying to give of their best) – started to pull in even rhythm. The ship began to make steady progress.

Rowing started to be more awkward, sea becoming rather worse than choppy. It was difficult to keep blades properly covered as the long-ship pitched and rolled. A wind sprang up, quite suddenly. Judging the moment, Guthrum called an end to rowing, oars to be shipped, sail unreefed. Smartly, oars were stowed, sail brought back into action and made secure. Skilfully manoeuvred to benefit from the rapidly strengthening wind, the vessel shook itself and began to leap, buffeting into the rising sea. Drenching spray everywhere, no refuge for anyone. Water streamed from the yard and trailed astern. On went the craft, curtseying and climbing through every wave, the dragon's head flinging off everything thrown at it. The canopy, aft, whipped and jerked in the wind. The mast held firm, shrouds humming. The two balloonists, more used to quiet, serene floating – in the dry – held on tight. They couldn't possibly know where they were bound but hardly had time to think about that. Waves mounted and lashed. Excitement or what? The wind roared. Even experienced members of the crew braced themselves and held on. Eyes half shut, keeping out the salt water, heads ducked, clothing drenched, much startled laughter, this was the life, surely. Through everything, Guthrum, unflurried, remained firmly steering his rolling, riding, bucking craft, with the skill of a lifetime.

All at once, the sea gave a mighty heave. A whale as big as a row of houses rose from the depths and broke through the surface. From the blowhole in its massive head, a deafening spout of air and water, wonderful to see, shot as high as a cathedral. Caught by the wind, the brilliant squirt was flung sideways, sweeping right across ship, passengers and crew. What a finale! Plunging again, the great mammal hoisted its massive, elegant fluke and with it gave the sea a splashing whack, slinging a drench of spray, bubbles and seaweed everywhere, then disappeared. There had been dolphins already, leaping and singing. One of them flipped into the ship, smiled and flipped out again.

Suddenly, the Viking craft bumped sideways, sharply heeling right over, gunwale almost under. All those aboard, jolted off their feet, fell over each other, arms and legs everywhere. Someone shouted: 'Man overboard.' It was Alec, catapulted over the momentarily submerged side of the vessel. Out from the deeps shot a massive black and white orca. Unwilling, it seemed, to leave the party, it had joined the others in leaping, plunging and diving everywhere in thunderous water-play. It could be supposed each creature was thoroughly enjoying itself at the expense of everyone on board Guthrum's ship, flinging water high and wide.

But where was Alec now? Nowhere to be seen in the heaving sea. Spread-eagled, he had been flung out to hit the sea like a sack of spuds. And sunk! Down he went, any old how, somehow managing to hold his breath after the initial gulp of salt water. It was difficult not to panic, everything had happened so quickly. He thought he felt contact with something solid, moving but solid. His tumbling mind groped for an answer. He imagined a figure of some old seaman with a stump of a pipe jammed in the corner of his mouth, slowly revolving and cart-wheeling, submerged near him in the gloomy depths. He held on, lungs beginning to hurt, bubbles dribbling slowly from nose and mouth. Oddly, a strange calm overcame him as he rolled and drifted. He half-saw, or thought he saw, a kindly, interested eye. He was lapsing into a dream-like state seeming to go on for a lifetime. Gradually, he felt carried upwards, something very solid beneath him. Up, up, so very slowly, he sensed being lifted up, almost for ever. Suddenly, gulping and half choking, he was out in the open air, shot clear of the water like a cork released from a champagne bottle. In a swirl of bubbles and foam, he landed almost alongside the long-ship, still grappling with everything the sea could throw at it. Boy! And weren't they glad to see him? Not half so glad as he was to see them! The great humpback, for such a whale it was, that had blinked at him and risen from the depths to save him, rolled over and delivered him like a shuttlecock into the belly of the vessel. The great leviathan leapt, flinging itself into the air, its whole body, barnacles and all – magnificent. With a mighty splash it returned to the boiling sea and was gone. Staggering!

Guthrum ordered Alec's wet clothes to be replaced with some dry ones from his own sea chest. 'Get some mead into him and let him sleep,' he said, before concentrating again on keeping his craft heading into the wind. It was still pretty furious, but showed signs of easing. As it continued to do so, the sun made an effort to reappear, gradually strengthening. Alec's wet gear, tied very securely to the rigging, billowed and tugged. It would dry before too long. Hardly aware of anything, Alec slept, beginning to warm at last. His borrowed Viking clothes – colourful woollen tunic and trousers – were very comfortable indeed. He wouldn't want to give them back, ever.

The voyage settled again, weather improving all the time. Precisely what o'clock it was, Ben had no idea, but the sun's position indicated that it must be well turned mid-day. It was warm and a real pleasure to be afloat. After all the excitement and turmoil of the threatened capsize, Guthrum's crew set about putting things to rights, making sure all the ship's gear was in good order and the last of the seawater baled out. There were unstowed oars wrenched adrift, sea chests lying scattered, shoved out of position, certain rigging displaced, fortunately not broken. Used to the sea and its capabilities, it nevertheless took the crew a spell to restore order on board. Ben made himself as useful as he could. After a while, food and drink was passed round. Very pleased everyone was for that! Alec slept on, too exhausted, perhaps, even to dream, but there lingered that watery image of an old, briny mariner, drifting and turning over and over in the churning sea.

The long-ship quietly ploughed ahead, swaying, nodding, bubbling in what was now an easy sea. Calmness, enjoyment of the voyage, had returned after the near turn-turtle. Jossund told some of the crew how their two passengers had arrived through the air. The balloon and its pilot took a deal of explaining, I can tell you. There was some head scratching and a lot of laughter. Thorgils, who had rowed next to Ben, shook his head in disbelief.

Still pondering, he seized two pieces of storm-damaged rope and began to show how to splice them together. He was still very much amused. The end of another rope had become split and frayed. He proceeded to back-splice it. Ben, paying close attention, was fascinated and completely awed by the skilful fingers at work.

Suddenly, a voice from the masthead shouted out in a burst of wild enthusiasm – 'Land ho, on the starboard bow.' It was Knud, one of the young and particularly fit members of the crew, who had climbed up to check the rigging and keep a lookout. He had hardly made this dramatic discovery before he was shinning down and striding across to Guthrum to tell him what he saw. He simply gasped out – 'that island.' Ben got to his feet and searched the horizon. Given a shove, Alec's recovery took a sudden upturn. Making an effort, he gathered himself and – perhaps a bit unsteadily – joined those gathered in the belly of the ship.

'What was the shout?' he said.

'Catch a look at yon island,' said Lars, a very jolly member of the crew and, you might care to know, a skilful oarsman, too.

Well, there it was, some way off to starboard. Even at a distance, it could be seen to be a fair old chunk rising from the sea. Lars, with Ben and the fast-recovering Alec, spied out from the long-ship's shapely bows. Even way off, the landmass vastly impressed: majestic rocks, craggy and pillared, seeming to support the sky, let alone a wide, grassy top-knot. Some seagulls – one in particular – displaying in wild aerobatics overhead, repeatedly dived down to inspect it. What was it that interested them, Ben wondered, are we going to land? But glancing back at Guthrum, no orders seemed to have been given. On went the ship at a distance from the rugged Hebridean coastlines. Slowly, persistently, anticipation was building almost to bursting. The broad sail remained comfortably filled and carried the vessel serenely on its journey. Even the dragon's head at the prow, usually hawk-eyed, seemed somehow to doze. Seagull Sam had quietly returned, found a bit of fish and a crumb or two and was resting up on the yard. On went the ship. Iona came and went, left astern. The Skerryvore lighthouse was just visible somewhere to port. Where was the destination to be? The ship sailed on. At last, the object of the voyage was right there, majestic, mysterious, challenging. The Isle of Staffa and Fingal's Cave lay before them.

Something began to happen. As if attached to a submerged cable, the ship was hauled irresistibly towards the island with its towering, massively massed columns of igneous rock. Insistence from the sea to get close and personal, left no doubt. Waves rising, heaving and swirling, rapidly gathering strength, at once went completely crazy. Gripped in a mounting frenzy, the ship began spinning and bucking. Very curious indeed – there was not much water flung about. It seemed the craft just had to do and go where it was told, with the least possible delay! Guthrum furiously wrestled with the steering. Everyone on board braced himself as best he could, clung to every and any possible handhold. Closer and closer, Guthrum's Viking long-ship was pitched and spun towards the Isle of Staffa's mighty cave. The craft, held in a whirl of spray, seaweed and stinging salty bubbles, darted into its gaping mouth, spun several more times, rubbing and bouncing against every kind of rocky obstacle, then was flung out into the open again on a mass of creamy froth, where it rocked and tipped in jerky dance with the force of it all. Its gleaming hull was untouched. But now, there was a stillness. Just a swaying and nodding of the plucky vessel.

Guthrum and all on board, at first laughing with shock and surprise, gradually relaxed, drew breath and looked about them. Odd, maybe, but nothing seemed to be amiss, awry, on board. Here was a long-ship as spruce and ready as you might ever expect or hope to find. Apart from the swish and occasional slap of the waves against the ship's side, there was now hardly a sound. An eerie calm, a silence. Would the dark cavern finally swallow them all up? How long the mood lasted, who could tell? It seemed to go on for ever.

Guthrum suddenly looked up, he'd heard it first. Listening carefully, very carefully, there it was again – a low laugh from somewhere deep inside the vastness. He gave the order to trim the ship, as a light wind stirred and began to draw the vessel forward. Erik, once again appointed steersman, looked doubtfully at the shoreline nearby. Pretty rough it was. No landing possible there, he thought.

'Now then, you two lads,' said Guthrum very quietly, 'I think there may be someone or something waiting for you. We must find a place to put you ashore.' He thought he'd heard a sound a while ago. Now, he was certain. Ah yes, now, everyone heard it – louder – this time, a full-throated laugh. The ship was eased astern, then steered to another part of the island where smaller rocks, shingle and seaweed ran out into shallow water. Just the place. Very gently, the long-ship made contact, bows rising up to come to a crunching stop in amongst tumbling pebbles and seaweed. There was no real conversation from Guthrum, he simply said – 'hop ashore, you two lads.'

Alec was first. He still wore the Viking clothes given to him after rescue-by-whale. They're yours to keep, he'd been told. Something shot through the air as he landed, hitting the shingle just ahead of him. It was the bundle of his entire wardrobe, dried a while ago on the ship's rigging. He picked it up and put it under his arm. Ben lowered himself from under the dragonhead bows. He was in his own clothes, minus socks, which he'd long since given up. His shoes were hung round his neck on the laces. He'd hardly squelched ashore and clear of the water when another bundle flew from the ship. 'Catch,' shouted somebody, Ben turned just in time to catch it rugby style and keep close hold of it. He scrambled up to speak to Alec ahead of him. Suddenly, such a squall burst out from absolutely nowhere, it really knocked both of them flat. Seaweed torn from the rocks whirled and flew up into something of a fog. It cleared. Where was the dragon-ship? No longer beached, it was now just a tiny dot fast disappearing over the horizon. A spearing glint from the dragonhead caught in the sun, the long-ship had gone.

The two friends studied the horizon for some time, changing their positions more than once, seeking a better angle. But it was no use

'Did you actually see the ship go?' Ben asked.

'Nope,' was the reply. 'Absolutely not,' Alec repeated from a stack of rocks he'd climbed as a high vantage point. Well, it was a bit of a facer for the pair of them, I can tell you. A brief glance at each other said it all – "What do we do now?" Disbelief, an emptiness, the situation had it all.

Chapter Nine

Rather absentmindedly, Ben started to open the missile that had followed him ashore. Landed and stranded, might as well do something. He found in it, Viking tunic, belt, "trousers" and shoes (which would fit perfectly). There was also a kind of light shirt. Ben had noticed Alec, after rescue, had been given a similar one to wear under his belted tunic, along with "trousers" and leather shoes. But he parcelled everything up again. Save for later, he thought. Alec joined him and, still astounded, they sat down and tried to grasp the situation, the two of them, with only Sam seagull for company. He had fluttered down some way off and now strutted about searching and pecking amongst any promising-looking rocks and shingle strewn about. Occasionally, he looked up and caught the two marooned dalesmen with a beady eye.

Ben came straight out with it: 'What do we do now,' he said.

Alec shrugged his shoulders. 'Can't help laughing,' he said, 'can't do anything else, and, er, where exactly do you figure we are? Strange island, cave and a half, look at it! Guthrum didn't spill the beans and neither did anyone else.'

'Jossund seemed to have a smile on his face,' said Ben.

'You're right,' came the reply, 'but before we go any further I must change out of these clothes.' Alec didn't hang about, carefully opening the bundle shied at him from the long-ship. Quickly, he was back in his own gear, Viking rig safely packed up. The seagull, stooping and probing at every step, gradually made his way towards the sitters, didn't stop but walked right past. Every now and again he fixed them with a sharp stare and jerked his beak back and forth, clearly sending the message – follow me. A brief hesitation, maybe, in grasping Sam's meaning (after all, they thought, he's only a seagull), they set off after him – why not? – in surprising haste, tripping over more than once amongst the scatter of loose rock and splintered fragments lying all around. A biggish rock sent Ben hopping, staggering (and him a fell runner!), almost falling. He caught his foot against a pebble, it leapt forward, jumping and rolling for several yards, finally clipping another and sending a piece of rock into a low, looping arc towards the sea. The missile hit the water – kerplunk – producing a depth-charge-like vertical splash right in front of the cave's wide open, rather surprised mouth, before sinking below, to leave an ever-widening circle of ripples tumbling over each other. As it plunged, the rock made a sound, rolling, reverberating, magnified, bouncing round inside the unsuspecting cavity! It was some time before the disturbance rumbled into quiet. The lapping of the sea alone broke the stillness. It was a calm, beautiful day, hardly a breeze, white clouds drifted across a wide, blue sky. The island of Staffa warmed in the sun. What now?

At first, from deep inside the cave a low chuckle stirred, to be followed by another and another, expanding into all-out laughter. It subsided. A voice called out – 'Come in, gentlemen.' Now that was enough to shake anyone. The two friends halted, stock still. The sudden disappearance of Guthrum and his crew had already left them stunned. What were they to expect next? No idea. Sam appeared to know, but he was a mere seagull – wasn't he? Although it was a little odd, perhaps, how he seemed to keep turning up. He wasn't telling. Anyway, it seemed they were being ushered – scrambling – towards some sort of entrance to the island's cave. Progress for Sam was easy, flying and fluttering over the really difficult bits of the way. Watching him planing and gliding as fancy took him brought Alva and the balloon back to mind for the two. Might they ever become airborne again, was the thought. But this was interrupted by that voice of the someone or something heard rolling out from the cave to greet them at first landing on the island. 'Come on gentlemen, welcome. Do be careful,' it went on, as if aware of the succession of trips and stumbles.

The broader stones in the path ahead almost looked to have been deliberately set out. As the terrain began to fall away, each stone lying there became wider and flatter. Together, they offered, quite clearly, a safe if rather rough flight of steps, curving away to disappear towards the unknown. A sizeable chunk of old timber, draped with crusty seaweed, lurched nearby, leaned, half-buried, where it had long since been washed ashore. It made a convenient, strategic perch for Sam. He looked all-knowing, in charge, even a little superior. He settled and adjusted a feather or two as he waited for his charges to catch up.

Alec was first to join the bird and, steadying himself against a jumble of rocks, looked back to call encouragement to Ben, struggling more than a little. What on earth are we going to find down there, he asked himself, giving the winding stairway rather critical inspection. 'Come on Ben,' he shouted, 'come and take a look at this.' Slipping for the umpteenth time, launching another shower of pebbles and small stones into the sea, Ben caught up. 'What a right carry on, all this,' he said to himself. Careering after seagulls – what the heck! It had been an effort trying to remain on his feet. The bundle of clothes he was carrying kept Guthrum, Jossund, the long-ship and the rest of its crew very fresh in his mind. (Fresher than dried fish!) Where was the ship now, he kept thinking. Might it turn up again? If not, we'll be stuck. He slipped again. 'Concentrate,' he told himself, as he covered the last few yards. 'Made it,' he shouted with a laugh, and was rewarded with a slap on the back from Alec.

'Well done. What do you reckon to this pathway?' Alec said, taking Ben by the arm and pointing down to the stones disappearing out of sight. 'Got any idea?'

'Only one way to find out,' said Ben, grinning.

Attention was now given to the patiently watchful seagull, whose beak arrowed, pointed very particularly towards, you could say – the way below. Both friends looked at him, trying to home in on his signals. Sam trapped them in a piercing look for, maybe, a full minute, demanding their attention. Satisfied, he solemnly, purposefully, nodded his head several times. A final, exaggerated nod, he paused, drew himself up, spread his wings wide and took to the air. Rising ever higher, he circled then dived, making a great wheeling draught, rose again, gave a wild urgent call, then shot away to become a distant speck in the wide Hebridean blue. The friends were alone.

'There he goes,' Alec said. 'There he goes, strange bird.'

'Yes,' said Ben. 'Very.' He clearly had something on his mind. The two adventurers would not be long in finding out!

Both young men glanced round at the infinite seascape. A wind was freshening. The sea slapped in easy rhythm against the rugged shoreline. They stood for a few minutes just taking in the remoteness of it all. Thoughts of any stairway and where it might take them, if prepared to risk it, were lost for a brief spell, very brief, the seabird could not be ignored. But there came another sound, faint, more positive – captivating. The two dalesmen fixed each other in a very long, thoughtful stare. Ben suddenly got it. 'Bagpipes,' he simply said. 'Bagpipes.'

Alec grabbed his sleeve. 'You're right,' he said. And very quietly – 'wonderful.' He didn't quite know why, but he felt the need to be quiet. Almost whispering, he said: 'Come on Ben, let's make a move.' Avoiding kicking any loose pebbles, they, step by cautious step, began to follow the descending pathway down into – they were not at all sure. They pressed on. The music, gradually swelling, came up to meet them. It was the loveliest pibroch – lilting, ever-changing tunes. Down, down what became a winding staircase, went the seekers, edging their way through a high, slanting cleft in the rocky strata. For a few very long unnerving minutes, they found themselves cut off, both from the outside world and anything that might lie ahead. Right then, they couldn't even hear the music. A last few steps, a final twist and, blinking in welcoming brightness, the two arrived in a vast, high, over-arching, warmly lit chamber. They looked all round in amazement. Flickering candles set in hundreds of neatly-chiselled hollows, winked and flared in every direction. The piper, ah, there he stood, kilted, resplendent, in the middle of his concert hall. Glorious music. Both visitors stood spellbound, wrapt in the magic of the sound. After forever, the music gradually quietened, steadied and mournfully sighed to nothing. Slowly removing the mouthpiece from his lips, the tartan bag from under his arm, expertly gathering chanter and drones, the piper carefully laid his instrument down on a small, polished wooden table standing on its own. Turning to his enthralled listeners, he said: 'Welcome to the Isle of Staffa. Fingal, at your service.'

Such a shock! It certainly was a shock. Perhaps his sense of humour, or wanting to create mystery for his two passengers, Guthrum had kept Fingal and Staffa right under his hat, as you might say. Some hat! The only reply Fingal received was a rather shaky 'hel-hello.' Talking about things and looking back later in their lives, the two Yorkshiremen said their reply must have seemed very weak indeed. But what might they, completely bowled over, have honestly been expected to say? I ask you?

The individual who had stepped forward to greet them seized their imagination. It was not easy, for a start, to determine his size. Was he a giant? Or had the extraordinariness of the situation defeated ordinary judgement? There he stood, great presence, geniality to match. His mighty handclasp shook the whole place, set every candle struggling to stay lit. In later years,

Alec wondered whether there had been a curious size adjustment and re-adjustment, ebbing and flowing in the mind during the whole astonishing encounter. Normality, meaningless. The great lair was, in itself, more than enough to take in: high, over-arching, rugged roundness, softened by the candlelight and its hovering shadows. In the ever-changing light, who could guess the size of the place? Plenty of room for the vast table at which Fingal had nimbly taken his seat.

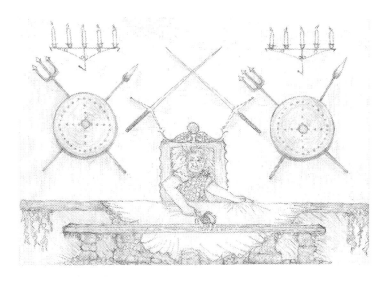

'Care for a crab,' he said with a wry grin. His table stood magnificently well-set on a sandy level a little higher than the broad sweep of the floor, rock worn smooth by many footsteps and Scottish dancing. Mounted all along the wall behind the table were shields, pairs of crossed claymores and different weapons, enough to deter any sea monstering krakens unwise enough to stray from waters far north. The whole armoury glinted sharply in every candle-burst, before returning to watchful shadow. Five metres long, two metres wide, ten centimetres thick, Fingal's table was something to see! Standing in front of it ran a sturdy bench. Amazing, at a distance burnt a fire of considerable size. It glowed hotly from a deep wall recess, spilling enough heat to keep the whole interior pleasantly warm. Quite what fuelled it was anyone's guess. There was a comforting peaty smell everywhere and not a hint of smoke. There must have been an efficient flue. But where might it be, Alec wondered. Did it have a flue? He pondered this many times in the years ahead. Such was the warmth of the place, his archaeologist mind even hinted at hypocaust. Anyway, there it was, and there they were, guests agog at the situation in which they found themselves. That was enough.

Evidently, their host was something of a mind reader. 'You're mebbe a bitty hungry,' he said. 'Weil, we'll see to that. Sit ye down.' Fingal pointed to the long bench and, getting to his feet, he put a hand on the shoulder of each of his guests and steered them towards it. 'Put your bundles underneath,' he said. They clambered on (took a bit of doing) and sat down. Turning to thank him, they were surprised to find they were alone. Where was their host?

'What happens now, d'you think?' Ben quietly whispered. He and Alec had been sitting for what seemed a rather lengthy spell. In fact, they probably hadn't. But who knows what anyone might be thinking in such remarkable circumstances? He looked along the long, empty table, then across to the little one on its own. Where were the pipes? They were no longer to be seen. He hadn't seen them go. 'Pipes, where are they?' he said, looking straight at Alec. 'Did you see them go? I didn't.'

'Search me,' was the only answer he got. At that point – more or less – came the sound of bagpipes, a little way off but steadily becoming louder. Turning towards it, the friends were stunned. Emerging from the shadows and casually floating in the air out into full candlelight, the bagpipes, streaming tartan behind them, were playing all by themselves. And they wafted in a cloud of the most wonderful savoury gravy. Savoury was hardly the word, I can tell you! Brilliantly lit in sudden candle-burst, triumphantly regal on a silver dish, floated a plump, quivering, steaming haggis. Close behind, a tumble of oat cakes revolved quite slowly in mid-air, accompanied by glasses, drinking horns and a glinting, winking, rolling, pot-bellied flagon. Round the arena went the crazy troupe. Twice. Both Alec's and Ben's heads spun clockwise, anti-clockwise, any old-wise, necks corkscrewing this way and that! The pipes quietened and slowly faded into the shadows. But there to behold, in pride of place and lordly in its might amongst everything else – the haggis! Sprawling luxuriously, it lay on its silver dish in the very middle of Fingal's great board. Who had been at the cooking? Fingal? You must guess! Set in his place at table were carving knife and fork. Glinting and ready. His guests found before them – drinking horns and the finest, Scottish silver place settings.

Not in his great seat, Fingal was just visible working vigorously in the shadows at a side table. Wonderment was cut short. 'Here, gentlemen,' he said. Out he came into the light. Each fist held a broad, silver dish. Before his guests could tell what was happening, there was one for each of them on the great table and piled with roast meat (venison?) along with a host of hot totties and other vegetables.

'Now gentlemen,' said Fingal, 'hold fast for a moment if ye please.' He took his position behind the table and stood by his chair; in his hand – skean-dhu held high above his head. He addressed the haggis in a manner his guests only just managed to comprehend. He started boldly: 'Fair fa' your honest-sonsie face, great chieftain of the puddin'-race.' With rising emotion, he went on to complete that verse and the remaining six. Flecks of perspiration flew from his chin as he prepared himself for the final lines. Exploding into the very last line of all – 'Gie her a haggis,' he gathered himself, rose on tip-toe, swivelled his shoulders, raised the dagger even higher, then plunged it into the heart of the steaming, quivering, savoury bundle! Such a spicy, oniony, meaty gush burst out across the dish. 'Help yersels,' he just managed to whisper as he sat down, exhausted. Rallying, he said 'nae, let me.' Brandishing a fine horn spoon of monster size, he served a generous dollop of haggis to each of his hungry guests. 'Ye'll be takking a dram, will ye no?' he said. Laying the spoon aside, he grasped the flagon and filled first Alec's and next Ben's drinking horn with the finest Scottish whisky. 'Let's eat, gentlemen, let's eat,' he said. 'But first, a toast. Scotland for ever! And welcome to my table.' His two guests stood to him. Three whisky-filled horns met each other – just – in salute across the great table.

The meal went on for some time, during which other place settings appeared along the table. A well-dressed figure walked noiselessly from nowhere, sat down at his and began to eat.

'All well with your lighthouse at Skerryvore?' called Fingal across the table. 'Ships will be glad of it, these rough nichts.'

'Aye, they will that,' came the reply. ''Tis a fearsome rock that once destroyed many a fine ship, out there in the North Irish Channel.' The diner quietly finished his meal, took a long pull at his whisky, acknowledged his host with a short bow and moved away.

'Lang may your lum reek,' called Fingal as his guest drifted out of sight. 'Great lighthouse builder, that Alan Stevenson, along with his family,' was all he said. The two Yorkshiremen nodded. Ah, right enough, was the quiet thought. 'Lang may your lum what?' Ben murmured to himself. Just catching his question, Alec whispered – 'reek. Lang may your lum reek. Long may your chimney smoke. That's what. Long may you live, you see.' He got a brief nod in reply. A lingering potato got speared and was gone. Fingal's mention of the Stevenson family tingled a faint recollection of all Robert Louis' family and their widespread, tough engineering. His, too, for a brief spell.

Someone with a rather familiar look came to the table and sat at his place, already prepared for him. He raised his glass to Fingal, took a dram and began to eat. Who might he be? His meal over, the diner stood, raised a final glass and quietly walked out of sight. He'd had a red, red rose in his buttonhole. 'Ah, guid nicht, Rabbie,' Fingal called. Ben tugged at an ear and scratched his head. 'Who next,' he thought. He steered a last little bit of turnip through what gravy remained on his plate, ate it, finished his whisky and sat back. 'Grand wee man, Rabbie Burns,' was all he heard Fingal quietly say to himself.

As if there wasn't enough already to keep the two Yorkshiremen guessing, from nowhere in particular emerged a remarkably striking, fresh-faced, dark-haired woman, in charming highland dress, all swirled about with finely-woven tartan. She moved up close to the table. Very calm and resolute, she looked. She held Fingal in a steady gaze, then quickly caught sight of his disbelieving guests. She paused, then said with a smile breaking right across her face: 'Any of ye care for a row over the sea to Skye?'

'Och awa, Flora,' Fingal guffawed. 'What about it, lads?' he enquired. 'Mebbe not, mebbe not, Miss MacDonald,' he said, without waiting for an answer. 'But thank ye all the same. Safe home to ye, now.' As the figure drifted away, she sang, very quietly, 'Will ye no come back again, will ye no come back again?' Flora was gone.

The two friends couldn't possibly have said, precisely, at that moment, whether they were actually coming or going! Who was that hunched in one of the cavern's darkest corners? Concentrating on a spider, was he? No! Must have been the whisky, Ben thought. Guid stuff! Fingal glanced across, 'Ah, Robert,' he said.

Both young dalesmen now sat completely relaxed at the great table. Fingal's hospitality had left them thoroughly content. Whilst they could be wondering what might be going to happen next, they weren't exactly bothered. Fingal, too, was happy enough, sitting back, with elbows resting on the arms of his great chair. He had an idea. He stretched out a hand, fingers closing round his empty drinking horn. A sharp tap on the table with it, and what a result: a skirl of the pipes, two pairs of claymores leapt from the wall and clattered to the floor in a fountain of sparks. The weapons skipped, slid and skidded to a halt, to form a perfect cross on the open floor. They lay trembling, glinting, exchanging fire – sword tip to sword tip. 'Dance if you dare,' they challenged. Four lively characters, appearing from nowhere, flung themselves into brilliant highland dance, nimbly heel and toe-ing in between the lethal blades. High sprang the dancers, feet hardly touching the ground. Round and round they went, back and forth between the tingling steel. Leaping high, higher still – never to come down again? On went the music. Would it never let the dancers go? One by one, other dancers, some familiar, some not, came from everywhere, moving to the rhythms. All blended into a mighty whirl. Fingal rose to his feet and almost out-danced the lot. A hypnotic blur. No other ceilidh was ever like this! Both young dalesmen were utterly hooked: reel, jig, hornpipe, sword dance, Strathspey, Dashing White Sergeant – away we go, away everyone went! Frenzy, exhaustion, delight. Phew! Could anyone survive?

Gradually, pace and mayhem slackened, slowed, music quietened, stopped, revellers melted, faded into the shadows. The original highland four were alone, left in eerie silence, broken only by echo and distant seagulls. Fingal had, after a final fling, returned to his seat. Now, he clapped his hands. His dancers gave a final leap – better than ever, to disappear out of sight high above. A flash, a ring like a bell, the claymores shot back to their crossed positions on the wall, where they might cool. They'd become red-hot. Ben blinked. A single figure remained in the middle of the floor. Alva!

Our balloon pilot was well acquainted with Fingal and glad to see him. The flying helmet must have been stuffed in a pocket, for he had upon his head his be-furred hat. Who could guess what might next come out from under its brim? Alva turning up, meant taking off again in the balloon to who knew where. Ben wouldn't have minded staying on the island for as long as it might take to learn the bagpipes, if Fingal would teach him. The big man got up from his chair to greet Alva. He shook his hand. 'Come and sit down,' he said. A drinking horn brimming with – I'll leave you to guess – slid right across the table and into Alva's hand.

'Your very good health,' said Fingal.

'Here's to thi,' said Alva.

'Would ye like some haggis to your dram?' enquired Fingal.

Alva politely refused, smiled and finished his drink. 'Ee, that were grand,' he said.

Ben, who had taken a turn round the cave, found a set of bagpipes on a small table out of candle-glare. With a single finger, he touched them, very carefully. They moved slightly and gave a low moan. 'Sorry,' he said. 'Nae bother,' Ben imagined the pipes to say. Returning, he walked across to Alva, seated at the table. 'Good to see you,' he said. But his mind was really on bagpipes. What might, back home, some of his hiking party guests say, entertaining them with a blast across the tops?

Alec had been looking at the swords, lost in thoughts about the courage, or horror, of pitched battle. Alva caught sight of him. 'Na then, tha two lads,' he said, breaking the spell, 'mebbe it's time to be off. But perhaps t' morn would be t' best. I've had a word with Fingal and he agrees. Spend t' night here. What d'you reckon?' Spend the night in Fingal's cave? Not many folk get the chance, would you say? Grand. Alva said he would snooze in the balloon, keep an eye on it. There would be Sam for company. 'Back first thing in t' morn,' he said. He snapped his fingers, spun round three hundred and sixty degrees and disappeared.

Fingal, comfortable in his great chair, stretched a leg out under the table and gave it a kick. From under each end shot a low couch. 'One for each of you,' he said, yawning. He sat back, composed himself, had a good stretch, rapidly dropped off and began snoring almost immediately. The flame of every candle flared and went out.

Morning broke. From all directions, high and low, brightness flooded into the cave. Daylight now in charge, the place was even more brilliant than before. Alva turned up, ready for action. 'Hello,' he called (maybe a little too briskly!). 'Grand day outside. Anyone hungry?'

Fingal had been up for a while, trimming the wicks of some of his speciality candles in readiness for evening. He smiled and shook Alva's hand. 'What d'you suggest?' he asked. 'Ham and eggs? Get up, lads,' he said, giving the nearest couch a sharp dig with his foot. He snapped his fingers. In no time at all, his guests, rather wondering where they were and what had shaken them, were wide awake, on their feet, couches back where they came from. Everything required for eating lay on the table, for everyone. 'Ham and eggs?' Fingal repeated to Alva, who laughed and with a flourish of his hat produced ham, eggs, oatcakes and jam for everyone, including himself. Fingal's appetite might not have surprised anyone! Just as well his plate constantly refilled itself. The meal was lubricated with the clearest water Alec thought he had ever seen, adding to Alva's remarkably tasty and definitely welcome breakfast, eaten to a standstill! Now what? Alva took off his hat, whirled it round like a Catherine wheel. Sparks flew off and so did everything remaining on the great table, till there it stood, gleaming, magnificent, crumbless and completely empty.

Ben, like everyone else, he supposed, was feeling relaxed and beginning to think life might be not at all bad, sticking about for a while longer with Fingal in his cave. After all, hospitality had been excellent. And even if Alva had business elsewhere, the bagpipes would handle catering, for sure. As for entertainment, what other characters might drop in from time to time! But such thoughts were shoved aside. Hovering in the shadow of a jagged crevice in the cavern wall: a figure! Ben half-closed his eyes, leaned forward and peered very intently. He walked several paces towards what he'd seen. Surely, it was the old seaman? Looked like it: rough blue jersey, trousers stuffed into well-worn sea-boots, cap on the back of his head. Why should this old guy keep turning up, Ben thought. Must tell Alec. But his sparring partner, still fascinated with swords and shields, was studying them again and imagining scenes of close combat. By gum, those claymores looked sharp! Alva and Fingal were in close conversation. Better not interrupt them. What were they talking about? Ben strained an ear, but couldn't catch much of what was being said.

Alva stood up. 'Time to be off,' he announced, and looked round to see if he had been heard.

Hearing Alva's voice, Alec made his way back towards the table. 'Come on, Ben,' he called. 'What's to do?' he asked Alva.

'Must mak a move, get airborne. Catch hold of Ben,' was the brisk reply.

Alec called to him, his voice echoing and re-echoing round the great cave. 'Over here, quick,' he shouted. His target, rather startled, took the hint, slowly turned and quietly walked back.

'Did you see that?' Ben said.

'See what?' Alec said. Ben swivelled round and pointed to the distant rift in the wall. But ….. nothing!

'What was I supposed to see?' Alec said.

'There was somebody. I'm sure there was somebody,' Ben replied. 'Somebody or something.'

Sam seagull flew in, round for a moment, and flew out.

'Ah,' said Alva.

'That it?' said Alec. He hadn't seen anything and, quite frankly, was rather wondering what was going on. Ben looked at Fingal right between the eyes, but before he could say anything, Fingal got up, came round to him and confidentially placed a hand on his shoulder. Very quietly, he said,

'I'll believe you, young man. All kinds of folk drop in here. Remember? I once thought maestro Mendelssohn might.' That had to do for the time being. Ben shook his head. He knew what he'd seen. Just knew it. And, now, he was not the only one. Hallucinating, half-drowning under the Viking ship, Alec, we know, had imagined the image of an old seafarer. There was the lighthouse incident and, earlier, quicksands in Morecambe Bay, though he'd imagined nothing on Staffa. All very odd.

But now there was something else to think about, something very definite, undeniable. One by one, all over the cave, the candles were beginning to flare into life. Brightness from the early, natural light had been steadily losing its sharpness. Maybe it had been constantly on the move, fooling Ben all along. But you couldn't have convinced him!

'Gentlemen, let's go.' Alva turned to Fingal, seized his hand and shook it firmly. 'My thanks for everything. You've been good to t' two young men. They'll not forget their visit here, ever. But I'd be glad to tak off fairly quickly now, whilst there's light enough. Gentlemen, are you ready?'

A quick search under the long bench, the two fished out their belongings. They were ready to fly wherever Alva took them, but would never, could never forget Fingal and his great cave on Staffa's Isle. They thanked the remarkable character as best they could.

'Grand to see you, grand to see you,' he boomed with such a laugh, setting every candle flame a-tremble sideways, almost out. Disturbed by the echo, bouncing round the loftiness above, a handful of bats took off, looped the loop several times before landing (or ceiling-ing) back again – upside down, of course. Fingal's handshake, to set the travellers on their way, left an impression to last them for the rest of their lives. 'Be off with you,' he said, 'and safe journey. There'll always be a welcome here for all three of you, whenever or however you can make it. But that might not be very soon, perhaps.'

At this, Sam seagull, who had flown in again, unseen, and was now perched on the back of Fingal's chair, gave an emphatic nod – just caught by Ben out of a corner of an eye. 'Correct,' he said to himself. A flash of white and black – Sam was gone.

Attention now turned to Alva. No sign of his be-furred hat. No, he was wearing his flying helmet, goggles pushed up, gauntlets held in one fist.

'Now, if you please,' he said to Fingal, 'if you would kindly show us where, we can make our way to my balloon.'

Trying to go back the way the two friends came in might have been the thing to try, but Fingal might well have in his mind his preferred departure gate! Fun to find out. Right. Their host shepherded the balloon party round the back of the great table. 'A moment,' he said. Carefully reaching past Alec, Fingal touched the hilt of one of a pair of gleaming swords held on the wall. Click! A shield mounted nearby slowly moved to one side (sending a mouse, gnawing at a bit of turnip it had found, scuttling for cover). The shield rumbled, boomed and trembled for a few seconds, a bit like a dinner gong, then fell silent. Fresh sea air gusted in, and there, stretching away down, was a wide, shallow staircase leading to a little ballustraded platform. A stout wooden ladder, thickly draped in seaweed, hung down from it directly to Fingal's secret back yard.

'Awa wi ye, lads,' he said. Seizing the moment, he slapped his three visitors on the back, shook their hands. This was no half-hearted Godspeed. It would be remembered for ever. 'Right, down ye go,' he said. 'Ye'll find steps ahead of ye to tak thi round and up to the top. Your balloon's safe and in good order.'

The three departing guests paused a few steps down to the little platform, turned and looked back. Fingal stood completely filling his "back door". He waved an arm and gave a wide smile. 'Guid journey,' he called, 'lang may your lum reek.' They all waved to him as the shield began sliding back into position. It was quite sad as the kindly giant disappeared from view. What a time they'd had! Bagpipes began playing from somewhere way back in his great cave. A bonnie piper was doing his best. (If an actual piper was playing!) The tunes broadened out into a fine burst of jolly pibroch. Turning to look in amazement, the three – soon to be balloonists again – could see their exit from Fingal's domain was now completely closed. Sheer rock surrounded them, but, remarkably, bagpipe echoes swirled round everyone and everything.

Down, now, to the little ballustraded platform, and tackle the seaweedy wooden ladder. In great spirits, Alva,

Alec and Ben went down, rung by (very slippery) rung, made their way to a curving strip of pebbles and shell (official guide books have absolutely no idea!) that trickled out for a short distance from the final rung, to disappear beyond a cluster of fallen rock.

Alva knew the way. 'Come on,' he urged, 'let's go.' A casual starfish winked at them as they splashed and crunched their way along the salty path overhung by the island's great mass, hugging them close.

'Look at that,' suddenly Ben said. What appeared to be a small octopus was seen, frantically wriggling about, optimistically hoping to slither and bubble its way out, escape back to the sea. A clatter of wings, seagull Sam appeared, landed and rather ceremoniously walked towards a handy rock, where he flipped to perch. He offered a beady stare. 'Come on, no time to waste,' he could have been saying. The three walked round past him, to discover right in front of them a staircase reaching up to Staffa's launch pad. At the very top awaited Alva's flying machine. Though tethered safely enough, its basket rocked and bounced a bit. Above, the bowler-hatted balloon swayed rather more than a bit. The whole contraption was eager to be off. No one in the basket, as far as anyone could tell, but the burner fiercely flared on and off. 'Come on,' it roared. The crew of three started to hurry, eager to fly. Alec began to run ahead up to the top.

'Steady, young man,' said Alva, himself at a smartish jog. Ben, rather sad to be leaving Staffa, paused for a moment to take a final glimpse behind him. He saw, sitting on a piece of driftwood, an old seaman, smoking his pipe and talking to Sam. (Ever talked to a seagull?) Got to tell the others, he thought. He turned to shout to them. He looked back to check what he'd seen, but there was no seaman of any sort, just Sam – preening. Oh well, forget it. No one would really believe him, not Alec, anyway. 'Not again,' he would say. Up the steps two at a time, Ben joined the others.

Alva was first to climb into the sturdy basket. 'Come on, Ben,' he called. 'Now then, you two lads, cast off. But first throw me your luggage.' All of it flew like rugger balls through the air and landed on the basket floor. Taking a mooring rope apiece, the two friends prepared to oblige Alva in releasing his aerial contraption from the island. Alec let go first and made a rush to the basket, clambered in and pulled the rope in after him. He'd made it! He started to sort his rope into some kind of order. It was all or nothing for Ben. He released his line and hung on. Whoosh! Up soared basket and balloon. Wildly swinging underneath like a pendulum, you might have thought Ben was having the time of his life. You might have had to try to convince him! Hand over desperate hand, he steadily clawed his way up into the basket. He'd made it too. Just. A last glance below, he saw nothing but sea, creaming, surging and heaving round the mysterious island. At last, he scrambled into the welcoming wickerwork.

'Glad you could join us,' Alva said with a wicked grin. 'Fettle t' rope oop,' he went on. And laughed out loud. Both mooring lines soon hung neatly on their respective hooks. 'Relax,' Alva said. He reached up and gave his burner a sustained burst. His two passengers were more than glad to take him at his word, and sat down.

Silently, serenely, carried ever higher and now caught in a persistent air-flow, Alva's wonderful aircraft found itself some distance out to the west. And there it was below – the Skerryvore lighthouse, buffeted and sluiced by rising sea.

'Give him a signal,' Alva said as he leaned over the basket side. His passengers got to their feet and looked down to the waters below. Yes, there was a figure waving furiously from the balustrade round the top of his great lighthouse, standing defiantly on the rocks of Skerryvore, way out in the Hebridean sea. A voice drifted up through the wind: 'Safe journey, safe journey.' It was Alan himself.

'Grand lad at building lighthouses, yon Alan,' said Alva. (He were right!) Everyone enthusiastically waved back and kept going for as long as they could, offering a shout or two of their own before distance defeated them.

Sam seagull (how did he get there?) nestling in the corner of the basket, preened for a moment and started to doze off. 'Some lighthouse,' he said emphatically. 'Completed in 1844, and way over forty metres high,' he went on, nodding knowingly to himself. 'Blow me down!'

Chapter Ten

I t was delightful, relaxing in the balloon's great basket and flying quietly and steadily far out into the blue. Complete contentment, good to be alive. But eventually, what about something to eat, thought the two young Yorkshiremen. To tell the truth, the pilot was, himself, beginning to feel distinctly peckish. All this flying, I ask you! Peering through his goggles, Alva took hold of his familiar, be-furred chapeau, at this moment hanging neatly inside the basket, and gave it an energetic swish. At once, standing firmly in an unoccupied corner, there promptly appeared a small, round, mahogany tabletop, sitting tight on a shapely stem held steady on its tripod foot. It was laid ready with a bright white cloth, except you could hardly see it for cheese rolls and bottled pickle, jostling each other for space. A tall, shapely glass flagon marked "Elderflower" stood firm and twinkling in a silver coaster.

The movement of the balloon offered no threat. Everything upon the table remained firmly in place. The stately flagon might just have rocked to the very slightest degree. But it sat snugly within the coaster's dainty gallery, almost smiling at three glintingly-cut glasses poised ready to be filled. Very quietly, Alva announced: 'Lunch is served.' Alec, leaning over one side of the basket, was trying to study the land below, as they smoothly floated and flew on. Alva had changed course to the east, he knew. They were now flying over the Isle of Mull. Alva had previously told him it was to be part of their route, but the sudden invitation to eat smartly brought his eyes and other interests inboard! Ben had actually dozed off. Alva's bursts on the burner hardly disturbed him at all. His swinging about in mid-air and trying to make it up into the basket had quite whacked him out. Glad to find a free corner, he had subsided to the floor, closed his eyes and quickly drifted into a state of exhausted bliss. He imagined himself floating off into space. The balloon flew on across the wide freedom of open sky, taking them all steadily, surely, unavoidably drawn to who knew where! Alva did.

Was it the pickles? Alec had, after all, unscrewed the lid off the bottle. But Ben's nose twitched. Lifting one eyelid, he – but before he could fully comprehend the loaded little table, Alec gave him a shove.

'Let's eat, come on, Ben,' he shouted enthusiastically. Alva joined in, grasping in one gloved hand a cheese roll, held high.

'Yes, help tha self,' he invited, as he took a bite. A few crumbs broke off and fell down to land on Sam seagull, still aboard. He hadn't been quite awake, but the spatter of food arriving on his head quickly put that right. You might like to suggest that in eating a cheese roll Alva had become a bit earthly. Surely, he was nothing of the sort. But he rather liked cheese and, after all, it was his balloon!

On his feet now, Ben joined the others in the feast offered by the table. The bottle marked "Elderflower" seemed inexhaustible. True, the elegant cut-glass goblets were hardly buckets, but no matter how often they were filled – and emptied – the bottle remained full. "Elderflower", yes, on its label. Champagne? Cordial? What other brew? Maybe you'd be hard-pressed to have a guess at it. The bottle kept its delicious and generous secret, which none of the balloonists attempted to solve. Why bother? They all felt absolutely terrific! The cheese rolls, too, kept coming. As soon as one was taken, another replaced it, until everyone was satisfied. At this, savoury was replaced by sweet. Now it was a grand apple pie, already cut in generous wedges, each half-submerged in its own crystal dish of fresh cream; silver spoon at the ready. Brilliant! Did any balloonist ever enjoy such an airborne banquet?

Alva, as ever, knew precisely what he was doing. He perfectly judged when the meal had run its course, noted the murmurs of satisfaction. Seizing his hat, he gave the headgear a quick spin. Instantly, spoons and dishes were claimed by the little table. Promptly, it, and all that remained upon it, vanished. Alva smiled. Gave the burner another burst. His balloon gently floated on. His passengers were smiling, too. What a meal! Ben, still a little tired, slowly sat down, settling himself on the neatly-tied bundle of clothes that were his. It felt quite firm and very comfortable. Had anything been added to it, he wondered? Anyway, leaning back against the basket, he was glad to relax and close his eyes.

Alec felt very well indeed. Such an excellent meal. He looked fit and ready for anything, surely. There he stood, contented and smiling, resting against the basket-side, which comfortably supported him, his arms outstretched along its edge. He took in a deep, satisfying breath. All was right with the world. This was the life!

But was it? Dark shadow spread across the basket. A deafening, rattling gust of feathers – a white-tailed sea eagle, fearsome golden eyes, yellow killer bill, lethally efficient black talons, dived and snatched Alec by the scruff of the neck. Hooked, he hadn't a chance! He shot skywards like a rocket. The awesomely, magnificent bird had its prey by the collar and swooped up high and away to the northeast. Too great a shock for the victim, legs flailing, to think straight. Trying to relax, he realised he was in no pain. But, horrors! Would his shirt manage to hold out? He didn't fancy a free-fall to whatever lay below. Calming at last, he just hung and dangled like a luckless fish snatched from the sea. His mind went blank.

Dragged high and higher in a sudden sharply dramatic movement, rush of air and just a touch of panic, breathing became almost impossible. Next, down, down, dropping like a stone. Ground rushing up. Collision certain! But his captor soared again in great sweeping curves. Almost blackout from G-force. Then a change to an easy floating, a lovely, lovely, sense of floating. Now, a hovering, almost to a standstill, frightening and restful at one and the same moment. The balloon, where was the balloon, fluttered in and out of Alec's consciousness. Ah, forget about it. Might as well now.

The eagle side-slipped into a steep dive, seeming to go on for ever. A turn, a brilliant upward swoop, the bird folded its wings, came to rest and opened its mouth.

Released, Alec suddenly found himself bouncing in a tangle of twigs, feathers and down. Dumped quite gently, as a matter of fact, face down in a right mess! The bird flew off with great, wide wing-beats and rapidly became a mere dot in the far distance, leaving prey, or passenger, if you will, to gather its wits as best it could. Not easy. Alec cautiously struggled to his knees, spat out a bit of feather, wiped away a dropping or two, and looked about him. He was shocked. Before he had a chance to think, a fierce gust of wind struck his position, forcing him to grab hold of anything within reach. Not much! Reality hit him. By gum, he was in the eagle's nest way up at the top of a tall, very tall, pine. Fortunate that the bird's headquarters, except for him, was empty. Alec grabbed again for whatever he could and shakily raised himself to a half-standing position. He looked all round. You could see for miles! And way beyond the rugged terrain lying below, with its trees, bushes and every kind of undergrowth, there gleamed a stretch of water as far as the eye could see – further still, even! The wind returned, to rise almost to gale force. Swaying crazily, Alec and his nest in total chaos, the tree was doing its very best to fling its "cuckoo" out! Something had to be done, somehow, to get to the ground and safety. Easier said than done. And what might "safety" be? What might lurk in the unknown, down beneath him?

The nest sat on top of a really magnificent pine tree. Uncomfortable as it was, the violence of the wind helpfully succeeded in shaking the nest apart, giving Alec the clue to his escape. He spotted that beneath the boughs carrying the eagle's nest, stumps of old branches stuck out at odd intervals down the length of the tree trunk. That was it! Bracing himself on an elbow and stretching a leg down through the disintegrating eerie, he managed to get a foothold on one of the stumps. Turning himself over – never mind the fluff and droppings – by shoving down his other leg, he was just able to find the same stump with his other foot. Twisting and wriggling, holding on to whatever he could, he corkscrewed his way out of his prison. Down the pine tree he went, foothold by handhold, stump by stump, clutching at the rough bark either where the stumps ran out or were awkwardly placed. Don't look down, he told himself, so he wasn't sure till the very last minute whether he'd made it to the ground. Peeling his face, at last, from the sticky bark after what seemed like forever, he glanced about him. He was nearly there. His foot met a stump, which promptly snapped. Losing his grip, he was suddenly too tired to care. He let go into an empty drop of a couple of metres and fell sideways into a clump of bracken, lay there a bit winded, generally sticky, but otherwise unharmed. And what was more – back on earth! The soft growth had mercifully cushioned his arrival.

Alec couldn't tell for how long he'd been lying flat out on his back, but gradually coming to, he felt for any broken bones. There didn't seem to be any, nor was he in any pain. He carefully got to his feet. All was well. What a relief! There was real delight in finding he'd succeeded in avoiding that prickly, straggling patch of gorse nearby! Even if he was – admittedly – a little shaken, Alec was pleased at where he found himself. The area, covered in shortish grass, gently sloped down and away from his position, losing itself between a scattering of trees intermingled with brambles, honeysuckle – climbing wherever it could – purple foxgloves and drifts of fern. Bright yellow gorse, lit by the sun on what had become a beautiful day, lay all about in challenging thickets. He'd missed all of them. Lucky old Alec!

Oddly drawn to the winding, welcoming landscape, Alec found himself quietly heading down amongst it, wondering what he might find. A noisy bird startled him and flew past to find cover. Sun glancing between the trees found reflection some way off. Alec caught it immediately and broke into a run. Into the open now, he saw it: a truly vast waterway – Loch Ness! Completely dazzling! There was no stopping him. He raced to the water's edge, came to a sliding halt, recovered himself and looked round in astonishment. He stood for some time, gazing across and beyond the vast stretch of water and the magnificent terrain that held it. He began picking out various features of the landscape, now brilliant under a cloudless sky. Almost to his surprise, as his eyes raked round, he caught sight of a building, way, way across the loch. Rugged, this building clearly appeared to be of some considerable size, although distance left much to the imagination. Battlements? Were there battlements? And, difficult to make out against background trees, surely there stood a tower! He leaned forward, trying to focus more carefully.

'Interesting, is it no?' came a quiet voice beyond some willows a little way along the bank-side. 'And would ye be liking to tak a look, mebbe?' the voice went on. Even before a rather startled Alec could frame any sort of reply, there was a movement in the curtain of willows trailing in the water. A small rowing boat nudged its way through into the open. Clinker-built and a-gleam with bright varnish, it was surely the neatest little craft afloat. Smoothly propelled by two oars, it made its complete appearance in wide, rippling circles, then headed towards

Alec until it gently nudged the bank and rocked lazily to a stop where he was standing.

'Good day to ye,' said its expert waterman, as he shipped the oars. All in dark blue, he had, Alec thought, an oddly familiar appearance. The peaked cap, tilted ever so slightly to the back of the head, carried a sprig of bright purple heather. This oldish individual was smoking a short pipe. After a quick draw, he took it from his mouth and puffed a tingling, aromatic cloud of blue smoke, which wreathed up about his head. Slowly clearing, it revealed a smiling, weather-beaten face of many seas.

'Come aboard, if you've a mind,' came the invitation. 'Ye'll be wanting to see the castle, will ye no? Ye'll be Alec, I'm thinking.' Seized by an eagle, having to escape at a great height from its nest, here he was being offered a lift across Loch Ness, Alec stopped looking for reasons to it all. He just said, yes. Could this be one surprise too many? 'Thanks,' he said, as he was helped into the stern. He shoved off from the bank with his foot, as requested, then sat down and tried to relax. Splash! The oars plunged in. The little boat gathered way and headed across the waters.

Back in the balloon, Ben had been totally shocked at Alec's sudden disappearance. Alva reacted quite sharply, but it would seem with rather more amusement than alarm. He calmed Ben pretty well and gave him a go on the burner, clapped him on the shoulder and said: 'We'll find the lad, don't worry, we'll head north-east.' Given the responsibility of the burner, Ben started to enjoy the drama of it all. And what's more, the speed of the balloon began to increase in a timely, helpful, following wind, so much so that, before very long, he was glad to have Alva back in control. Down below, water gleamed from river and loch. Ben certainly didn't fancy the idea of a ducking. But what had become of his mate? Had he survived? Where was he now? Ben turned these questions over and over in his mind. He chewed them over with Alva, who merely raised an eyebrow and focussed harder on piloting his craft. 'Don't worry,' he said, 'we'll find him in a bit.'

This would do for the moment. For, whilst concerned for his old sparring partner, Ben knew Alva well enough to be reassured. Not thinking too much about danger from eagles, he leaned out of the basket and looked down as the balloon flew quite low over one of the many inviting stretches of water. Any salmon down there, he wondered.

Voyage across Loch Ness was going well. Untroubled serenity might have described it. Alec became mesmerised by the regular click of rowlocks, smack of oars hitting the water as the rower heaved, smiled and puffed at his pipe. Bubbles chattering against the hull, the little boat was laughing. Calls from wild fowl echoed and drifted away. The old Scot (well, to Alec he seemed a little old) pulled in easy rhythm. The boat gently bowed to him, to rise again at every stroke. Ahead, Urquhart castle, yes, and getting nearer.

What now? Serenity ripped to shreds! Utter disaster! What's happening? Bows were suddenly dragged down – almost submerged, stern half out of the water, oarsman on his back in the bottom of the boat, legs in the air, oars flailing wildly in every direction, giddy rowlocks just holding out. (Don't ask about Alec!) Boat suddenly airborne, spinning, flung high in a great arc. Over and over it goes. (I said before, don't ask about Alec, confused, holding on.) Now, he doesn't even know if he can trust his eyes. Was that a tremendous, twisting, scaly tail flinging water everywhere before thrashing back into the loch? It was gone, hardly a bubble disturbing the surface. A mighty gush, splash, a drenching fountain of wet, unbelievably the little boat came down and landed with a smack, right-side up, back in the water. It slowly revolved once or twice, gently rocked, then came to rest in the shallows. They had arrived, safely moored. The castle lay before them. Alec, completely shaken, tried to stand up, wobbled violently, grasped a gunwale and sat down, with a bump, in the stern. He said, very loudly, WOW! What of the oarsman with the heather in his bonnet? A figure in blue, and a cloud of pipe smoke, disappeared between some trees. As to his boat, oars now neatly stowed, it was as if nothing had happened at all. It swung a little at its moorings, at moments tugging a bit. Hinting at further adventure? But no, on the whole, just now happy enough where it was.

Alec wasn't exactly unhappy, but still rather shocked. He remained sitting in the little boat, gathering his wits and wondering what might happen next. More to the point – what was he going to do next? He knew he couldn't just hang about. And what about the others? Where were they? Would they be looking for him? He glanced a little nervously across the loch. Might something else leap out? He knew all about being grabbed! The boatman, what about him? Sea boots, old pipe, something familiar about him. Here one minute, gone the next. Is it him, or someone like him, who keeps turning up as if he knows something? Whoever it is, he keeps it to himself. Enough! Come on, magnificent Urquhart castle standing there demanding to be visited. The salty old boatman knew. Alec heaved on the mooring rope, pulled the little boat close enough in, jumped ashore and started walking. He hadn't far to go, the castle was now only a short distance away.

He was getting quite near. The thrilling structure reared up ahead. What was that sound? Bagpipes! Right up close to the castle, now. It was on top of him. Taking a chance, he edged across the drawbridge and on through an archway that took him into a small courtyard. In full highland dress there stood, alone, the piper. On Alec's approach, the imposing figure turned away and slowly entered the main building. It was quite impossible to see who the piper might be or what he looked like. Alec followed him in, the music swelling and echoing, through empty candlelit passages and dark, mysterious galleries. There was a fascinating glimpse past a half-drawn tapestry revealing just a little of a great banqueting hall, richly hung with banners. Weapons, set against the walls, glinted under candelabra suspended from lofty timbers arching above. Shields and trophies caught the light. Alec wondered what might be served at the mighty table glittering with silver and glass. On and on went the piper, Alec at a discreet distance behind him.

A flight of steps, a winding staircase held close in curving walls spoke to Alec of a tower. But how tall? He stumbled, missed a step and painfully barked a shin. Must be more careful. Up and up went the piper, his tunes changing from pibroch to lament and back again, several times over. Must be some tower! Alec was glad of the dim light offered by occasional flickering brands reaching out from the walls. Was this staircase going on for ever? Suddenly, ahead, a door burst open. Bright, almost blinding light exploded in a gush of air. Thank goodness, top at last! Through the doorway went the piper. Alec followed, catching sight of the amazing view. Now, he would be able to get a real look at the musician, views could wait. But there was no one at all. Astonished, he found himself completely alone. Piper disappeared. Abseiled? No! Disappeared! Shock? Disappointment, certainly. Was there another exit from the tower – a hidden door? Search, fruitless. But the encircling battlements were handsome enough. Poking his head through, Alec peered down below. No piper, no nothing. But, briefly, he heard his music hanging in the air, gently trailing, fading away across the kindly breeze.

Alec felt kind of stuck at this point. And he wasn't all that keen on finding his way back down the staircase. Oh well, the all-round vista is spectacular. Count your blessings. View across Loch Ness – very special. Enjoy it. But hold on, isn't that something bursting through the surface? Hope not! He braced himself, looked closely and waited. Nothing happened. At least he felt safe where he was, and the weather was good. Sun out, sky pretty brilliant, plenty of light, although it struck him that some of the glorious colours beginning to spread from the west hinted at evening. More to the point, he was hungry. Fascination with the music had drawn him here to the tower. Had the piper ended his recital and remained present, he could perhaps have had a word or two about food. Hard cheese! The banquet below might be fun, he said to himself. Great idea. Wonder what Alva's serving right now, in the balloon. Where is the balloon? Alec began to dare himself to give the staircase a go. He quietly opened the door to it and took in the flickering dimness that led away out of sight. Was there a gorgeous smell of cooking, or what, wafting up? That great table, the silver, the glass, brimming tureens, he could picture it all! Supposing he was to quietly sidle in? Exciting? I'll say! What about it? In later years, he often wondered if he'd pondered too long. His foot had been on the first step down, when he took a last look at the beautiful evening clouds. Well, would you credit it, he thought, that particular cloud to the right looks uncommonly like a balloon. Is it a balloon? It is, and it's coming this way. He would be pleased to rejoin the crew, but he couldn't help feeling slightly done, as he breathed in a last incredible waft of Scottish broth! He stepped back and, with a sigh, closed the door.

Slowly, really slowly, yes, the balloon sporting a bowler hat drifted across on the evening breeze until it was right over the tower. It and the basket looked enormous. A voice shouted, 'Grab hold,' as a long rope snaked down and almost knocked Alec on the head. 'Come on, come on,' urged the voice way up. Alec did, took firm grasp of the line, wrapped his legs round it, held on and began to climb. 'Lift off,' shouted Alva, giving his burner a burst. Alec was yanked from the battlements and swung like a mad wild pendulum way out and over the water. WAH-HOY!

Balloon and basket, reacting to Alec's weight, dipped a bit, and in that moment the extra length of rope swinging and twisting beneath his feet, flapped and splashed into the water. A massive phosphorescent streak burst up from the depths, water furiously boiling. Alec turned white. Anxious to help, Ben only made things worse, leaning dangerously right out of the basket, ruining balance and bringing the whole rescue operation face to face with – how might one describe the creature that reared up to present itself, full-faced: all jaws and teeth, to rip the basket bottom right out? Stylish, I'd give it that – and such eyes! Amused, almost kindly, 'Room for one more on top?' the beastie enquired in broad Scots. With a huge wink, the resident monster was gone.

Whoosh! An unstoppable spurt of water gushed and spouted high into the air. Alec was soaked. Water rained down on balloon, basket, everything and everyone in it, including Sam seagull, aboard, still cadging a ride. There was a sudden, violent gust of wind, but thanks to the skirt rigged above the basket and Alva's masterly touch, the burner just remained alive. Be quick! Give it a good sustained roar. Balloon and basket, Sam, Alva, Ben, Alec, rope and all shot high and clear, flinging long trails of water scattering and splashing right across the loch. In a minute, it was calm as a millpond. Was Alec ever going to make it up into the basket? It didn't look like it. He did his best, but soaked through on a rope itself pretty wet, hauling himself up seemed hopeless. Gritting his teeth, with frantic encouragement shouted from within, he finally arrived and, grabbed by Ben, toppled over into the basket and lay in a heap on the floor. Darkness was creeping in. A night's rest would do nobody any harm, Alva thought, especially after recent events. He caused the basket to warm up and, after providing a meal, advised his passengers to shake down, get some sleep. He set his balloon on a long, steady drift into the night sky.

Quite early in the morning, conversation between Alva and Ben resulted in a decision to return to Urquhart Bay and make for the land. Alva decided he'd drop his passengers off and leave them ashore, if only briefly, to recover themselves, relax a bit and get properly dried out. He manoeuvred his balloon and brought it down close to a reasonably flat area a little beyond the water's edge.

'Jump out, you two,' he said. Both did, with just a bit of a scramble, but glad enough to feel solid ground beneath them at last. 'I'll be back,' Alva called. The burner roared, and he was away.

Chapter Eleven

'Didn't say when he aimed to be back,' Ben said. 'Not too bothered right now, but at least the weather's warm,' Alec answered. 'Glad he left us these bacon sandwiches for breakfast.'

The sun had actually begun to come through. Finding a sunny spot between some trees, shirts were soon off. Draped across helpful gorse bushes, they would be given a good dry airing. A patch of soft grass made a great place to lie flat out, take off shoes and socks. Alec was more than glad to do this. He dozed off and began dreaming of an invitation to a banquet. Might he make it to the table this time? He managed to get halfway down some half-remembered staircase ..... Ben, who had been on his feet for some time looking for wild plants, quite unintentionally woke him. 'Look up there,' he said.

Alec, blinking and stretching, 'What, where,' he said, struggling to stand up. Pity, missing all that food, he reflected. Might have been great. 'What's to do, Ben,' he said, yawning.

Pointing a finger Ben said, 'Look right up the hillside.' Somewhere way above, at a fair distance, could be seen a rather handsome-looking house. It was hard to pick out much detail. Might be interesting to find out about it, thought Ben. 'Come on,' he said, 'Alva has given us time, let's wander up there. Could be worth our while.' Both shirts were good and dried. Get 'em on, shoes too. Ready for anything now.

Looking to the hillside, movement of a person could be seen amongst the trees. Seemed to be, as far as could be made out, a figure of a man, moving away from the house. He took a zigzag way down against the steepness. Down he came, to disappear and re-appear at intervals between trees and bushes. From time to time he paused, as if inspecting some of the things growing around him. At one moment he stopped for quite a while, looking right across and beyond Loch Ness.

Ben turned to Alec. 'D'you think he's spotted our balloon?' he said. It was perfectly likely. Hot air balloons in flight, no longer any wonder in that. But what might the man think about a bowler hat sailing across Loch Ness? Watching his leisurely progress down – they hoped towards them – the two friends tried to decide what they might say were he to stop and speak. For a start, were they trespassing? But there hadn't been much option as events had turned out. Nearer now, and easier to make out emerging from a fringe of greenery, the individual appeared to be a man of middle years. He was well built and looked very fit. He held a stout staff in the crook of his left arm. Over the opposite shoulder he carried a pair of long, slender fishing rods. A wicker creel, secure on a broad canvas strap, bright with brass fittings, hung across his back. He wore a collar and tie, tweed jacket, kilt and sporran. His thick socks, skean-dhu, robust leather brogues, would see him right for whatever the day might offer. The angler, if that's what he was, would be ready for anything!

Looking slightly more respectable, shirts and shoes – maybe a bit tatty – back on, both adventurers stood ready, perhaps to explain or apologise if they had in fact been spotted. But almost upon them, the man abruptly veered off and headed down towards the loch. They followed at a distance and, moving clear of the trees, were just in time to catch sight of a rather familiar figure in dark blue. His little boat – that some while ago had ferried Alec across Loch Ness – was no longer at its mooring, but heading across the loch, him pulling at the oars. Hunched in the stern and rather alarmingly weighing it down uncomfortably close to the bubbling waterline, sat the man from the hill.

'Who d'you imagine he could be?' said Ben. Alec shrugged his shoulders.

'Search me,' he said.

'Try asking her,' Ben said. He'd caught sight of a young woman, possibly a stable girl, leading a horse –

equally young, you could say – out from between the trees. She looked nineteen, or thereabouts, slim, bright, fair-haired, attractive and just a little over five feet tall. 'She's probably a local.'

'Heard you talking,' she said, walking towards them. 'Do you not know? Why, that's Sir George, the Laird of Drumnadrochit. And where might you be from?' the girl went on, looking just a little puzzled. 'I haven't seen you round these parts before.' Great question. The two dalesmen smiled, quickly glanced at each other, obviously more flummoxed than puzzled. Who was to try and spill the beans? But how to produce a simple explanation? Been hot air ballooning – hardly enough!

Taking the bull by the horns, Ben quietly said: 'Well, I'm Ben. Alec, here, and I have been doing a bit of a tour (he supposed this might just describe events!) by hot air balloon, starting some time ago in the wilds of Yorkshire. I don't know if you've ever been there, have you?'

The girl thought for a moment, shook her head and said: 'No, up to now I never have.'

'Ah, you'd love it, would she not, Alec?' said Ben. 'Great countryside – hills, tops, mountains, tremendous caves, potholes and waterfalls. Can't tell you, I suppose, here in Scotland, much about mountains and such! Could see you smiling. Called in at Staffa on our way up here. You will know all about the island, of course. Ever met Fingal in his cave? Great fun, you should try it some time soon.'

At this, the girl could only give what you might call "an old fashioned look". Quite unaware, Ben ploughed on with a brief remark or two about Vikings and lighthouses without actually going into detail. Surprise, disbelief, interest and perhaps a little indulgence, at intervals spread across the young horsewoman's face. Her eyes lit up, however, at the mention of Loch Ness and a creature. She gave a firm nod. Here was a believer, nae bother!

'It's been grand having a talk,' said Alec, a little ruefully, having patiently waited to get into the conversation. 'Could we possibly ask your name, if that's not too rude?' Everything had been going so well, he didn't want to spoil it by being a bore. He needn't have worried.

'You may,' said the charming young female. 'Morag, now there's a good Scottish name for you.' She smiled. Happy conversation promised to open out, everyone now perfectly relaxed.

'Lovely animal,' Alec said, running his eyes over the handsome horse's form. 'Is there a name?'

Morag noticed his pleasure. It pleased her. 'I call him Murdoch,' she said, smiling. 'He's really grand, I ride him as often as I can whilst down from university. But there are so many other things to be done. Looking after him and keeping him fit takes time too.'

'Haven't ever been a rider,' Ben remarked, 'but I'm fond of all kinds of horses. Way back, my family bred shires and the like: magnificent, and such gentle giants.'

Morag nodded in agreement. 'Yes,' she said.

'By the way, which university are you at,' Ben asked.

'St. Andrew's,' Morag said. 'I'm reading medicine. Great university, and St. Andrews itself is splendid. You can recognise medical undergraduates by their scarlet gowns, you know.' Conversation was going really well.

Alec's attention was suddenly captured by something high up in the far distance. Morag noticed, too, and attempted to follow his gaze across the loch. She half-closed her eyes and concentrated on the tiny speck just

visible. The sun, which had been playing fast and loose amongst drifting clouds, blazed right through.

'Look,' she whispered, 'it's a bowler hat. A hot air balloon wearing a bowler, and its heading our way.' Alec and Ben shared a grin but said nothing. Morag studied the phenomenon more closely. 'And what a bonnie colour,' she laughed.

There it flew, a gleaming, beaming, custard yellow. Was there ever such a balloon? Sun, now more than ever glancing off it with dazzling effect, the balloon steadily grew larger in its silent drift towards the spotters. Pilot Alva was quickly picked out in his sturdy basket held triumphantly below. But what's this? The whole contraption was beginning to come down! Was Alva intending to land? Surely, not in the middle of Loch Ness! The basket, with its pilot fully rigged in helmet, goggles and gloves leaning over the side, was now very close to the surface.

'Hey, steady on,' shouted Alec. 'What does he think he's doing?'

'Maybe checking on the monster,' said Morag in a quiet voice.

The basket was now skimming across the water and flicking up beads of spray. Sam seagull, perched on Alva's head, was peering into the depths. Splash! Touchdown! But no, a nudge to the burner and the aerial wonder gently began to lift.

Now whether it was the streaming spatter of moisture trailing from the basket, or whatever it was, who could say? But the waters heaved, and for a second time, a fiercely beautiful head reared up. Its long, serpentine, dark blue, rather elegant scaly neck swirled round the basket, to grip it. But Alva was on his game, gave the burner such a blast that balloon and basket drew clear, leaving a corkscrew neck with, on the whole, not an unfriendly face – water dripping from everywhere – looking to see where its prey had gone. This second appearance offered the chance for everyone to take a closer look at – wouldn't really want to call it a "monster"! See the face. Part sea lion? Part shark? But better fangs by far! Part dragon? You will have to make up your own mind. Friendly, or what? It rolled its large, intensely emerald eyes fringed with waving, weedy lashes. A grin spread across its wide mouth, which closed for a moment and gave a long, low sigh, to echo and re-echo all round the loch. As the sounds died away, the neck coiled down, drawing the head beneath the waters. A great bubble rumbled and heaved up. Was that a rather liquid "Goodbye", or was it "Och ae", that washed right across and round the loch? On the whole – surely, rather fun. Never to be forgotten. Anyhow, just then a long, deep blue, powerful scaly tail whipped up from below. It just managed to give the bottom of the basket a farewell flip and a great boost, causing Alva to hold on very tightly indeed and wonder what on earth had got into his burner when given the last blast. Some gossiping wildfowl took off in a flurry of feathers. It sounded just like laughing; whilst an uncomfortably familiar-looking sea eagle hovered overhead, in hopes, perhaps, for a minute or two. It seemed very interested, indeed, and after a very long look at Alec, swept away. Alec didn't notice. Probably just as well!

Of the three young people ashore, Morag seemed almost completely unruffled. She had burst out laughing at one point and still had a smile on her face. And what was she making of her two new acquaintances? Astonished, maybe, but doing their best to look for her benefit as if it was all a matter of course, wondering at the same time what Alva might have in mind. Caught in the upheaval, he'd steered his balloon away a short distance. And was pondering. Ben explained, at least a little, to Morag about pilot Alva. She had been rather intrigued by the helmeted, goggled, gauntleted individual in charge of a yellow bowler hat. But as we know, that was less than half of it!

Our ostler-turned-pilot now allowed his craft to drift back towards dry land and came to a gently rocking halt sufficiently clear of trees and just half a metre or so from the ground. A handy height, you might say, for conversation with the three below, fascinated by his skilful manoeuvre. Heaving out two ropes, he shouted: 'Anchor t' basket to those trees yonder, if you will.'

There was no telling whether Morag was feeling at all hungry, but there'd been a lot of chat, and her having been exercising her mount, she must surely have worked up an appetite. Her two new companions were, right now, feeling distinctly peckish. The little table likely to appear in the corner of Alva's basket would surely be able to help out! What might appear on the menu would have to remain to be seen. Without doubt, anything would be welcome. Whatever it turned out to be, delicious. Any such hopes and expectations were cut short.

'Climb aboard,' called Alva. 'It's time to be off. Took a little trip over Braemar. Grand fun going on there. You'd surely like to tak a look, the pair of ye. And what about the young lady? Morag, isn't it?' How did he know? 'She'd fancy to drop in too, I reckon, enjoy t' pipes, dancing and all.' Morag's face lit up. 'But first we should be properly introduced, don't you think, gentlemen?' Quite right! Shoving off in a balloon with three strangers (albeit from Yorkshire), what sort of sense was that? Arrangements needed to be correct. And Morag would certainly have to let the stables know what was afoot.

'It would be grand,' she told Alva, 'but the young horse is due back at the stables. In any case, I must leave proper word with the other people, too. Could you possibly hang on for a bit?'

'Reckon I could,' Alva said, 'but look sharp if tha can.'

'Do my best,' Morag said, had a confidential word in the horse's ear and led him off at a trot. 'Shan't be long, shan't be long,' she called back excitedly. The pair were very soon out of sight.

'It'll be grand to have extra company,' said Alva. 'And t' lass is doing t' proper thing. And we must look after her.'

'Reight lads,' Alva began again, to the two friends. 'Suggest tha comes aboard.' From his weskit pocket, he fished out his pocket watch. They remembered when they had first seen it, in the great barn unexpectedly discovered near their village, when they were young boys. How it glinted! It gave a ringing "ping" as he set the timer. 'Hope she'll not be long,' he said. First one, then the other of his accustomed crew climbed in and sat down in the bottom of the basket. In the corner opposite him, yes, the little circular table began once more to appear. It presented sausage rolls, casually piled on a blue and white china plate. Next to this, another, offering crisp bread rolls already split and buttered. A deliciously savoury haze, steaming from two shapely soup-filled mugs, drifted wonderfully into all four corners of the basket.

'There you are, lads, fill tha faces,' said Alva. No further invitation was necessary. Getting to their feet, his guests thanked him and made short work of everything the little table could provide. No saying where it all came from, except that Alva's be-furred hat, hanging inside the basket, was seen to be all of a tremble. Funny, nothing ever came out of his flying helmet! And Alva himself seldom seemed to eat. Time was ticking. It was good not having to rush the meal. After offering water, to send everything down, the table disappeared. 'Hope t' lass found a bite to eat,' said Alva, considerately, looking at Sam pecking and tidying up the crumbs. 'Bit more than that, though,' he said, smiling.

'Hello, hello,' Morag was calling. There she was, bright and smiling, resplendent in most elegant highland dress. Everyone was glad to see her. Alva had been looking at his watch several times and beginning to hum, appropriately enough – 'Will ye no come back again?' under his breath.

And even for him, it became tricky firing the burner on and off over a period, to keep the bowler full.

'Sorry to be so long,' Morag said rather breathlessly. 'Had to change and grab a bite to eat.' She smiled prettily at Alva.

'Tha's all reight, lass,' he said patiently. 'Come on in. Help her, you two lads. Careful now.' Shown where to put her feet in the gaps woven into the basket-side, and offered a steadying hand, the young Scot was soon on board. 'Hold on,' Alva said, 'and we'll be away. You two lads, release yon ropes.' Ben jumped out and loosed his from one of the tall pines which had served as an anchor. Alec, releasing his from the trunk of another pine, found he'd got a bit of sticky resin on his hands. Did this remind him, unpleasantly, of his eagle episode, I wonder? Taking them in turn, first one then the other rope was scrambled back into the basket, to lie neatly stowed. Second man out, Alec, held on till the last minute, trying to steady the whole rig. With Ben, he made a run for it, determined to get back in good order. No more crazy swinging about underneath for him if he could help it. Not on your life (or his)!

'Thanks, lads,' Alva said, took extra grip of the throttle, and gave his burner a steady burst. The yellow bowler gathered itself, rose skywards and began to drift across the famous loch. By compulsion, perhaps, or somehow lured, Alec rather unwisely leaned right out of the basket. The journey hadn't been going very long, when he suddenly felt he just had to do it. A sort of a challenge to what fate had delivered before. He looked deep down into the water. No bother, no bother, safe as houses. Crikey! Ooer! A great silvery-green bubble, eerily lit from below, was wobbling its way very slowly up from the depths. What now? What now! Whoosh! Splish! The bubble dramatically squirted up, producing a fountain almost high enough to hit the bottom of the basket and left behind it wide ripples, repeating and repeating, smiling. Was something from the depths having a laugh? Some of the spray, all whirled about by the commotion, caught Alec in the eye. Next time, next time, waiting for you! Was that the message? Alec drew back and caught his breath. Phew! That could have been a close one! He smiled, everyone smiled, especially Morag. She knew the loch well. Alva's balloon sailed on.

The ever-changing countryside below kept everyone interested enough. No small table to be seen in any corner of the basket, but a very comfortable chair quietly appeared. Morag was small, it was small. It was for her. How very thoughtful! Invited, she said 'thank you very much,' and sat down. Alva busy with flying, navigating, checking his altimeter and rise and fall indicator, didn't talk a great deal, apart from making occasional remarks about drift and weather, which right now was really bonnie. During a lull in everyone's conversation, Morag suddenly said, 'What do you two guys do, back home?'

'Archaeology,' Alec said, and talked enthusiastically, especially about some of the field digs in which he'd been involved, along with lecturing at university. 'Hadrian's wall, spent a lot of time working there. Terrific.'

'Always been fascinated with that,' Morag said.

Ben quietly mentioned his one time career as a botanist. 'Great,' he said, 'and it's such a help to me as a guide. I take all kinds of folks, young and old, right across the Yorkshire Dales, back home, in all seasons. I live there, anyway.'

'Sounds really grand,' Morag said.

As to precisely when, no one might have been able to say, but gradually there came music rising from a distant point below. Bagpipes! Alva smiled. His apprentice balloonists, who had sunk to the floor of the basket and dozed off, didn't at first hear anything. Morag's head was dropping. But – her toe began to tap. Instantly, she was on her feet, listening, and craning her slender neck over the side of the basket. For sure, way down below in a wide grassy arena, it was all happening in a frantic swirl of music, movement, colour and excitement, crowd and sound all wrapped and woven together on a sunny, windy highland afternoon. The games! Morag glanced at the sleepers. 'Och awa,' she said gently. With her toe, she gave Alec a nudge. His eyes opened in surprise, saw her smile and gave Ben a shove. Result? All three young people, now wide awake, up on their feet, you could say, and ready for anything. What fun, below!

Alva was way ahead of them. 'OK,' he said, 'we're going down.' He sized up the position. He had no permission to land. Certainly mustn't interfere with the highland gathering obviously in full swing. Not that many folk would be aware of his very singular balloon as it came to ground. But he would find a sensibly open, reasonably flat area, clear of trees, where he could make his landing. Ah, there's the very spot, and close enough to all the activities. Under his expert hand, yellow bowler, plus basket, smoothly descended and came to rest with hardly a jolt in a small, secluded field. The basket did tilt over somewhat and gently bump along for a short distance. But the grass was lush. Nobody's teeth were rattled, elbows bruised. Perfect landing.

'Well, here we are,' said Alva, 'hop out wi' t' tethering ropes, you two lads, if you please. Yon hedge might do for one. Mebbe that old stone gatepost would hold t' other.' It didn't take long to do the job.

Chapter Twelve

Beyond a clump of tall trees, which Alva had so skilfully avoided, cheerful shouts rang out, bagpipes going at full throttle. How could anyone resist?

'Off with all of thi,' Alva said. 'I've one or two things to do. Will call thi back later.'

'Come on, you two,' said Morag. 'Let's take a look.' A quick glance round, ah – a handy gap in the hedge.

'Here we are,' Ben said, pushing branches aside. The three ran through and across a small field. 'Over there, right over there.' Through a sturdy five-barred gate (closing it behind them) Ben, Morag and Alec headed for the action. Down a grassy track, wild flowers dotted everywhere, and finally through a wide, inviting opening between trees, the companions arrived. Boisterous crowds, wearing tartans of every pattern, were having the time of their lives amongst the stalls, flags and tents scattered all round the sporting arena. The sound of the pipes echoed around the hills. And what a delicious smell of cooking drifted across the entire field of play.

Back at the landing field, Alva made careful adjustments to keep his balloon just sufficiently inflated. (He knew exactly what he was about, you may by now have gathered.) He made sure there were no cattle near the landing ground (those horns!), got back in the basket, lay down and closed his eyes. Even pilots, such as he, were sometimes glad of a zizz. Sam seagull flew out and round for a bit, enjoyed some sandwiches discarded near a refreshment tent, then returned to the balloon. Full of sandwich (ham, I think), he perched on the basket-side and put himself on watch. Helmet, goggles and gloves abandoned in a heap on the basket floor, Alva was lost to the world.

Well, Alec had seen it often enough, one way and another, but never tried it. Egged on by Ben and with encouragement from Morag, he, on impulse, took hold of a fairly substantial pole found lying idly at the edge of the field. 'Go on,' they laughed, 'try and toss the caber, bet you can't.' Alec just about managed to get the timber upright and balanced between his head and shoulder, his hands under the butt of the unwieldy thing. Heavier than he'd imagined, it lurched about alarmingly. Steady, steady, a few inexpert steps forward and – heave! The pole tried hard, managed half a revolution, hit the ground and fell sideways. Tough luck!

'Well, at least I gave it a go,' said Alec.

'Good man,' Ben said, and thumped him on the back. 'But that's how it's done, look over there.' Way across the field, the burliest Scot you might ever expect to see, took off his glengarrie, sporting a sprig of fir, and seized a monster pole. A rising pitch of crowd excitement coming to a frantic crescendo, he staggered, half ran forward, bent his knees, straightened them, and sent the caber flying into a completed spin. It came to earth on the proper end. Deafening applause!

The hammer throwers were amazing. Watch out! A heavy metal ball on a length of chain thudded into the ground just clear of Morag. Well, not that near, but seemed almost too close for comfort. Way across the field, shot putters, grunting and sweating and heaving their own particular missile, strove to out-do each other. Must have been some strong porridge at work! Slinging a heavy weight, backwards, over a high wire, drew a good deal of gasping admiration. More porridge, obviously. People milled about having a great time on what was a lovely summery day. Drift in and out of refreshment and sweetie tents. In others, admire crafts and merchandise. So much to see, eat, nibble and buy. Sit down, perhaps, to salmon and salad, scones and jam, haggis maybe. Try sausages at the barbecue – hopefully not burnt – smoke billowing out in welcome. Drink what you like. And there is always ice cream.

Bagpipes kept squeezing out their merry skirl, pipers' faces getting redder and sweatier in the bright sunshine. On an open platform, rigged for the occasion – highland dancing, kilts whirling, repeated in relay with hardly a gap for breath. There were silver cups to be won. Morag found her way into a brilliant group of dancers. The two Yorkshiremen were entirely captivated. Heel and toe, tiny feet leaping, spinning, fleet, precise. Necessary, where swords glinted just like the silver dazzling from velvet jackets. She was stunning! Nearby, on their own platform, several highly polished silver cups and trophies winked in the sun. Who might claim them?

Pipes and dancing slackened, gave way to accordion, also orchestral and band music, further diversity and delight. Relax, relax, enjoy. But what was this? A purple tandem shot into view from a cluster of trees. Two figures, crouching low, pedalling furiously, made a wide circuit of the field, then screeched to a stop in a spectacular skid. Off jumped the front man. He stood and helped his "rear gunner" to alight. Surprise, surprise? It was none other than Sir George, Laird of Drumnadrochit; last seen sitting perilously low in the stern of a little wooden boat being rowed across Loch Ness! Spontaneous applause from the crowd. Sir George had come to present the cups. He mounted the trophy platform, to sit in Braemar's ceremonial seat. He took out a large red handkerchief and mopped his face. Eyebrows bristling, he was ready to greet the winners. As to the tandem, the front man wheeled it away. His dark blue rig and sea boots – hmm.

Wandering amongst everything, everybody relaxed, with not a care in the world on this blissful, highland day, you could say time really ceased to exist. One or two contented dogs snoozed in the sun. A lively border terrier scampered up to be petted. It was a cheerful breed of little animal that Ben determined to have one day soon. Crowds seemed to be thinning. There was still much fun, but quieter, and music more or less fallen silent. The three friends were now sitting on a wide bench set under a tree, offering room enough to lean back against its trunk. Lured by the smell drifting from a small tent, they had bought a piping hot, finger-nipping bundle of fish and chips to share. What better?

Something began to appear in the sky. Couldn't see it all at first, as it disappeared behind trees. But it had a familiar roundness. A seagull dived in, pinched a fat chip and was gone. 'Sam,' Ben said. The aerial object, rounded, distinctly yellow, came into full view. The bowler hat. What else? Alva was arriving to collect his passengers. Alec wondered who had assisted him to get airborne, let go ropes and all that. Alva was Alva. He had probably enlisted a friendly haggis – wild in those parts. Anyhow, the balloon, triumphantly inflated, flew ever higher and closer. Huge, overhead now, it began to come down. Its pilot called, 'Get ready, everybody there below.' His craft grounded within fairly easy reach. Helmeted, goggled and gloved, Alva leant from the basket and beckoned to his three passengers to join him. Perhaps just a little unwilling to end the fun, Morag and by now her two adopted Scots, slowly licking their fingers, ambled to the basket and clambered in. Oh yes, be sure, a litterbin had already claimed the fish and chip remains.

'Now then, young Morag,' Alva said, pushing up his goggles, 'we really should be getting thi back. The lads and I have a fair journey ahead of us. We mustn't tak thi any further from home, I'm thinking. What about t' stables?' At this, Morag looked rather thoughtful.

'There'll not be a problem,' she said, rather wanting to see where the next balloon flight would land. 'A friend of mine runs them, said she'd look after Murdoch till I got back. I told her about everybody and the situation and that we were off to Braemar. Wished she could have come too, she said.'

'Reckon she would have, at that, but we must see thi right,' Alva said, climbing out from the basket. 'Be back shortly. Keep an eye on t' balloon, gentlemen. Give t' burner a boost from time to time if you will. Just fasten t' anchoring ropes one at a time round yon trees before I go, then nip back. Don't leave Morag on her own, tha sees.' Trusting us with the balloon, thought Ben, wow! At a brisk pace, Alva headed straight off across the fast emptying games arena. Not much left to see, but a heavily churned muddy strip remained to tell of tug-of-war. Were wild shouts still echoing? The trophy platform stood abandoned, silverware long since presented. Sir George, quite exhausted from smiles, congratulations and yet another handshake, had been loudly thanked by officials, then shepherded away to enjoy Braemar hospitality. Would he ever get back to Drumnadrochit! Alva disappeared behind the platform.

Moments ticked by. No Alva. His three passengers waited. The longer they waited, so curiosity grew. They'd been given no hint. Sam was no help, perching nearby, eyes half-closed, dreaming of chips. At last, 'Here he comes,' shouted Ben – duty lookout.

Alva, goggles down, was heading at speed, straight for the balloon. He was not on foot, nor was he alone. There was a co-pilot riding in front of him, crouched almost double over seriously racing handlebars. Screech of brakes, wild skid, Alva bundled off a rather familiar-looking

purple tandem. Chest heaving, 'Are you there, Morag?' he called. He walked to the balloon and leaned against the basket, pausing for a moment to catch his breath. 'Now then young lady, transport has arrived. Let me help thi out of t' basket.'

There had been much conversation whilst Alva was away. Morag realised that, for her, ballooning would for a while be on hold, although it would be grand to ride Murdoch again. Everyone was a bit sad. As to the ballooning crew, where might the next flight take them? Anyhow, addresses were exchanged, you may be sure.

'Come across and see us, maybe stay, in the Dales,' Ben said.

'Don't leave it too long,' Alec said, 'we've so much to show you and you'd love it.' Ben wondered what she'd make of all the goings-on which had taken place with Gilbert and his gaping pothole, let alone everything else alive throughout the great mountains. They each gave Morag a hug, a peck on the cheek, and helped her over the basket-side. Alva removed both gloves and lifted her down. There it was, the machine, the purple tandem, back seat waiting, driver astride and ready for racing, his old cap reversed and halfway down the back of his salty neck. All aboard! Ship ahoy! Alva helped Morag to perch on the rear saddle.

'Cast off forrard, cast off aft,' came the shout. Morag, a little unnerved, perhaps, waved and shouted 'Scotland for ever.' A brief wobble, she found her balance and began to concentrate. Steering a wide preliminary circle to build up speed, both riders at last pedalling furiously, the tandem with Loch Ness in mind shot off in a cloud of dust, flaxen hair, tartan and navy blue and rapidly disappeared from sight.

Chapter Thirteen

The yellow bowler hat was anxious to be away. Alva climbed straight back into the basket, took command and reached for the burner. 'Right lads, let go t' ropes,' he said. Helmeted, goggled and gloved once more, he was ready for any action. Tethering ropes, one after the other, smartly cast off and secured inboard, full crew back in the basket, the balloon took flight. Food? Good idea. Befurred hat given the nod, there once more stood the little table with its white cloth. Except the cloth was hardly visible beneath omelettes, apple tarts and a bottle of white wine in its silver coaster, merrily clinking and rattling with accompanying glasses eager to be filled.

'Help tha sels,' Alva said, reaching for the throttle handle and giving the burner a long go. Who might say what he had in mind, but, encouraged, the balloon gathered itself and flew south-east as fast as it could, scudding across the sky and shoving aside every cloud sufficiently unwise to be anywhere near. Away went the wondrous contraption. You might say bowling along! Such was the pace, this flying object was sometimes almost horizontal. By gum, it were in a hurry! Somehow (gimbals maybe) the little table remained perfectly steady. And nothing ever fell off. Alva and his crew held on for dear life, eating quite happily! Sam was a winner in all manner of crumbs.

Temperature, for long enough so agreeable, dropped sharply for a moment, before managing to recover. Noticing the change, Ben glanced across to Alva, who looked back at him and merely gave a nod. 'Nearing Dundee,' was all he said. He allowed the balloon to settle down to a more leisurely speed. A gleam of water came into view, far down below. Alva knew. 'T' Tay,' he said, 'River Tay.' He considered the burner, looked rather thoughtful, smiled to himself and allowed his craft to steadily, slowly, lose height. Lower and lower, almost drifting now quite low along Dundee's waterfront. "Discovery Point." "Discovery Quay." And there, gently stirring at her moorings – Royal Research Ship "Discovery", Captain Robert Falcon Scott's vessel, taken on his 1904 Antarctic expedition. Built in Dundee in the year 1901, there she lay, back, it could be said, where she belonged. 'Grand ship down there, lads,' Alva remarked, 'tak a look.' His crew of two leaned out and spent some time letting their eyes and imaginations roam over every inch of it. Glancing further afield, they could see people about their business in hot sunshine, comfortable in shirtsleeves and summer dresses. But what was happening? Returning again to the three-masted barque, the sun that, before, had bathed it, now glinted off frozen ropes and rigging. The deck looked icy, slippery enough, and the stumpy funnel, aft, to serve the engine below, was rimed with frost. Dundee wasn't anywhere near. Frozen terrain stretched as far as the eye could see. Further. Awesome! A mighty glacier reared up in total domination, towering almost out of sight. In the distance, a crowd of penguins, nodding advice to each other, shuffled off into misty dimness. Half a dozen angry seals loudly argued between themselves. The temperature had dropped almost out of the bottom of the basket. Alva steered very slowly till the balloon drifted right over the ship. No one on deck, just a lone lookout, crouched and huddled, in the crow's nest high up on the mainmast. And maybe cursing his luck. The balloon was almost on him. Horrors! The figure suddenly reared up, grabbed at the basket, took hold of it and swung a sea-booted leg over the side. In he came, the whole lot of him, and stood staring-eyed, as stiff as a board, motionless, completely rigid, hunched so awkwardly with cold. Stubbled face blue with cold, grim, this ice-bound example of misery was frozen solid. A glint of encrusted sea salt edged the peak of his old, crumpled cap.

With a low moan and a shudder to shake the whole universe, this figure of a seaman in remnants, only, of dark blue, vanished. Alva's two apprentices shivered, blew on their fingers in some hope of warming them. Circulation? Forget it. Along the basket edge ran a crisp edge of rime like cut glass. Alva released a smile into the corner of the basket. Instantly, there was the little table. It offered hot soup and, of course, there were oatcakes! A touch on the burner, up went the balloon, up went the temperature. Alva steered his craft in a high, wide circle. Down below, RRS Discovery rocked gently in the Tay, gleamed warmly in the sun. The crow's nest? Empty! Relief all round, basket really beginning to warm. Bowler balloon headed for Edinburgh.

Apart from essential interruptions from the burner and occasional navigational checks, the balloon floated silently on a smooth, level course. In time, Alva gave it an easy lift to clear the Lomond Hills and before you knew it, there lay the great city, Auld Reekie. Alva had skilfully managed to avoid the wonderful Forth Bridge. Watch out for Edinburgh castle, mister pilot, best not to bounce off it! Breezing into Edinburgh, sailing down Princes Street, who's that below? Sir Walter Scott jumps up from his monumental seat and, with one hand tightly gripping the masonry, he swings out on one arm, waves with the other and shouts, 'speed bonnie boat.' (Where had he heard that?) Peering below, Alec just had time to see the great writer sit down once more, with a laugh and a shake of his head. Who'd have thought it? Away, now, from the great city. Steer south-east, head for the coast. Before long, feel the strengthening breeze, smell the salt. The open sea!

Ah, yes, the open sea! Romping and jostling along high above the shoreline, balloon buffeted by North Sea winds, Alva did a grand job keeping his jaunty craft on a reasonably even keel. Sam seagull was, of course, in his element, taking to the air, skydiving, wheeling, soaring in expert flight, keeping a sharp eye out for food. Fish and chip eaters along the seafront needed to beware!

Berwick-upon-Tweed, with its turbulent history, rapidly left behind, Alva steered close to Bamburgh castle. Way off out to sea on this bleak north-eastern coast: the Farne Islands, which could tell of Grace Darling who, with her lighthouse keeper father, William, on the seventh of September 1838, rowed out in their open, flat-bottomed fishing boat, through a raging sea, to help the battered, broken merchant ship, "Forfarshire", run aground and wrecked. A great wave leapt up to the bowler's basket, knocking it sideways. A rope of wet seaweed looped up and almost throttled the burner, which coughed just briefly, shrivelled the intruder and continued on duty. Alva smiled, his crew gasped. That was a close 'un! Make for Alnwick castle, now, (was that a skirl of pipes, clash of battle?) then after a longish flight, float over Durham, contemplate its mighty cathedral commanding the River Wear. Ghosts enough here, too. And such architecture! No time to land and explore. Be sure to return sometime. Look in on the Venerable Bede and St. Cuthbert. It would please them.

The balloon journeyed southwards to Darlington. 'Just look at that,' Alva said, peering below. Trailing thick black smoke, belching and swirling from its tall, stovepipe funnel, the Stockton to Darlington passenger train, its locomotive cranking, clanking, wheezing and steaming, was making its way along the track, rattling the rails at a breathtaking, swaying, bone-shaking, maybe twelve miles an hour! Darlington, quite near now, would surely be quaking at its arrival! The train slowed, slackened, finally arrived at its destination, where it rumbled to a halting stop, locomotive hissing and steaming. Jostling and chattering, the passengers spilled out. Such excitement amongst the top hats, bonnets and shawls – sooty faces. Wonderful! The balloonists, by now right overhead, saw it all. The mechanical wonder at rest, its gasping driver climbed down from it, leant against one of the great wheels, wandered a short way from the heat, wiped his sweaty face and beamed with satisfaction. His mate, already at the trackside, prodded and inspected some of the couplings, soon joined him, then began to enjoy a pipe. Engineer wearing sea boots? Interesting. Simmering heat, smell of hot oil, remnants of smoke rose up and drifted into the basket. 'By 'eck,' Alva gasped. The burner given the nod, he and his passengers soared into clearer air.

'That railway, some way to travel,' Alec said, wiping a streak of grime from his face. Along with Ben, he'd been hanging over the basket-side for a better look at the marvel below. 'Interesting, that.'

'Aye, reight interesting,' Alva agreed. 'Grand way to travel for folks on their day out. Reight exciting adventure it was in those days,' he went on. 'Can you see t' poster on t' station wall? See what it says. Tak a look.' Grand Darlington Show, Fruit, Flowers and Vegetables and Big Brass Band. There it was for all to see. Actual day not clear, but, in bold figures, the year – 1833. 'Wow,' Ben said.

It hadn't been exactly dull up here so far, Alec thought, wondering quite where Alva might be going to steer them all next. A bit of a clue, perhaps, from Samuel seagull,

who'd been half asleep in a corner of the basket. Now he lifted his head and began to sniff the lively breeze, steadily building as Darlington faded astern. A brisk flutter and he upped and perched on the basket-edge, shivered his timbers, stretched his wings out wide, settled, preened his feathers, put each neatly into place. He took a careful look all round at the world, gathered himself and, with one or two steps along the basket, for balance, flung out his wings and took off. He knew, he'd sniffed it, he headed for the sea.

'I know where he's bound,' said Alva, as Sam became a distant dot. 'Any idea, you two lads?' he said.

'Might be Whitby, d'you think?' said Ben. Alva smiled, glanced up into the bowler hat, checked his compass and roused the burner.

The three flyers could really smell the sea. Increasing wind-speed had the balloon racing along at a fairish lick. Every now and again, the basket was whirled, swung and jerked about. The whole contraption was at full-stretch, eager, you could guess, not to waste time. Alva simply rode with it, as you might expect. His crew found it best to sit on the floor, but were cheerful enough, especially when the little round table appeared again, this time offering ham sandwiches and cups of tea. As usual, there was no slipping, tipping, wobbling or slopping. The table stood, rock solid.

Suddenly, a thumping gust of wind put all catering arrangements really to the test. Whoof, whoosh, wow! Wer-hoy! Whacking, tilting, rocking and spinning, the balloon basket certainly knew what had hit it! Even Alva gasped a little. His usual smile burst right out into a laugh. 'By gum, that were a big 'un,' he said, recovering his breath. Ben laughed too, as he slid across the floor of the basket. Alec couldn't help giving a shout, suddenly finding himself upside down, feet in the air. Well, what was that all about? They'd arrived over Whitby, to be blown, hurled and blasted with almost gale force, right across the harbour. A sudden stillness. Then – crack! A violent squall made Alva and everything under his command almost loop the loop. What next? What next?

Uncanny calm, a gentle rocking. Whispering breezes fan in and out of the wickerwork. Odd. Hardly a sound. Voices faintly rising from below? Ben got to his feet. Alec disentangled himself from a jumble of mooring rope jerked off its hook. He got up too. Both stuck their heads out, looked down to whatever lay beneath. Moored at the quayside was a ship, a three-masted, cat-built Whitby collier of long ago. Clearly, something significant was going on, important preparations being made. Figures could be seen humping bundles, packages, barrels and bulging sacks, toiling with them along gangplanks sloping up from quay to ship; heavier loads causing everything to bounce rather alarmingly. Safe on board, at last, the humpers staggered off in different directions across deck, to disappear into cabins and holds. Plenty of other activity along the quay: artefacts and ammunition of sorts, all to be taken on board. Here and there, men appearing to be carpenters, maybe shipwrights, worked with timber. A busy forge glowed and spat. Alva brought his craft down low enough for a closer look.

It wasn't possible to hear exactly what was being said, listen to orders, perhaps. Someone, obviously in command, probably the purser or his assistant, stood at the top of one of the gangplanks, checking each item as it was taken aboard and directing where it should be stowed. Quite clearly, it was to be no ordinary voyage, no ordinary ship being prepared and provisioned. What might she be? Skies were a little dull, but an unexpected shaft of sunlight half revealed the craft's identity, gilded right across the galleried stern. Almost in the same instant, the sun disappeared. Was this ship the "Endeavour", skippered by Captain James Cook? Was she shortly to leave? Had time slipped to 1768? Crew members began nimbly climbing the rigging and taking their positions way out along the yards to ready the sails. When towed clear of the quay, the ship would be eager for the open sea and wide oceans. Ben's mind became lost, looking at all going on below.

Wouldn't mind giving something like that a go myself, he said, thinking out loud. How he got aboard he'd no idea, but, unbelievably, he found himself right there on deck, beside the mainmast.

'Get thee aloft, look lively now.' It was the bo'sun, in rough breeches, open-neck shirt, striped brass-buttoned reefer jacket and tarred hat. Stocky and weather- beaten, there he stood. And not a man for any argument! 'Get thee aloft,' he again ordered sharply, taking a quick pace forward. Ben jerked back and leapt for the ratlines. Was that a rope's end that swished behind him? Up, up Ben went, clinging to the rough shrouds. Up, up. At last – relief – the crosstrees. Would that do? He was really sweating. No chance. Don't look down. Again – 'Oop the mast,' the bo'sun shouted more harshly. 'Out on t' yard.' Scrambling more than a bit, barking his shins more than that, missing his slippery, panicking footing, Ben at last made it to the upper cross. How much further? He was trembling like a jelly. A gust of real Whitby almost tore him from his position, clinging to the topmast. He slipped backwards and hit his head on something hard. "Out on t'yard"? How was he going to manage that like the men out there already, waiting for orders?

'Stop daydreaming, matey,' Alec said, 'sorry I caught you on the head with my elbow. But look across there – Whitby abbey.' Ben came to, astounded at finding himself back with the bowler hat, slowly tried to focus, first on his companion, then, very slowly, in the direction Alec was pointing, he just managed to say 'Oh yes,' in a lost kind of voice. He was still up a mainmast heading out to sea.

Stark, high up in its commanding position above the harbour, stood the ruined old abbey of Whitby. History and legend, familiar bedfellows! Even at the very moment both friends beheld the ancient pile, dark, brooding clouds began blotting out the sun. The balloon flew lower.  Temperature plummeted. It was very chilly now. Even Alva blew on his fingers. Was that a dark, menacing bat-like presence hovering over the ancient ruins? Did any of the three travellers glimpse a black, rangy, wolf-like animal, all fangs and fierce, wild, staring eyes? It had slunk from cover amongst the abbey's crumbling arches and glanced hungrily up at the balloon, before making off looking for prey. Who or what would fall victim?

Really awake now, Ben thought he'd seen the flash of greedy eyes, heard a snarl. Alva was ahead of him, and from his weskit pocket, threw overboard a handful of garlic, smiled and said: 'Don't worry, lad, nobbut Count Dracula out and about. Bit peckish, happen.' From his other weskit pocket, he produced a large slab of Kendal mint cake and hurled it like a discus after the departing hound. It was a little brighter, now, what a relief! Garlic redundant? But make the most of the daylight. Soon, first stars would be glinting. Already, there was just a hint of a moon. Up rose the balloon.

Alva attended to his duties. His craft began to leave behind – rather reluctantly, you could feel – Whitby, with its bracing history and tingling mysteries. Lewis Carroll liked it, and would holiday there. Alice stirred in her wonderland, Alec knew, under Whitby skies. 'She'd have enjoyed our bowler hat,' Alva said with a laugh, when Alec told him, as they drifted on down the eastern coast, to float awhile over Robin Hood's Bay. Haunt of smugglers long ago. "Brandy for the parson, baccy for the clerk." Give your imagination a rest would you say? Surely not.

Chapter Fourteen

Hold fast! What was that full-bellied old ship's boat all about, clearly to be seen in the sea below, being rowed stealthily shore-wards: four oarsmen a side and a coxswain (on his head a stylish tricorne hat) at the tiller. The boat was very low in the water, not just because of the crew, you could guess. They looked a tough bunch as they heaved on their oars through the choppy waters. And what a bunch! Some were bare-headed, others in stocking caps, all in rough sea-going clothes, rough enough to match their wild-haired, weather-beaten faces. Was that an oath joining the rumble of oars as they were shipped, dripping, inboard, as the boat finally hit the beach, rode up to be crunched to a standstill by the shingle? One man leapt out and gave the boat an extra heave, which jerked his tobacco pipe from between his teeth. The heel of a merciless sea boot trod it deep into the sand. It would never be found. He spat and returned to his crew for unloading. They all scrambled out, stumbling and muttering. There were bundles, maybe barrels to shift. Smartish! Glow from dark lanterns ready for the road home, signalled from heavy shadows higher up the shore. Where might be the customs men, the revenue cutters? Not this time, mebbe.

'Belay talking,' came a hoarse command. A quiet clink of harness, muffled snorting there in the dimness, meant horses and covered carts – waiting! Sea mist began creeping in, damp, drifting, rolling, swirling. An ear-splitting shot, a curse, instantly put paid to secrecy for the contrabanders. Then there was nothing either to hear or see. Time died.

At last, bowler and basket drifted on. But neither Ben nor Alec could forget what they had – leaning out as far as they dared – been able to hear, witness or believe during the whole desperate action. Darkness was closing in.

'What if you were to hold her steady, Alva,' said Alec, 'for Ben and me to go down and scout round?'

Alva looked at him, just a little surprised. 'Dost tha think tha should, lad?' he said.

'Bring her down as low as you can and we'll drop a rope. Why not?' Alec replied with a wink.

'Well, by gum, young fella,' Alva said quietly.

'Got to give it a go,' insisted Alec.

Concerned, 'Tha'll need to go a bit canny, happen,' Alva said in a low voice, as he slowly began to bring his balloon down. 'Try that now,' he said. Alec trailed a short rope from the basket, climbed out and swung himself down, letting go to fall clear the last metre or so to the beach. He sprawled sideways into a patch of soft sand, lay there for a moment, listening. He peered all about, but could see almost nothing. Barely any light, now. Hardly able to breath, he slowly got to his feet.

'Come on, Ben,' he whispered. 'Quick, let's have a look round.' Go just a little bit careful, he told himself. It was all a bit eerie. Even the waves, slowly tumbling and rippling into the shingle, sounded thoughtful. What did they know? Whatever it was, they were not telling.

A great cliff reared up above the beach and, in the fading light, it was all dark menace. The sea, in constant rhythm, washed and slipped ashore in whispering quiet. Further out, a roller crashed and thundered. 'Be with you soon, catch you out,' it seemed to say. Ben dropped down from the basket. The two friends drew breath in an attempt to stay calm, then groped their way forward, at times tripping over rocks and splashing into unexpected pools all along the shore. At first, there was not much to see. Ben suddenly pulled up short. 'Look at those,' he whispered to Alec, 'hoof marks, surely!' And that smell, he said to himself, sniffing the air – horses I bet, yes, for certain, horses.

There came a break in the foot of the cliff, crumbling away into a deep, dark hole. 'Got to have a look,' Alec whispered. As if on cue, the moon, which had been teasing in and out amongst scrappy clouds, suddenly delivered full power – a piercing spotlight, which now revealed something of a cave, a secret hiding place, with, half buried in the sandy floor, something of an old, sawn-in-half, upturned sea boat. A battered, rotting piece of wood hung crazily, trying to do duty as a front door, helped by a rag of old sailcloth nailed to one side. It stirred very slowly back and forth.

With a grip that made his victim wince, Alec grabbed Ben's arm. 'What d'you make of that,' he whispered, pointing at the mouldering lair.

'Dunno,' was the only, muttered reply he received.

'Come on,' Alec said, 'let's look.' They both edged up to their discovery. Ben reached out and gently pulled aside the dirty canvas. Frightening! Shattering! What remained of the rotting sea boat flew apart, the two intruders flung flat on their backs, where they lay for several tense minutes, hardly daring to breathe or speak. Gradually recovering, they shakily got to their feet, slowly pulled themselves together.

'You or me?' Ben said.

'Both of us,' Alec said sharply, dusting himself down and spitting out bits of sand. Together, they moved to inspect the refuge, its wrecked and scattered remains. What a sight! Lying there was a skull, teeth grinning wickedly and just about connected to a dirty, yellowish skeleton, half-buried up to its waist in the sandy floor. The skull had a musket ball star-split hole, right between the sockets of its eyes! At this precise moment – no moon. Eclipsed. Gone. Blackness. Mouths went dry. Hearts thumped. Palms sweated. Such a rattle of bones! Where is it? Where is it? What's the matter with it? The moon, where has it gone? Pitch black. Deadly dark. Terror!

Must have been listening. At last, bright moonlight shafted down, picked out the rotting devastation. Got to go right in. Got to. Grinning still – perhaps even wider – the owner of the teeth hadn't shifted, had it? Why think of such a thing? Reaching for something half hidden at his feet, Ben accidentally nudged the skeleton, jolting its leering, shattered mask. Its teeth, rattling like scattering dominoes, the skull wobbled, threatened to fall off right on top of Ben's sweaty hand. With a shout that nearly turned Alec inside out, Ben jumped backwards and fell over.

'For goodness sake keep your voice down,' was the politest remark that a rather shocked Alec could muster right then. Recovering just enough, and hastily scraping away the sand hiding a half-hidden object, Ben on hands and knees at last pulled out what looked like a seaman's ditty box, rotted right through. It completely fell apart. Out of it dropped a little black glass bottle, tightly sealed. It felt very full.

'Look at this,' he gasped, as his nervous fingers took hold of it. But Alec was fascinated by what seemed to be a heavy buckle tangled in shreds of a very tired old leather belt, close to the skeleton's collapsed rib-cage. Reaching out to touch it, his hand closed on rough metal. Out slid the blade of a murderous looking rusty cutlass. Were those bloodstains clinging still? With a rasping cough, sharp clatter of bones, the skeleton remains fell forward, bony fingers seemed to grab at Alec's arm, as if to stop him. Was there life in the old seadog yet? That cutlass would be needed for the next boarding!

An angry shout! Was that the figure of a man, sharply silhouetted against the bright moon, suddenly brighter than ever? Quick! Clear out! Had enough of this place. Run like crazy! They did, as best they could, the pair of trespassers, hoping to be able to find Alva and his balloon. With the moon half hiding in and out from bits of clouds, it was not at all easy to see. Who were the pursuers? How many? Fierce shouts, shots. Were those musket balls ricocheting, whining, pinging off the surrounding rocks, humming past their ears? Of course they were. One splashed into a pool right under Ben's foot! What else could they be, stupid! Stumble, stagger, trip in the dark. (The moon had its own business.) Run, run, run, like forever!

At last, there's the balloon, burner flaring. Good old Alva. Grab at the rope, somehow get back aboard. The two dalesmen did, and fell on top of each other in the floor of the basket. They'd made it! 'That were a close 'un,' they both managed to gasp. Ben found he still had the little bottle tightly clenched in his fist. He glanced up. His hair stood on end, and he grabbed at Alec. A row of crazy skulls, grinning and cackling, danced along the basket edge. 'The bottle,' screamed one, 'the little bottle.' The screams changed to a whining, then choked to a stop. The skulls vanished.

Rip, whizz, fizz! A musket ball shot through the basket side, hit the floor and rolled into a corner. The missile, stinging hot, lay there smoking. Alva said, 'By gum, we best get cracking.' He got to work and the balloon soared. His passengers scrambled to their feet and cautiously peered out of the basket. They were shocked and exhausted. The last shot had been a complete surprise and too close for comfort. Wind whistled through the shot hole, but – musket ball? It was nowhere to be seen. Scorch marks? Yes. Shot? No! Maybe Alva had picked it up, though they hadn't seen him. They didn't ask, he was busy.

'We're heading south,' he said. It was now rather cold, there was hardly a star and the moon had really got lost. The only light came from the burner whenever Alva encouraged it. 'Here, you two lads.' As he spoke, Alva heaved towards them a bundle he'd been sitting on. They hadn't fully clapped eyes on it before. Maybe it wasn't there before. It was now. 'Open it up' he said. Soon, Alva's two exhausted and rather thoughtful crew were dozing very gratefully under warm sheepskins. Was that a tiny label declaring: "Dales Fleeces by Mick the Shepherd"? Surely not! Temperature never seemed to affect Alva, but he changed helmet for be-furred hat, and felt the better for it. Balloon slowly drifted on.

'It's getting light.' Ben heard Alva's words first. He roused himself, rolled out from under his sheepskin, got to his feet and looked out of the balloon basket.

'Where are we now?' he enquired.

'Just off Scarborough, reckon tha'd best be giving Alec a shove,' came the reply. Easier said than done to wake Alec, never an early riser unless on some really interesting archaeological dig. Making a great heave, he finally did awake after a rather harder prod.

'Where are we,' he said, yawning and stretching. He stiffly got to his feet. 'By gum, I'm hungry,' he said. Alva was ahead of the game. There was breakfast for all three balloononauts, wafting deliciously from the little table in its usual corner position. It offered bacon, eggs, toast, tea and coffee.

'Fill thi boots,' Alva invited. He'd heard the expression somewhere. Meal eaten, not much left, everything tidied, little table disappeared. A great flutter, delighted squawk,

Samuel seagull, his food detectors continuing in full working order somewhere out in the blue, dives back to assist the clean up and attend to crumbs. 'I'll bring t' balloon down,' Alva said, 'you can tek a look round, see what you can see – something of the castle, mebbe.'

With a sudden bump and lively tilt, Alva's basket grounded on Scarborough's great headland. There was a fair old wind blowing which, on hitting the balloon – trying to knock its hat off, might you guess – had rather spoilt the usual efficient landing. 'Off with you two lads,' Alva said, 'tek a look round. I've one or two things to fettle oop.'

'Want any help?' Alec offered.

'Nay, it'll be reight,' was the reply. The basket had dug in and dragged. Ben looked at the considerable gouges across the grass and wondered what could be done about them. With a bit of effort, maybe, they might be trodden back in. But it would be a little different to half-time repairs on the rugby pitch, he thought. He and Alec scrambled out from the rather crazy basket and just managed to heave it more or less upright.

'All right, Alva, if we leave you to it for a bit?' called Ben.

'Aye, it'll be reight,' came a voice from deep inside the wickerwork.

'Come on, Alec, let's be off then,' Ben said. Wonder what Alva's arranging, he thought to himself.

Regal, dominating, commanding, what largely remains of Henry the Second's Scarborough Castle – the keep – stood foursquare before them; massive stonework firing all manner of imaginings! Alec was in his element. Anyone entering the structure of the ancient pile surely experiences more than enough to get them thinking.

Both balloonists became lost trying to recall the turbulent history of the place. As if aware, the wind contrived to blow its head off, the sea thrashing ashore as if it really meant business! Disturbing. And there were other sounds – thunder of guns, faint but sharp cries of men. Gusting in across the wind – acrid smoke. What was going on? The day was fine: sun, blue sky, banks of high white clouds rolled and chased. But there was a change. The sun disappeared behind darkening clouds. A little way off in the semi-dimness, a shortish, stocky figure appeared: rough shirt, loose brass buttoned reefer jacket, breeches and sea boots, weather-beaten face – a man of action? A dark blue bandana more or less held his tangle of unruly black hair. He walked over, chuckling to himself. Even as he did so, a specially heavy thunderous roar echoed round, ricocheted off the castle keep's unflinching old stones, then faded away. Could that really be cannon smoke that, brought in by the wind, wrapped its way round the two adventurers, stinging their eyes?

The figure spoke: 'The admiral, that's what I calls 'im, at it again. That John Paul Jones, won't come 'ere, now, see 'im off, I will. Always see'd 'im off, I did. Couldn't beat me – t' master gunner!' When Alec got over his astonishment, he tried to speak. The sun burst through. No gunner to be seen! Ben was stunned. He and Alec searched for a bit. But, wait! Surely that's him again, way off, standing firm, looking out to sea with his telescope focussing intently on the horizon. What is he studying? Don't hang about – ask, decided the friends. At that moment, the master gunner faded and was gone. They ran over to where they'd seen him. Looked everywhere. Nothing.

Below, the sea stretched as far as the imagination could drift. What was that, half-remembered, about John Paul Jones and the sea battle off Flamborough Head, a few miles south of Scarborough? Think hard. Think 1779. Recall the very gallant action taken by HMS Countess of Scarborough and HMS Serapis, under the command of Captain Richard Pearson, escorting a convoy of forty or more other ships returning from somewhere along the Baltic. Remember how they were intercepted by Jones aboard his big old ship, Bonhomme Richard, along with the French frigate, Pallas. Such a battle! The old gunner must have been forever watching for any possible further threat to the castle by the piratical Jones.

Alva would be sure to know all about it, but right now, having "fettled oop" what needed fettling after the bumpy landing, he'd taken off on a short test flight. Nowt seemed amiss, as he might say, in fact he was enjoying a trip under the yellow bowler hat comfortably floating over the briny. He spotted his two young dalesmen and was pleased to see them treading like mad, attempting to finish fettling oop the turf where the basket had first grounded. He steered towards them and landed as light as a feather. 'Hop aboard, you two lads,' he said. They did. And Alva's kettle were on!

Relaxing with mugs of tea and gazing round at nothing in particular, still pondering t' master gunner, they hardly noticed the distant shape of a fully rigged man-o-war. Blown off course? Sound of cannon fire, closer this time. Mighty flash! Roar! Blast of wind! A howling, humming, great red-hot cannon ball hit the sea just offshore and plunged in with a hissing, heaving splash which, whipped by the wind, drenched the balloon and everything around with salt water and seaweed. Alva's burner spluttered a little, but shielded by the balloon's firmly rigged skirt, flared in defiance.

'Well, by gum,' said Alva, 'we'd best be off directly. Get shut of the seaweed, you two lads, and happen we'll be more comfortable.' He reached for the burner and gave it the hint. Wasting no time, his whole wondrous contraption, dripping just a bit, took off into the late evening and the light of a rising moon. Excitement? Shock? You name the atmosphere! Welcome breezes and more of Alva's hot tea helped a bit to dry out matters and calm the crew on board. A flash of black, white and grey, a rattle and flutter of wings, seagull Sam arrived back to settle, home from the sea. Were those wings just a little bit singed? Alva set his course westward, inland, and headed for Ripon. Be-furred hat off, helmet and goggles on, he was fully alert. His passengers settled on the basket floor and tried to relax, not easy with minds full of gunners and wild roundshot. There was enough to talk about and try to believe. Time rolled on. Maybe, there'd soon be supper!

Chapter Fifteen

There had in fact been some supper. The little table had delivered in due course. Darkness settled. The two friends dozed whilst the balloon flew steadily on. After a while: 'What time d'you reckon it is?' Ben said, rousing himself for a moment and giving Alec a nudge.

'Look at your watch,' was the drowsy reply.

'Where are we?' Ben hardly had time to juggle with the question when a warm, fruity musical sound floated up from the ground way below.

'We're over Ripon,' Alva said. 'It's nine o'clock and that's t' town horn-blower doing his stuff, like it's been happening every night at nine for centuries.'

Leaving the cathedral city behind, on floated the balloon. Alva was glad of the bright silver moon. Navigation was easier. Such a night! It was warm, the steady breeze in just the right direction. Flying was bliss.

I can't tell what feelings balloons and their baskets may possess, but there started up a real quiver in the wicker. Was there a sense of heading for home – Ingleborough? Flying over beautiful Fountains Abbey, there were lights here and there, glinting from dark stonework. The gentle, rounded voice of a solitary bell floated into the night. Later in his life, Ben said he'd seldom heard a more honeyed sound. And, surely, just caught by the moon,

there had been a hooded figure, head down, legging it to vespers. Hope he made it!

Sail on through Nidderdale, offer a respectful nod to Great Whernside. Away to port, pick up the distant glint of Malham Tarn, but head on to Pen-y-Ghent. Even Alva was now becoming excited as his craft coursed home over the Pennine Way. All of a sudden – well, by gum, Ingleborough was below. Would you believe it, they'd made it, full circle. What a trip!

'Look lively, gentlemen,' Alva called. 'Brace thaselves, we've landed back.' Message received and understood. After heaving themselves fully awake, brace themselves the gentlemen did. Alva smiled. The yellow bowler descended majestically, touched ground as softly as you like. Brilliant! And the landing site was hardly billiard table smooth. Alva really smiled. 'Mak t' basket fast,' he requested, 'then nip back for a mite o' breakfast!' Grand idea. Sun were coming oop and it were gurring a bit parky, as he might have put it. His crew obliged, attaching mooring ropes as best and firmly as they could to whatever anchorage they could find. Yes, it was a bit nippy!

Once more, the little table in the corner didn't disappoint, offering breakfast – a right grand fry-oop, in generous north-country style. It could be imagined that even Alva was just a little impressed. Sure that everyone was finally satisfied, he snapped his fingers. At once, there was nothing to be seen. 'Grand,' he said. 'Na then lads, if tha's fit, I've to tak t' balloon to be serviced, so hop out if tha will and let fly t' ropes. I'll gather 'em in. Must get off, tha sees.' He seemed to be in some hurry, so the friends did as he asked. No sooner were the ropes let off, back they whipped like greased lightning straight into the basket, where they hanked and hooked up all by themselves. 'Thanks, lads,' Alva called. Before there was any moment to say much else, the balloon was away. So was Sam, well fed, too, and now wide awake. Better get off back to Morecambe, he thought to himself; might be a snack.

It was just possible to catch sight of Alva waving and to hear him shout: 'Look out, lads, catch!' Two heavily loaded rucksacks and a couple of bundles flew in tumbling arcs from the basket and thudded to the ground nearby. 'Grand, grand, see thi in a bit,' was the final shout and, quick as you like, the airborne bowler was but a tiny dot at altitude. The early bright-eyed sun just caught it – a brilliant pinpoint of lively buttercup yellow that dwindled and was gone.

The sudden disappearing trick was a bit of a facer. 'Well, I'm,' was all Alec could muster. Ben was too flabbergasted; couldn't speak at all. There was such an emptiness. Was this to be the end of everything they had witnessed – certainly been through – and enjoyed, sometimes tempted to disbelieve? They even felt a touch exhausted right now. Waft of bacon, egg and fried bread fry-oop still hung deliciously on the morning air. That, surely, was not imagination. Ah, by gum, no! "Methinks I scent the morning air" – different story altogether.

The two adventurers – they certainly had been – rather startled, I must say, quickly retrieved their kit and just managed, rather optimistically, to shout 'thanks' out across the breeze. A child wandering just within earshot asked its dad who "that man" was shouting to. Dad didn't know, how could he? Not in the know, was he! It was time for sitting down and trying to adjust to the sudden change of situation. Felt a bit lost, they did, to be frank. Would have been the same for anybody. But there was clearly no future in hanging about scanning the heavens, or pondering for too long the next move. In actual fact, it took some time to fully sort themselves out and realise they were back again on Ingleborough where their adventures and ballooning had begun. How long ago? Not easy to say.

'Maybe we should go home,' Ben said quietly. This suggestion absolutely shocked Alec. Jerked him up good and proper, as you might say.

'Can't go straight away, surely,' he said. 'Come on, let's take our time, have a look round.' Then a thought struck him: exactly where had they come out from Gilbert's staircase, that had led them from his banqueting hall back up to Ingleborough? 'Come on,' he said, 'that staircase. (However long ago was that?) Why don't we look for it?'

'Calm down,' Ben said, 'let's just think and get orientated.' Both started to concentrate. Now where was it? A few degrees westward floated the pale, pearly disc of the retiring moon. What might it know? No knowing. Pity we didn't mark where we came out way back, was the thought that entered both minds at once. They got to their feet, gathered their belongings and moved off from where pilot Alva had set them down. Was this to be another challenge to amuse the wily fellow? Not easy to fathom, our Alva, but a good lad. The two dalesmen, glad to be back on home territory, began to cast round, decide where to look. It was good to be on the move, stretch their legs, take in familiar views, perhaps catch sight of Morecambe. What extraordinary memories that would trigger off!

'What's that over there?' Ben suddenly exclaimed. 'Look!' He'd noticed in the distance a rather loose pile of stones. Could that be anything to do with Gilbert's staircase? What about the tubular slide, where had they found that? They remembered a slight hollow where the staircase had come out, that was about all. But the tumble of stones, take a look at them. Were they beckoning?

'Come on, then,' Alec said. The two of them made a hopeful dash across to the intriguing heap. Arriving a little breathless at their target, they stood for a moment, then slowly walked round it; stopped and considered the chances. It was in just a bit of a hollow, after all, wasn't it?

'Don't reckon much to that,' Ben said after they had considered at some length the debris of cobbles and stones. Disappointing. He certainly didn't think much of it at all. 'See any more piles of stones anywhere? Come on,' he said, pointing, 'look, there's another bit of a heap over there.' He was ready for off.

'Shh a minute, wait,' Alec said, listening. They both stood in silence for several long minutes that seemed to go on forever. But bird-call on a lazy breeze was all there was to hear. A curlew glided round, landed, nodded, pecked round for a bit and flew off. Glancing in its direction, yes, surely, there was the tiniest glimpse of the sea at Morecambe in the very far distance. It took their minds, at least for a minute, off everything else. It certainly had been fun there. Ben idly poked a stone with his foot. A frog, to his great surprise – and lts – sprang out, croaked, gazed solemnly at him, and dived for cover again, close by. Had he been trying to communicate? After all, he'd come a long way, normally living in the lower reaches. Could have been offering a hint of encouragement? Quite spontaneously, the untidy heap seemed to shift just a little. A rough old chunk towards the centre slipped and fell.

Alec said: 'Can you hear anything? Ben, can you hear anything? Surely you can.' To be sure, from where the piece of stone had tipped out, there were sounds. What kind of sounds? You might very well enquire. Hardly daring to do so, Alec, leaning forward, gingerly took hold of the stone, which to his surprise was slightly warm, and laid it on the ground beside him. It was Ben's turn. Were they on to something, he wondered? Tensing somewhat, he slowly stretched forward and put his ear to the gap now revealed. He concentrated for what seemed to Alec like a lifetime. There were sounds, faint but quite definite. Ben was sure he heard them.

'Shh, hang on a tick,' he whispered, 'there are definite noises from somewhere below.'

'What kind of noises?' Alec said, maybe a little impatiently.

'Sounds like someone is having a right good party down there. I can hear music. Mighty good party I'd say it is,' Ben said with a laugh. 'Wow!'

Now, you might reasonably ask – what music and who could be making it? And if it was way below, how could it be heard above ground? Well, those were Alec's thoughts, too. He and Ben abandoned guesswork, just focussed on the heap. 'Let's get cracking,' they said together. Looking around, no one else seemed particularly near. Didn't matter anyway. It had to be action, now. Slowly, methodically, all the stones, one by one, were carefully laid aside. Something of a hollow actually began to form. Did it seem at all familiar? I'll tell you, if you like, how the music from below was able to make it to the surface. It came circling and bouncing up Gilbert's grand staircase, that's how. You've surely heard of the whispering gallery at St. Paul's? Yes, you might say, but what about that heavy tapestry that hung across the foot of the stair? Such a good party at Gilbert's dive. Phew! You can be sure someone pulled it aside for some fresh air. Good idea!

Piece by piece, stone by stone, flakes of old walling, handfuls of shale, the toppled old cairn was dismantled with much care and anticipation. The work was steady and very, very deliberate; all the time listening, listening, stopping and listening again. Yes, the sounds were still there, ebbing, flowing, rising and falling; with the occasional "whoop". But eventually, there were no sounds at all, just a silence that seemed to go on and on. Oh well, was the thought, maybe we got it wrong this time. At last, Ben said: 'We can't hang about, let's do something else.'

'What about these stones,' Alec said, 'shouldn't leave them like this. Let's put them in at least some kind of order, make a proper job of it, maybe make a decent cairn for Ingleborough this time.' They did. And, indeed, were really quite proud of the result. It had taken some time, but was definitely worth it and a lot of fun.

'Who's to put in the last piece?' Ben laughed, wiping away a final streak of sweat.

'Come off it, this isn't a jigsaw,' Alec said, a little impatiently. 'But go on then, at least we've made a pretty good effort.' They certainly had. There remained a slender gap to fill.

'OK,' said Ben, 'here we go.' Selecting the very best of the remaining chippings, he reached out, taking care not to jog the masterpiece. With the tiny fragment held between finger and thumb, he aimed for the vacant chink and let go.

It was hardly airborne – wow! Wow-ee! A gale of singing, laughing and bagpiping going nineteen to the dozen with "Auld lang syne" burst out into the open and the whole new creation flew to pieces.

'Duck,' shouted Ben, quickly glancing round, though not in the least bothered about anyone within earshot who might have heard. Debris scattered in all directions, whirled wildly in clouds of bits, chunks, chips and dust like mad confetti. Five figures, one after another, zipped up like rockets from the hollow, there now for all to see, and so fast you couldn't track them.

'Blow me!' gasped Alec. The eruption blew Ben off his feet and left him totally speechless. (Funny thing, emerging from the chaos, neither he nor Alec had any bits, or the slightest flicker of dust, dropped on them. Clean as a whistle – or two whistles – they were.) The whirlwind funnelled down, rather sedately, you could say, close by. Every piece of building material joined up into the neatest structure ever. The perfect cairn!

'Never mind blow you,' shouted Ben, recovering, 'look behind you!' Just a few yards off, basket gently nudging the ground, was Alva's yellow bowler balloon, its pilot just a bit squashed, but poised to blast off at any minute.

Don't know how they all piled in, but straining the plucky wicker way past splitting and beyond, crammed into the basket with Alva, all with smiles as wide as the Forth Bridge and gamely holding on, were Fingal, Flora

MacDonald, Robbie Burns, Alan Stevenson and Robert the Bruce. Sending them off with a mighty wave was Gilbert himself. With a blast, Alva and his craft shot to the sky and, with a trailing echo of "Will ye no come back again," it was gone.

Looking up, in the hope of following the balloon's progress as Alva and his passengers arrowed into the blue, Alec thought he just saw dashed right across the bottom of the basket, in bold letters: "Alva's Grand Celtic Tours." What! Had he really seen the legend, read it properly? By gum, yes! Hadn't been able to take his eyes off it. 'Hey, Ben,' he shouted, 'quick – look up there. Hurry, or you'll miss it.' He grabbed Ben by the shoulders, swivelled him round and pointed a finger skywards. 'See it, see it?' Alec said, frantically. Ben did his very best until a large white cloud drifted in and completely swallowed everything.

'Well, whatever it was, I missed it. What was I supposed to see?' Ben said, and thought it might have been some bird, perhaps rare in those parts. No, it wasn't, he was informed.

'Didn't you see the bottom of the basket?' Alec asked. 'I'm sure, right across it in big letters – you better believe it – was a sign saying clearly: "Alva's Grand Celtic Tours." Couldn't quite make out the mobile phone number – bit of a smudge.' Then he burst out laughing.

'You're having me on,' Ben said.

'Well, you saw who rushed out and jumped into the basket, I suppose. Work it out for yourself,' Alec said. 'When did you last see them all?'

'Well, Staffa, I suppose,' Ben said. 'Gilbert must have invited them all round for a meat pie supper; special meat pies, probably from Denby Dale. They'd only need one of those! Canny old Alva. Bet he delivered it. Pity you didn't get the number.' The two friends looked at each other and began to laugh so hard they only just managed to stop. Good old Alva, good old Alva, indeed!

Chapter Sixteen

All over again, it was suddenly a case of – what do we do now? Here were the two of them back in Yorkshire, some time since landing, standing on Ingleborough, balloon nowhere to be seen. Unreal. Someone in the distance flew a kite. A couple of children ran past chasing a dog. 'Out for a picnic?' one of them shouted cheekily. The kids had absolutely no idea! Once again everyone and everything was ordinary. It was going to take a bit of getting used to. The last few minutes had been a right shock. And now the friends were rather hungry. Forgotten about food. Hardly surprising, would you not think? A bite or two of Kendal mint cake from the bottom of a rucksack would have to do for the moment. It tasted grand. They sat and rested against their bundles for a while. Alec just about dozed off. Why not? Everyday life would kick in all too soon. And there was this curiously boring consideration of finally heading for home. Didn't really want to think about that.

After a while, not at all sure of a plan of action, and just hanging about half-wondering if Alva and his balloon might suddenly re-appear over the distant horizon, Alec was struck by the thought of the two collie dogs who had, way back, almost started everything off. Apart from the mysterious and very jolly meeting once more with Alva – how long ago? – in the hawthorn tree, such a surprise to meet the two lively dogs out of nowhere. But where were they now?

'Remember the two collies,' he said to Ben, 'what if they just turned up again? D'you think Mick the shepherd still has them?'

Startled by the question, Ben had to think for a moment. 'Suppose so,' he said, 'wonder if he's trained them for trialling? We'll have to watch the local press when we land back home. Would be interesting.'

'Good idea,' Alec said, 'though Alva might have other ideas.'

'You could say that again,' Ben said, getting to his feet. 'Shall we make a move?'

Alec gathered himself and belongings, stood up, stretched, sighed and said – 'let's go.' Looking skywards I couldn't say how many times, rucksacks on their backs, Viking bundles under their arms, the two of them headed down and away for the time being at least, leaving Ingleborough to its own deep thoughts and mysteries. There was now a slight chill in the air, hardly noticed during all the excitement. But consider, autumn was now not very far off.

The homeward journey took them wide of Gaping Ghyll – what a temptation to rouse Gilbert! Trow Ghyll and Giant's Hall gave them much to think on and remember, the rusty old entrance to Clapham Cave, too. Ice-cold Clapham Beck, remembered since childhood, couldn't forget that on their way back to pretty Clapham village and its fine church. On, next, above, to the high ground, meadows and drifts of windy trees. The steady amble continued, gently easing down across familiar, ancient grassy lynchets – remains of terraces worked by mediaeval farming peoples – and so through the five-barred gate (leaving it closed) down into the Dales village of their boyhood. It was great, felt real but kind of unreal. But home is home, is it not?

'Good to be home, eh?' Ben said as they walked along the green. Alec was just about to reply, when a voice floated perfectly clearly out from somewhere behind the Gamecock Inn: 'So, tha's gitten back, then?' The sound pulled the two homecomers up with a jerk, they turned towards each other and uttered one question – Alva? Finding their way up behind the building as discreetly as they could, they glanced carefully all round, but drew a complete blank

'What about going inside? The voice could have come from there,' Alec said. 'Catch him out!'

'Best idea you've had so far,' Ben said with a laugh. 'And we could have a meal while we're at it. Come on, I'm hungry.' Alec was as hungry as he was, and the landlord was able to provide a great home-cooked meal.

'Never lets you down, doesn't the Gamecock Inn,' Ben said, after they'd finished eating and were sitting back comfortably. There were a few other people eating and enjoying their own fare in the friendly old establishment, but all strangers. No Alva in sight. The voice – if they had actually heard it – remained a teaser. There was, however, one individual, clearly a military man from times past and evidently an old friend of the landlord. They talked closely. Alec and Ben had a word with the landlord, complimented him on and thanked him for the meal, which they had really enjoyed. A kindly man, he was pleased and asked them how their day had gone. He would hardly have been able to believe them, I fancy, if they had dared to tell him! He couldn't help them with the mystery voice, but seemed very thoughtful and scratched his head.

Daylight was beginning to fade. Bright lights in the dining room increased the appearance of darkness out beyond the window of the old inn. Relaxing in the warm, friendly atmosphere and able to rest awhile was great. But very soon it was time to go.

'Stay with me for a few days if you like,' Ben suggested, 'get sorted out a bit. I've got plenty of room.'

Alec had rather hoped Ben might invite him for a day or so to unwind, and was very glad. 'Thanks a lot,' he said, adding quietly, 'we set the landlord thinking, you know. He won't sleep tonight.' Smiling a bit guiltily, the two friends heaved themselves upright, gathered their belongings and, after settling the bill, made their way out into the fine evening. One or two welcome stars had made it through amongst streaky clouds high over the tops. There were makings of a moon. In no time at all, the two were at Ben's inviting front door.

The cottage had been built so as to offer more room inside than seemed likely from the outside. A great place it was. The pair must surely have been expected. A full can of milk on the doorstep offered them welcome, Yorkshire style. Given a prod, the front door very slowly swung open, with a low kind of wheezy squeak. Was it suggesting an oil can – or something else?

'Come in,' Ben invited. The unlocked door? He'd long been used to old village ways – but….. The two picked up the can and entered the cottage, closing the door behind

them. They went through to the comfortable kitchen, warmed by its old, black-leaded range. It was well lit and glinting in the firelight. Odd? On the hob, a kettle sang. Ben didn't reach for the electric light. Instead, after shrugging off his gear, he groped for matches, lit a candle and placed it on a saucer on the kitchen table. Flickering, caused by a whisper of breeze from a window crack, winked and signalled to an old, glass, ship's decanter picked up by Ben at an auction a while ago and now in command of his kitchen dresser. Always treasured it. Standing in front, plush with a great sheepskin, stood Ben's favourite Windsor carver. In the candlelight, it seemed to change shape – become larger, then dwindle to nothing, appear again, disappear. Such luxury in the deep fleece that filled it, the chair was Ben's delight. But had someone beaten him to it? Shadows went completely black, then slowly changed. Look again. Was someone sitting there? No, of course not! Ben turned to the kettle. Make the tea, think straight. No good, the chair wouldn't let him go. There, surely, in the wavering light, the figure of an old person – sea boots and all – lolled sideways in the chair. Was that a whiff of tobacco adrift?

'Lit t' fire for thi, messmates,' spoke a very quiet, gruff voice.

Ben instantly flicked on the electric light. His carver stood empty. Not quite empty! Crouching there, purring loudly with supreme pleasure and total ownership was a sleek, black animal with big, unblinking yellow eyes. A cat, and such a cat! Yes, it was Ben's own cat Marius, who, it might be remembered, walked uninvited and from absolutely nowhere into his cottage – how long ago? And more or less took over. The creature stood up, tested its claws (much to Ben's dismay), slid to the floor and continued to purr its head off. Couldn't that be a dusting of tobacco ash on one paw? Don't know whether either of the friends noticed. Both were a bit stunned. Could have been nothing at all.

'What d'you make of that performance?' Alec said, after recovering a bit. 'Many ghosts operate round here, do they?' Ben mumbled something, but didn't remind him of the Vikings, roundheads and Romans they thought they saw when they were boys. Tell you the truth, fair flummoxed the two of them were. They made a close inspection of the chair, walked round it, lifted it up, looked underneath, set it down, stood back and looked at it again. Well, being rather tired, you can imagine almost anything, can't you? Ben took a quick look out of the front door. Didn't help. No one about, not in sea boots, any road.

'I'll nip upstairs,' Ben said, 'just to check.'

'Get on with it,' said Alec, just a little uneasily.

Ben was soon down. 'Nothing different up there,' he said with a thin laugh. 'Oh well, better try and find something to feed the cat, I suppose.' He snuffed out what was left of the candle, now merely a stub wallowing in its saucerful of melted wax. 'Did me best,' it could have been snivelling. Marius seemed in a world of his own, had something on his mind, stared at Ben, then slowly stalked to the front door, asking to be let out. Barely opened for him, he slipped through and disappeared. Ben closed the door. 'Oh well, press on,' he said, took hold of the teapot, warmed it from the kettle, still boiling merrily in encouragement, found the caddy and made a cup of tea. Of course there was milk, you will remember about that. The table was laid ready for a meal. Had he done it? Couldn't remember. Never mind, was there food to complete it, if required? The beautifully cool-slated shelves of the larder provided ham, pickles and cheese and best part of a fresh, crisp loaf. Extraordinary!

Ben moved from the larder and looked back at the table, wondering, then very slowly walked to the front door, opened it and looked out along the village road. It was good and dark outside. All was quiet, except a breeze was beginning to get up. Wonderful smells. Better get horizontal, he said to himself. It's been quite a day, after all. He closed the door and found himself turning the key in the lock. There was a handy bolt. He slid it home.

'There's a spare bed upstairs, it's not the Ritz, but not bad if you'd like to shake down there,' he said to Alec.

'Sleep anywhere tonight,' Alec laughed. The table put to rights, the kettle filled, returned to the hob, and singing again, Ben helped Alec to take up his gear and showed him to the spare bedroom.

'Looks grand,' Ben said, 'shouldn't be damp, weather's not been too bad and there'll be at least some warmth up from the old range. I'll make sure. So, I'll leave you to it now.'

'Thanks very much, it looks all right to me,' Alec replied. 'See you in the morning.' What a day it's been, he thought to himself, went in and closed the door. Ben returned downstairs and stoked the fire. The cottage would be good and warm through the night, the fire glowing and ready to host a good breakfast in the morning. After switching out the light, he stood for some time looking at his great carver chair. Banked up for the night, the fire seemed dozing, as you would be entitled to expect. But it flared up, just once, brightly lit the room. Surely, sprawling in the chair..... Come on now, be sensible. Trick of the light? Of course. He stood quite still, took a deep breath, shook his head, and with more than just one more glance back at the vacant carver, gathered his own belongings, took to the stairs and headed for bed. Halfway up – the slightest hint, a sniff of baccy? Course not. Get a grip! Ben went straight to his room, firmly shut the door and, without bothering to undress (except for his shoes), flung himself on the bed, pulled half a blanket over himself, shut his eyes and breathed a long sigh. He'd really looked forward to a good sleep after all that had happened. At first, his thoughts jumped about on top of each other. Tired as he was, just dropping off became beyond him. The earlier breeze had gathered strength. Suddenly, sharp rattlings of his half-open window jerked and disturbed him. Branches from a tree, close by, flung themselves about, making jagged shadows across his ceiling. The old building creaked. He'd never heard it creak like that before. Moonlight, shafting through the bedroom window, hit the glass of a framed picture on the wall. Reflected light splintered into the room, over his bedclothes and across the floor.

'Thanks very much,' he muttered, 'about all I needed.' Draw the curtains. Shut it right out! He stumbled his way to the window. He'd take one more look down the road before trying again to sleep. There wasn't much to see. Nobody about. All was very quiet, very still. Where had the breeze gone?

About to close the window, he couldn't quite bring himself to do it. Something caught his attention. Not sure at first, he pushed the little window open a bit wider, looked harder. There was something along the road, something moving, definitely moving. What was it that slid out from the dark shadows of the parish hall? Whatever it was, it seemed to draw the blackness into the road with it. The moon knew its business, revealed the secret and shone down with full lunar power, scattering the dark – there was Marius, a rather different Marius, no longer black, but silky silver, brilliant in the light, and he clearly wanted to make a signal. His eyes, flaring diamond fire, zipped like lasers straight at the astonished Ben. Sleep? Huh! No chance of that! It would have to wait. Totally drawn in, Ben couldn't take his eyes off the animal. Had to half-close them against the piercing stare. Was something odd really happening, or was imagination twisting his brain? The cat, bathed in moonlight, began to walk away. His tail seemed longer than ever, held high, it swayed – almost floated – was this the signal? As he stalked on down through the village, was he changing shape, or had someone joined him from the shadows? Sleep could certainly, completely, go hang now!

Ben leant out of the window as far as he could but, quickly, there was only one thing for it. Quietly grabbing his shoes, he tiptoed from his room. Alec was snoring hard, which though awful was, at this point, rather handy. No fear of disturbing him! But did the staircase have to creak quite so loudly? Downstairs at last, Ben put on his shoes, unlocked and unbolted the front door, slipped out and closed it behind him. Feeling like the worst of amateur sleuths, he crouched low and followed the cat. Hoping nobody – perhaps squinting through their curtains by chance – would see him, he kept to what shadow he could find for himself. He hadn't wasted much time, but now cat Marius could only just be picked out, for clouds had, at that point, rather unhelpfully drifted across the moon. Slowly, carefully, Ben edged his way down the road until he could just make out the bold, dark stone column of the old village cross in its patch of grass opposite the church. So that was where Marius was heading all along. Just in time, Ben was able to make out a shape looking like him, disappearing behind it.

The moon now cast a weak beam through strands of thin cloud and, just to be seen moving near the cross, were human shapes. Ben was suddenly a boy again. Weren't they roundheads, Romans, Vikings, mixing and mingling all round it? Was that the clink of a weapon? Maybe here were some of the characters who had sparked his imagination when he was a lad. Or had he actually made their acquaintance then?

For a moment, the sky cleared, moonlight glinted, surely on helmets, armour and such weaponry! Low murmurs and gruff laughter made all seem alive. But, what! Just then, he fancied, he clearly saw, seated on the worn steps at the foot of the column, a bent figure not at all like the others. Moonlight shot through. There, completely at his ease and preparing to light his pipe, was the old, sea-booted seadog himself.

Chapter Seventeen

It was morning. Ben found himself in bed. The question was – had he been there all night? What about the window? Sunlight, searching through the curtains, demanded he got up without delay to find out. He flicked the curtains aside, to find his window only just open. Ben scratched his head, he could have sworn he'd been up in the middle of the night and shut the window to end the rattling and banging in the wind. Oh well, maybe not. Funny, though – odd! Head to the bathroom, sort yourself out, start the day. Good idea. Before going downstairs to fix breakfast (see what he could find – couldn't guess at that under the circumstances) he called to Alec to "shake a leg". 'Bathroom's empty and I'm off to the kitchen. You'll find a clean towel,' he called. Leave him, see if there is anything appropriate for us to eat. Or not! They didn't go hungry, there was all manner of breakfast. Over a cup of tea, Ben said, as casually as he could: 'Sleep all right?'

'It was grand,' Alec said. 'By gum, you make a great cup of tea.'

Leave it at that for the moment, Ben thought. 'Tell you what,' he said, 'when we're ready, I suggest we go out and stretch our legs, enjoy the sun. Good lord, the morning's half gone. Marius hasn't been in for breakfast yet, bit funny that, we'll put something down for him and leave the window ajar.'

Fresh and bright, what great weather to be walking out in a Dales village, maybe pass the time of day with other folks busy about their own business. Ben didn't say much, certainly didn't invite Alec to choose a direction in which he might prefer to go. There was only one that he himself was determined to take: a quick glance towards the Gamecock and across the green to the smithy (the anvil was ringing as loud as you like). What boyhood memories there! Walk past the post office and parish hall, so down to the village cross. Alec was interested at once.

'So many echoes of the past, all manner of imaginings here,' he said, his archaeological juices beginning to stir. 'The grass round this one looks pretty well trodden, something recently been going on, I wonder?' Ben nodded and murmured in an absentminded kind of way, which could have meant anything. He said nothing. His mind was suddenly, however, jerked alive. On the ground near one of the steps at the base of the cross, he was amazed to see an old tobacco pipe (familiar?), well used and charred about the bowl. Nice bit of cherry wood, he thought. He hoped, didn't think, Alec had seen it. Good, might avoid awkward questions.

'Things going on?' Ben said, picking up Alec's first remarks. 'Yes, interesting,' he managed to agree, in an offhand kind of way. 'Good,' he said briskly, to alter the mood. 'Let's go and take a look at the bridge, might catch sight of a trout.' Turning to go, something caught his eye. Undeniable. Settled in the corner of one of the steps was a small but quite distinct heap of tobacco ash. He'd almost missed it. Ben felt he should now come clean with Alec about what he'd imagined so vividly had taken place during the night. Jokes about cheese – or pickles – were not going to do. Shown the tell-tale remains, Alec took a close look, left them undisturbed and merely said 'humm.' What might he be thinking?

Leaving the cross behind, the two friends sauntered on down to the bridge spanning the beck, a little way off. Comfortably leaning over the parapet, it was fun peering into the water slipping gently beneath, and hoping to see a fish or two. Watercress and bright yellow musk, so nice to see, were doing very well in and around the shallows. Interesting, any observer could see how well puddled the surrounding mud was, with deep hoof marks. Whose horse, or horses, anyone might ask. They were quite fresh, perhaps left early in the morning. Or could it have been in the middle of the night, do you think? Our two investigators left the bridge, quickly went down and very carefully inspected the evidence. There were clear imprints of heavy boots, too. Nip back to the cross, look again at the trodden area there. Might there be some connection? Walk right round the cross, think hard, but touch nothing. Get on with it! They hurried back to the cross, trying not to attract too much attention. Arriving in a fair state of anticipation, they looked closely all round and beyond. Anything to see? There were nowt! There wasn't a trace of anything whatsoever, not on the steps, nor nearby. The grass looked thoroughly fresh. Back to the beck: watercress, yes, yellow musk, yes, trout, not too sure, mud, yes, oozing, plenty of it. Hoof and boot marks – none. But, that half-buried, rounded piece of metal, what might they make of that? Butt of a pistol? Not likely. As for that pole sticking up through that elderberry bush; maybe a busted pike shaft? Maybe not. Anyway, tough to get it out, probably break off, looks half rotten. Forget it. The most exciting thing was half an old bucket gently nodding and dipping in the watercress. Nonplussed, that's what the two dalesmen certainly were.

'Well, would you believe it?' Ben said. He and Alec had been surprised and mystified so often throughout all their journeyings, what a silly question! They both, often enough, believed it, whatever it was. Had to, but on the whole – great fun. So, what the heck?

'Search me,' was all Alec said. Thinking hard and rather disappointed, they wandered back up through the village. It was time for lunch at the inn.

Back in the old Gamecock, and happily trenching through grand meat and potato pies, at first they were both still very puzzled. But at the finish, after apple crumble, custard and a good Yorkshire cup of tea, they began to relax. Ben had an idea.

'Back shortly,' he said, 'I want something from home; leave you here if I may.'

'OK,' Alec said, 'I might have a bit of a read.' He'd seen a copy of the Dalesman magazine looking at him from a side table.

Letting himself into his cottage, Ben went on through to his tool-shed, where he chose a garden fork. Down the road with it, he headed for the beck. This will probably do it, he said to himself. He'd had an idea, couldn't let earlier matters rest. The mud down by the bridge was his destination. Now, where was it? Where was it, he asked himself when he arrived; you could say – hotfoot. Calming down, he tried to concentrate, looked everywhere. There it is, there it is, he said to himself. And there it was, at last, the mud-bound, rounded metal object. With his fork, he very carefully probed and dug round it. It's coming, it's coming – it did! There, lying at his feet, was the object of his search, muddy still, but no doubt as to what it was, no doubt at all. He picked it up and with his fingers prised away some of the mud. After a brief swill amongst the watercress in the shallows of the beck, it almost shone. His heart thumped. Who might the object have belonged to? That might come later. He put the ground right and cleaned the fork. With it in one hand, his prize in the other, he rather thoughtfully, and as casually as he could, walked home. The fork back in the tool-shed, he returned to the inn.

'You've been a long time,' Alec said, putting down the magazine. 'Nearly finished it. Where've you been?' Ben smiled, and without answering, slowly brought his hand out from behind his back and held it out.

'What d'you think of that, then,' he said. 'Went down to the beck, had a bit of a dig.' Keeping firm hold, it was a bit weighty, he held out to Alec a no-nonsense military-looking steel stirrup. 'Found it there in the mud.'

Alec took the stirrup, gauged its weight in his hand and turned it over several times. 'Well done,' he said, 'well done, bit of luck finding that.' He was thinking hard and trying to put two and two together.

Catching sight of the Gamecock's landlord, 'Found it down by the beck,' Ben said.

'Oh aye,' the landlord replied, with moderate interest. 'Haven't lost one of these, has ta?' he called, directing his question towards the diners beyond the bar. After what seemed like a rather long pause, a very quiet grunt was the only response he got. 'Tak care on it, lad, might come in useful,' the landlord said to Ben. No one need have worried, Ben still knows where it is. It was time to thank the landlord, settle the bill and return home.

Back in the cottage, one of the first things they noticed was that cat Marius's food, put down for him last night, hadn't been touched. He wasn't there, either.

'Must have found something elsewhere,' Ben said. 'He's a knowing old cat, likes to be left to his own devices, like most cats. Those eyes!' Cats in general were briefly discussed, but conversation soon turned to the events of the previous night, mysteries of the morning and the discovery in the mud. No joy-ride kind of stirrup, it was very solid, totally business-like and big enough for a serious boot. If only it could talk. Maybe if rubbed and polished enough, might it not yield like Aladdin's magic lamp? Such thoughts, fancies of all kinds, occupied much of the conversation between the friends. Ben, of course, had the advantage of what he thought he'd seen at dead of night. He'd certainly seen a staring cat (Marius or not?) lit by the moon. Alec, understandably a bit sceptical, did his best. The stirrup certainly got him thinking. Archaeologists like facts, are patient in seeking them, nevertheless are not entirely short of imagination. No fun without it! And what of the hidden voice at the inn? Anyway, chat went on happily for some time, including plans for the morrow: what might the day bring?

Tea – and strange delights bought from the village shop along with some discovered by Ben in the larder – came and went. Supper occurred and eventually it was time to "crash out" for the night. A snack was left for Marius, a window left ajar, and after leaving everything ship-shape, the two dalesmen friends went to bed.

Morning arrived, fine and clear. Nothing at all had gone bump in the night, Ben and Alec had both slept like logs. They were ready for the day and, after breakfast, were eager to be off. Plans laid last night would have them heading for the tops. But first, there was something they just had to do.

Outside in the sunshine: 'I'd like to have another look at the village cross,' Alec said, 'go down to the bridge, have another squint at the mud.'

'Right with you,' Ben said. Recent happenings and events had left them more than wondering. Wasting no time, off the pair of them went down past the parish hall and so to the cross. Not much at all to see there. Not even a toffee paper lying where it shouldn't. All was well at the bridge. Mud, musk and watercress, the beck rippling on its way. In all, everything was as beautiful and normal as you like. Rather disappointing, you could say, there wasn't even a trout to be espied – or tickled. Carry on with the day, drop by the inn, see if the landlord could put up a couple of picnic lunches. They had a word with him.

'You'll be wanting to take advantage of the fine weather,' he said. 'Aye, we can mak thi oop a picnic, no bother.' Ben knew he was right about Pennine weather. It had more than one trick up its sleeve.

They returned to the cottage for rucksacks and walking gear, and quite soon were back at the Gamecock. What a picnic there was for them. Good thing the rucksacks weren't small! The landlord was thanked, the bill settled, picnics stowed, it was the moment to shake hands and be off. Funny, thought Ben, that figure sitting back in the shadows behind the bar, couldn't see him clearly. Didn't it look uncannily like that old roundhead he and Alec had seen in the village when they were boys? Of course, it could have been a Viking, lots of them all over the place round these parts once upon a time. Boyhood experience, ticked. Lost in thought about such things – suddenly he was jerked back to the present.

'You're a bit quiet,' Alec said.

'Sorry, something half caught my attention at the inn,' Ben told him.

Up out of the village and into the hills they went, Oxenber, first, then way beyond. On, on, they hiked, climbing higher all the time. A glance back, the village was far below. A curlew wheeled and called. "Boys" again, they were back in their element. Both were now warm enough, but a brisk wind chased and chilled.

'Let's keep cracking, move on, keep the circulation going,' was Alec's advice. They did, and, d'you know what, before long they found themselves right where they wanted to be; had been heading that way all the time, almost without thinking, kind of drawn.

Round a low scrag of hawthorn, it was there – the ideal spot to rest for a while, unload rucksacks. Sheltered it was, partly by the run of the land, partly by a kindly old hawthorn tree, twisted and fashioned by weather over many seasons until it overhung a wide, flattish piece of limestone, quite perfect as a picnic table. It was uncommonly like the very stone they'd picnicked on goodness knows how long ago. I won't tell you what the Gamecock landlord had put up for the trip, but there was plenty of it. Reight grand it was, including a generous thermos flask. You can guess for yourselves what was in that!

'Reight grand to see thi,' said a voice. The tasty food, much enjoyed, a bit of a doze had begun to settle. The voice put a stop to that all right. The two picnickers sat bolt upright, staring up into the tree. There was something of a nest there! Immediately, one combined thought exploded ….. Alva! Focus on the tree! Focus on the nest! It slowly began to fade, drift, mesmerise. It was gone. The wind dropped – completely. Silence. All at once, that voice again: 'Hello lads, how is 'ta?' Out from the tree, and wearing his be-furred hat, there stood pilot-ostler Alva, large as life! At a distance and very slightly tugging at its moorings – a yellow bowler hat balloon, with its remarkably expanding wicker basket. Thoughtfully rubbing its neck over the basket edge was the head of a horse, a magnificent piebald horse. Well, would you believe that? It was Articulus, Alva's fine, very eloquent horse, who had advised and flown them everywhere and anywhere among the mountains and the tops when they were young lads. It was so good to see him again.

Alva didn't say a great deal more by way of general conversation. All a bit overwhelming, really. But shared thoughts were rich and would continue that way forever.

Quite soon: 'It's been reight grand, but better be off,' Alva said. 'Don't fret, will keep in touch.' How good to hear him say that. Both former members of his crew thanked him in any and every way they could. It was difficult for them to know what to say. Alva completely understood.

He warmly shook hands with each of them, gave a wink and, before you could even think about saying "ay-oop", there he was back at his balloon to rejoin his remarkable animal. Ask Alec or Ben, any time, they'll tell you all about him. Alva leapt nimbly into the basket, changed hat for helmet and gave the burner an encouraging reminder. With his free hand, he offered a wide and generous wave of his very singular, be-furred headgear and, after a slight lingering, maybe out of kindly consideration for those left behind, he raised his burner to a triumphant pitch and pulled down his goggles. Away went Alva, horse, yellow bowler hat, waltzing up into the blue.

The two friends kept their eyes on the balloon for as long as they could, then, quite frankly, a bit overcome (well wouldn't you have been too?) sat down again at their limestone table. Propped up, one on each side of the fat old thermos, were two, gradely, absolutely enormous packs of Kendal mint cake. Ah, Alva, that hat! What mint cake, cheese sandwiches and goodness knows what else it had produced for them at any time, any place all through their unpredictable travels.

So, at this point feeling decidedly flat, what were they to do now? Could go and knock old Gilbert up, perhaps, except he might be entertaining more guests. Catch sight of shepherd Mick, have a word with the dogs. No, leave them in peace. Tell you what, pack up here, head back to the village, see what's going on. Look in at the Gamecock. Any chance of a word with a roundhead? Thoughts were firing off in all directions. There wasn't really a lot to pack up, they'd eaten practically everything that had been provided by the inn. The landlord had very excellently filled the big flask – now empty. Must get it back to him in good order. A brisk trudge, rucksacks feeling very light now indeed, the two rather downcast individuals were quite soon back at the inn. They thanked the landlord for his kindness and excellent food. They would stay on into the evening if convenient, have a meal and then head home. Apart from saying they had enjoyed the day, nothing was said of its quite extraordinary events. Explanations, where could anyone possibly begin? So, quite late, it was back to Ben's place for a night's rest. There were dreams. Oh yes, you can be sure there were – very extraordinary dreams – till at last deep sleep drifted through to a new day.

Waking next morning took more than a bit of doing, I can tell you, but somehow it was accomplished. After sorting themselves out, their bedrooms likewise, it was – spick and span – down to breakfast for the two almost fully awake dalesmen. Ben had just had the energy to set the table before he turned in last night, so it was now a case of finding something eatable to put on it!

'Join me in the larder,' Ben said, 'we'll see what we've got.' The old range had remained warmly lit, so cooking a grand fry-oop would be no problem, neither would be the eating of it. But something intervened. Caught in the sun, shafting through a window left slightly ajar, there in the middle of the table were two small stones. How they glinted! One was red, the other green. The two friends were astonished. Apart from the surprise, they thought, for sure, they'd become lost on the long-ship. Well, anyhow, here they were! Ah, the two rather special collie dogs which had sprung from them, were they still with shepherd Mick? There was such delight in being reunited with the stones, first found long ago, when boys, along the beck-side near Clapham cave.

'Shall we give them a rub?' laughed Ben, slowly revolving his between his fingers, 'perhaps meet the dogs again?' But no, get on with the day was thought best. The stones were pocketed. It was time, after managing to eat t' grand fry-oop (invent the menu for yourself!) to really begin the day. Alec had to return to Lancaster University and matters archaeological. A party of eager (oh dear!) hikers was gathered outside the parish hall for Ben to guide them over the tops. Heigh-ho.

* * * * * * *

Existence for both friends unravelled in future times pleasantly enough. Ben headed for Loch Ness a number of times to see Morag. On these occasions, he made opportunity to exchange the time of day with Sir George, Laird of Drumnadrochit. Before too long, Morag and

Ben became happily married. Sir George gave the bride away at the wedding, Alec was best man, the reception held at Sir George's ancestral manor – bagpipes in full voice – a very good time was had by all, I can tell you! After a short honeymoon on the Isle of Bute, the couple returned to live very comfortably at Ben's cottage and are thinking that sometime they might need an extension. Never a dull moment, you could say, in village life season by season. Such fun when jolly summer events like the Cuckoo Festival come round; always enjoyed, sometimes inspiring Ben to wear his Viking attire.

Hot air balloons of every shape get out and about in Craven skies. They bring back a crowd of memories. One balloon flew low over our couple, out for a day on the tops, a while back. Hadn't really noticed it until the pilot's voice drifted down: 'Ay-oop, you two.' They looked up – wonderful. It was Alva and the yellow bowler hat. Still flying, Alva must be maintaining it in very good nick. So good to see him. 'I'll keep in touch,' he called down cheerfully from that extraordinary basket of his, as he sailed on. He did. At the Great Yorkshire Show that year, there were many magnificent heavy horses on view, their owners in bowler hats, mostly of right sombre old colours. Only one cheerful one raised a smile. It was bright yellow. Only one animal, a magnificent black and white piebald, cut all general conversation. Get it? Got it? Good. Whether the crowd saw the pair, I'll leave to you!

* * * * * * *

Alec eventually gave up full-time archaeology. He took on a little Dales pub and restaurant. Morag and Ben visit often and say the cuisine is excellent. Alec doesn't intend to remain single. But who knows? Hazel, a friend and fellow archaeologist, is a regular patron.

I forgot to tell you that, after a certain moonlit night, cat Marius was not really seen ever again. And there is something else you'd be interested to hear, I think, about the little black bottle which fell out of a grubby skeleton's old ditty box, found in a cave along Robin Hood's Bay. Well, Ben still has it. It stands on a little round table in an out of the way alcove in the cottage. Nobody has ever been able to break the seal; too difficult. Too dangerous? Most often the little object is stone cold. But sometimes when the moon is up and the weather turns wild, or when it's specially dark outside, the bottle becomes kind of agitated, quite warm. It trembles, shudders, rocks, tries to revolve. Wisps of bluish vapour sneak out from the impossibly tight stopper. One day this will have to burst!

Ben gave the stirrup to Alec for safekeeping and as a memento of curious happenings in his life. He has resisted all temptations to polish it. Archaeologist, you see. It sits on a shelf behind the bar, catches the light sometimes, drawing inquisitive remarks from some of his customers. It has been known to jog itself right off its position and to hit the floor for no clear reason. Any guesses?

* * * * * * *

'Well, lad, not much else to tell thi,' said old Ebenezer, leaning back on the garden bench in the sunshine. 'What does tha reckon to some of that? Tha might want to know what happened next, I suppose?'

'What did happen next?' demanded his listener, wide-eyed and eager to hear.

'Nay, young man, tha'd better go ask grandmother Morag,' was the reply, 'when she's back from t' village shop.' That would have to do.

At that moment, a large seagull flew over. From its beak fell a small, round object, which bounced and rolled slowly to old Ebenezer. He bent down and picked it up, felt it for a moment, nearly dropped it, nigh on dropped it! He seemed shaken.

'Musket ball, well by gum,' he murmured to himself. The lethal missile was still warm! He slipped it into his pocket. Instantly, the smuggler skeleton's little black bottle, sitting on its round topped table, started to fizz, just a hint of smoke drifting from the cosy alcove and beginning to curl up to the ceiling. The small boy's question was to take an unexpected turn.

'What d'you think of that?' suddenly said a voice. Throwing down her shopping basket with one hand and brandishing an unfamiliar object with the other, home from the shop came Morag. Fair flummoxed, she was. She held up a lively green, squarish, round-shouldered glass bottle, I would say about five inches tall.

'Found this down in the beck,' she said, 'not far from the bridge. Went to gather a little fresh watercress.' She held the bottle up high for inspection. 'Why, look,' she burst out, 'there's something inside, all crinkled up.' It looked like a piece of paper (or could it have been sailcloth?). Peering through the teasing glass, it was almost possible to make out one of the words which the remnant seemed to carry, but none of the rest of its fellows; any chance of deciphering the message they may have conveyed, defeated by the twist of the fragment. 'Now then,' laughed old

Morag, with a Scottish twinkle that made you want to dance, 'what d'you ken?'

To begin with, it was difficult to think of anything to "ken" concerning the new find, and certainly about any message – if it were a message – right out of reach and impossible to guess. Message in a bottle, you don't come across  such every day of the week! The landlord of the Gamecock Inn was called in for his opinion, and the green teaser passed round from hand to pondering hand – rubbed, fingered, weighed, inspected and considered by each of the amateur detectives. Of course, it was tricky. The tantalising, squat little green bottle had been expertly sealed against all weathers: cork firmly thrust home into the short neck, very tightly, purposefully, neatly bound round – almost throttled – with oiled silk and tarred twine, finally finished off with a serious blob of red sealing wax.

There was a silence. Who might be going to break the seal, discover what the message – if, as I said, it was message at all – might say? Could anyone dare? And, anyway, how did the bottle find itself in the beck midst trout and watercress? Slipped out of a midnight, moonlit pocket a while ago, do you think? There were some fair old guesses, I can tell you. Maybe, what was to happen next in the story was the message in the green bottle. Someone would have to find out. But who?

Grandma Morag called a halt. 'We'll have to think about all this,' she said. 'Hand it back to me, if you please.' Giving a final polish to it with her apron, and the landlord thanked and gone home, the rather chuckling, you could feel, green glass prize was placed inside the long-case kitchen clock, for safekeeping.

The young grandson lay awake in bed that night. Sleep impossible. There'd been no chance to consult with his grandmother. What might she have said in answer to his question about what happened at the end of his grandfather's story? He came to a decision. With as little noise as possible, he crept out of bed and, very slowly, shocked at every creak, made his nervous way downstairs and into the kitchen; silent, except for the steady, rhythmical beat of the tall old clock, its moon face, half in shadow, half suddenly lit in firelight from the kitchen range, and saying nothing.

A few tiptoed steps, he was touching the tall mahogany case and feeling for the little key to release its door. Wait! Were those sea boots he momentarily thought he saw in the shadow of the timepiece? Whose were they? Grandfather's? Quiet! What an awful, shattering click as the key turned and sprung the lock. Someone upstairs must surely hear. Don't move! Wait, wait, listen, nothing. The boy felt icy cold. Gradually, warmed again by the fire, his courage returned. The little door in the belly of the clock swung open with barely a sound. Cautiously reaching inside, the boy's fingers closed on his small, squat, round-shouldered quarry. The bottle, out it came, green glass glinting in the firelight.

The kitchen window had been left ajar. Suddenly, there was a movement, a dark shape appeared in the slit, dropped noiselessly to the floor, moved swiftly and

jumped into the big old kitchen chair, quite filling it. Such a cat! This large, benign old black cat, purring loudly, settled in for the night watch. Just lit by the fire, quieter now, was there ever such a knowing smile? One small boy, however, was rooted to the spot! The glass bottle, only just within his grasp, slipped from his fingers and shattered in a blaze of splinters as it hit the old stone kitchen hearth. The secret message, if such it were, lay amongst the debris and slowly uncurled. Shocked and in a daze, Ebenezer's grandson picked it up. Was there now a whiff of tobacco, hint of rum? In the glow of firelight, the boy slowly began to read .....

* * * * * * *

Look out everywhere for the old seafarer. Any time, but especially maybe on stormy nights. On warm days, you could find him eating fish and chips (after, of course, he'd first tapped out his pipe and stowed it under his hat) as he sits on your particular favourite summer holiday's seafront. Join him, by all means. But watch out! A certain hungry seagull may suddenly dive down with your own chips at his mercy! Of course, you may really be in the company of a very fat, black cat. Check for sea boots.

Are you sure you'll be locking your front door tonight! What about leaving a window ajar and providing a large plate of something tasty? Because, who knows! The skeleton's little black bottle sitting on its table in the cottage is, right now, trembling, rocking, whirling round and seriously fizzing. Listen!

Will Riding

About the Author

The author spent his important growing-up years in the Yorkshire Dales. Following service with the Royal Navy, he began a professional career with Harrogate Parks and a further studentship at The Royal Horticultural Society's Gardens, Wisley, to qualify. After experience in the seed trade, mycological research, commercial carnations and roses, he founded his own garden design business. Writing for foremost gardening publications, lecturing, judging and contributing to a number of gardening books, proceeded over many years. Occasional writing for theatre augmented his activities, as did actual performing in the field of music and drama.

The spirit of the Dales took firm hold very early on - its topography, character, history over the aeons and certainly its remarkable weather in all its wide variety and caprice.

Life took the author, who has lived in Hertfordshire, now, for a number of years, away from the North, but affinity has never faltered. Frequent holidays in the Dales with his wife and three children - now grown up, with families of their own - were essential. Travelling there will always remain very much a 'going home'.